THE
DISAPPEARANCES
OF MADALENA
GRIMALDI

THE DISAPPEARANCES OF MADALENA GRIMALDI

A Claudia Valentine Mystery

MARELE DAY

WALKER AND COMPANY
NEW YORK

For Nick Masterman (1948–1994) and Cybele

First published in Australia in 1994 by Allen & Unwin Pty Ltd; first published in the United States of America in 1996 by Walker Publishing Company Inc.

Library of Congress Cataloging-in-Publication Data
Day, Marele.
The disappearances of Madalena Grimaldi: a Claudia Valentine mystery/Marele Day.
p.   cm.
ISBN 0-8027-3277-1 (hardcover)
I. Title.
PR9619.3.D382D57   1996
823—dc20   95-48782
CIP

Printed in the United States of America
2 4 6 8 10 9 7 5 3 1

THE
DISAPPEARANCES
OF MADALENA
GRIMALDI

The Kid felt the small round pressure in the middle of his back and the lightness at his hips as the man from Pinkertons deftly removed the pearl-handled guns from the holsters. 'The slightest movement and I'll blast a hole clean through your body,' the man breathed down his neck.

From the outside it appeared as if the Kid was rooted to the spot. But inside the blood was whipping round his body as if he was about to leap into a ravine. He wasn't afraid of dying but he didn't want to be shot in the back. Goddam city man, didn't he know the rules? Thirty-seven men he'd killed. He didn't want to be shot in the back by a goddam city man.

Behind him, the man was doing something. 'OK,' said the man, 'you turn around nice and slow.'

The Kid turned around nice and slow. The man was pointing a gun at him. As well as that, the Kid's pearl-handled guns were stuck down his trousers. From out of his coat pocket he produced a pair of handcuffs. 'OK,' he said, 'you put your hands out nice and easy.'

The Kid put his hands out nice and easy, just like he was told. The man slapped on the cuffs.

'Now you and I are going to take a little ride in my car.'

That was the last thing the Kid wanted to do. 'What about my horse?'

'No room for the horse,' said the man, untying the animal.

1

'*It can take care of itself.*' *He slapped the horse on the rump and fired a couple of shots in the air. The horse hightailed it out of there.*

Shit, thought the Kid. Now the horse was gone. If he refused to go with the man, would he die alone out here in the desert? He knew what would happen if the job wasn't done properly. If the man shot him and just left him here, the vultures would come circling. And vultures didn't wait till a man was properly dead. He didn't want to watch the flesh being picked off his own bones. But better to die out here a man than let himself be captured.

'*You want me to git in that thing, you gonna have to put me in it yourself,*' *he challenged the man. The Kid kicked a flurry of sand up into the man's face.*

The only other time someone had kicked sand in the man's face was when he was a boy of fourteen. That very same day he sent away for the Charles Atlas body-building course. No-one, but no-one, did that to the man from Pinkertons. He knocked the Kid to the ground and beat him till he was unconscious.

The woman sitting next to me in the plane gave me a dirty look and moved the book away. It probably wouldn't have helped if I'd explained that my interest in her reading material was strictly professional. I'm a private investigator. I wasn't particularly interested in how the man from Pinkertons went about solving his cases, I wanted to see what happened when it came time for him to send his client the bill. Because I'd just finished a case and I was wondering whether I should itemise the expenses or just give a total. If I specified this return airfare to Melbourne the client would want to know what I was doing there. And I wasn't sure I wanted to tell her about Melbourne.

There'd been no guns involved, I hadn't beaten anyone unconscious. Not this time, anyway. In fact, if there was a place in the golden west to which old PIs retired, this certainly wouldn't be the case I'd reminisce about as I sat on the verandah in the rocking chair.

I was following a man to make sure he was sticking to his diet.

His name was John Larossa. He supplied books to country libraries in New South Wales. He had a heart problem and was on a strict diet. On his return from one of his country trips his wife, Anna, had found a paper napkin with Delightfully French printed on it. She thought it sounded as if it might be a patisserie. He wasn't supposed to eat cake. I suggested to Anna that perhaps he just called in for a cup of coffee. She told me he wasn't supposed to drink coffee either.

John Larossa's library run encompassed the New South Wales south coast as far as Bateman's Bay, then inland to Goulburn, Braidwood and Bowral. I'd set out to follow him, looking forward to a week in the country. I'd hired a car because my own was in the garage getting a new head gasket. My mechanic was in love with the car. If ever I wanted to sell, he'd buy it. I'd been thinking about that a lot lately. I was only keeping it for sentimental reasons—I mean you can't really follow someone for hours on end in a car as conspicuous as a 1958 Daimler.

He came out of his front door in Strathfield, waving goodbye to Anna. He was a short balding man in his mid-forties, fifteen years older than his wife. He got into a jaunty little station wagon, in the back of which were boxes, presumably full of books.

But he didn't go to the country.

It started off OK. I followed him onto the Princes Highway, heading south. But at Rockdale he turned off and stopped outside a block of flats. He went up to the flats and pressed the buzzer. About ninety seconds later a young man in a shiny grey suit came out, carrying a small suitcase and eating an apple. They got into the station wagon. The young man dropped Mr Larossa off at the airport.

Then Mr Larossa and I got on the plane to Melbourne.

At Tullamarine airport John Larossa went through the hire car formalities then got into a blue Toyota. A little way down the line Otto sat purring in his fawn Subaru.

Otto is an old friend. I'd phoned him from Sydney, as soon

3

as I realised what was happening. He said he'd be at the airport waiting.

'So what is it?' said Otto, when I'd got into the car. 'Murder, drugs, international espionage?'

'Diet.'

'Ah,' he exclaimed knowingly, as if I'd just used a code word known only to a select group of people.

'No, Otto. Diet. I'm following the guy to make sure he is sticking to his diet.'

His expression changed completely, like someone who'd just spent a lot of money buying a shirt only to find when he gets it home he doesn't like it.

We passed Melbourne Travelodge then got onto the freeway through a grey–green Australia of scrawny gum trees and puffy-clouded sky. Gradually the trees were overtaken by built-up areas. In the nineteenth century Melbourne had been the richest city on the continent. It was the establishment city. The gold they'd dug out of the ground had been converted into solid buildings and solid citizens that were going to last forever. There was no convict stain here as there was in Sydney. Citizens were upright, honest. They believed in law and order. I guess that's why they acquitted members of their police force when they shot people.

Trees got greener, more European, the closer to the city we came. Along Flemington Road were banners announcing the Spring Racing Carnival. I didn't have time to see whether it had been and gone or whether it was yet to come. Other signs whizzed by. Whilst I kept my eyes on Larossa, Otto told me his tale of love gone wrong. 'So here I am, celibate once again,' he concluded.

Otto still had illusions about meeting his prince and living happily ever after. One prince after the other. Although the idea would have shocked him, he was an addict. A romance addict. He wasn't one to go after rough trade, not anymore anyway. He'd be clean for months, then he'd get a taste and get hooked all over again. He actually functioned well on his own. During those periods of celibacy he was at his best. He went to the gym and got fit instead of using the gym as a pick-up place.

But there was nothing like the fiery breath of passion. I remembered it well.

'How are things with you and Steve?' he asked.

My turn now. 'They're not,' I said, as briefly as possible.

Otto looked like a boa constrictor trying to swallow an elephant. 'So what happened?'

I kept my eyes on the blue Toyota, three cars ahead. 'He irons his underpants.' I abruptly changed the subject. 'My mother's getting married.'

I reached out to steady the steering wheel as Otto almost lost control of the car.

'Mina's getting married?! Oh my God, who's the lucky man?'

My mother was something of a pin-up girl for Otto. She used to dance at the Tivoli. 'Brian Collier.'

'The journalist?' Otto seemed to be scrambling for words. 'But I thought he was an old friend of the family.'

'Didn't we all?'

'Well,' he said, after a small silence, 'I'm very happy for her.'

'Yes, me too.'

We both stared straight ahead, thinking our private thoughts. It was fine being happy for someone else. A lot easier than being happy for yourself.

By the time we'd struck the Children's Hospital I'd sighted my first tram. We stopped alongside it, Otto now familiar enough with Melbourne to understand the protocol. People got off in the middle of the road and crossed to the footpath. To me it was like taking your life into your hands. There was a 'ding' sound and the tram started up again. We followed John Larossa through the top end of the city, past Kings Pool Room and men working on the road in bright red safety jackets. I made a mental note of the pool room in case I needed a quick game. Made a mental note of the men too, just in case.

'You wanted to see sights? There's the National Gallery of Victoria,' Otto pointed out.

The waterfalls and the ceramic dragon were pleasing to look at but by the third time we'd passed the gallery I'd had enough. We were going round in circles.

'He's lost,' announced Otto.

'How can he be lost?' I said. 'No-one gets lost in Melbourne, it's laid out on a grid, easy to get around. The most liveable city in the world. I saw the sign on the way in.'

'It's the new casino they're building. They keep closing off streets. It looks like he's trying to get into Southgate. The car park's over there but this approach is blocked off. Maybe I should pull up beside him and give him directions.'

'Oh, yes, and who are we supposed to be? Good Samaritans?'

We must have driven around Melbourne for an hour, before an increasingly frustrated Mr Larossa finally found his way to Southgate Car Park. What delicacy was he going to reward himself with after all that? In his position I'd be having a stiff whiskey or two. Was his version of whiskey a nice rich cake?

Once in the car park he struck it lucky, finding a parking spot straightaway. 'Just let me out here,' I said, as I saw Larossa heading for the lift. 'Where will I meet you?' asked Otto, suddenly panicked.

'I'll be around.' And left him to enjoy the adrenalin surging through his veins.

Southgate was full of shops and restaurants, not unlike Darling Harbour, except that instead of being on the harbour it was on the river. There were lots of tempting little cafes and restaurants and, sure enough, Mr Larossa entered one of them. It didn't come as a surprise to me to read the name on the awning—Delightfully French. I had my miniature camera in my pocket. There were lots of photo opportunities here—the humped pedestrian bridge, redbrick Flinders Street Station across the mud-brown waters of the Yarra. Men from Sydney coming all the way to Melbourne for a piece of cake.

Although he had so much trouble finding the place, now he was here he seemed to know his way around. He went straight to a table by the counter and sat down. The guy at the espresso machine greeted him then turned his head as if speaking to someone out the back.

In about three seconds a woman came out, planted a lavish kiss on John Larossa's cheek and joined him at the table. She was a striking woman in her fifties, black hair pulled back in Spanish style, well made-up, lipliner. A big woman who knew how to dress. She spent a lot of time stroking his hand before the guy at the espresso machine put a coffee down in front of her, and a bottle of mineral water in front of John.

I became aware of the sound of impatience and looked up to see a waiter hovering, blond hair, each curl crisp, perfect and rock hard as a Greek statue. 'I'll have the blueberry bavarois with cream, thanks,' I gave him my order.

His lip curled as crisply as his hair. 'You won't need cream,' he said.

'I'd like cream,' I countered.

Louder now, as if I hadn't heard the first time, he said: 'You won't need cream. The bavarois is rich enough already.'

I didn't want to draw attention to myself, especially not now when things were becoming so interesting, but I was really starting to get a strong desire for cream. 'I'll have cream,' I said in a voice meant to wither his curls. He looked at me for a long time, lips pursed so tightly they turned white.

'And to drink?' he said finally, stretching the lips across his teeth.

'Short black. No cream.'

I was sitting in the outside part of the cafe, which meant I could keep my sunglasses on without looking conspicuous. John and the woman were obviously pleased to see each other and seemed quite at home in each other's company. Judging by his hand movements he was describing to her the roundabout way he'd taken to get here.

The waiter and Otto arrived at the same time. The blueberry bavarois had an enormous mound of cream beside it, as big and white as a snowdrift. The waiter stuck it in front of me and gave me a look of challenge, defying me to eat that amount of cholesterol. I picked up the gauntlet. Before he'd even taken Otto's order—an apricot juice—a huge spoonful of cream had disappeared into my mouth. He looked at Otto as if to say, how can you bear it? About ten minutes later Mr Larossa and the woman stood up. They said something to the guy at the espresso machine then, even though he barely came up to her earlobes, Mr Larossa ushered this striking woman out with an air of authority.

I stood up to leave too, which brought the waiter over in two seconds flat. He looked at my plate, aghast. I'd eaten all the cream and left the bavarois untouched. 'You were right,' I said, handing him a ten-dollar note, 'it was rich. Keep the change.' Well, hell. Let him think what he liked. Where I come from, when you have cake, you have cream.

We followed Larossa and his companion to a big white duplex in Toorak, separate entrances upstairs and down. I took a photo of them at the gate together, the woman checking the letterbox and pulling out three business-sized envelopes. She handed them to him and they slowly walked towards the steps leading to the top entrance. A woman in a well-tailored jacket came out of the downstairs door, carrying a briefcase.

'Hi. Good trip?'

'Same as always,' Mr Larossa said cheerily. 'How's the university?'

'Exams,' she grimaced. 'Marking.' She got into a dinky little yellow sports car.

Larossa and the woman waved her goodbye then disappeared into the house.

I stayed three full days in Melbourne and never once did I see Mr Larossa break his diet. In fact I didn't see him eat anything at all. A couple of times he returned to Delightfully French but mostly he stayed in the house, the doors shut and curtains drawn.

In five minutes we'd be landing in Sydney. The woman beside me put away her book and started adjusting her hair, so I never did get to see how the man from Pinkertons billed his client. I wondered now whether subconsciously Anna Larossa had more than food in mind when she referred to her husband's 'diet'.

But I'd done the job she'd asked me to do. By the time the plane touched down in Sydney I had my letter to her composed:

Dear Mrs Larossa,

re: diet, Mr John Larossa

I have followed your husband for the agreed period of time. During this time I did not observe him partaking of any of the items in the list you provided me. I conclude from this that, to the best of my knowledge, he is sticking to his diet.

Best Wishes

Claudia Valentine

I would include travel expenses but not specify each item. If she thought that was too much for petrol for a week in the country she could query it. And then I'd tell her about Melbourne.

As the passengers waited to get off the plane I picked up a Sydney newspaper to see what had been happening during my absence. A twenty-one year old woman had been bashed to death in a doorway in Kings Cross. Politicians and police were arguing about who should oversee an enquiry into police corruption in New South Wales. An investigation was finally being opened into the drug-trafficking operation centred around Sweetie's Icecream Parlours.

Ah, it was good to be home.

'Claudia Valentine.'

'Hello, dear.' It was my mother on the other end of the line. She asked me if I could come over and see her. 'It won't take a minute.' For something that wouldn't take a minute her tone sounded ominous.

'Everything OK?' I asked. It was the day before the wedding. I hoped she wasn't getting cold feet. 'I'm picking the kids up at 2.30, I'll call over on the way.'

The front door was open, with just the screen door protecting Mina from the outside world. I nevertheless knocked and called out to her. The neighbour watering his garden looked up and gave me a friendly wave. Mina came to the door absentmindedly carrying a teapot.

The house was in chaos. There were clothes, packing boxes, crockery and newspapers all over the place. If you hadn't known what was going on, you'd swear the place had been burgled. My mother's orderly, calm life was in upheaval. Not only was she about to remarry, she was also selling the house and moving. 'So that Brian and I can start out afresh,' she'd explained. Mina's life was in eruption and some of the lava was coming down on me. This was the house I'd grown up in, my grandmother had been born here, it was the home we came to after my father had pissed off.

Mina had discussed the matter with me—I thought it was a great idea for her to cut loose from the past. But coming back here, probably for the last time, I felt the twinge of change.

It wasn't on account of Mina. She was only going to the next suburb. It was on account of the house. I'd assumed she'd live here forever. That the house would always be accessible to me. But next week there'd be new people with new furniture. They'd probably renovate, paint it Federation colours. Put Polyfilla in the hole I'd drilled in the wall to see if I could get through to China.

Despite the pot in her hand she didn't offer me tea. Nor did we go into the kitchen, as we usually did. We stayed in the dining room, where the biggest mess was. There were three piles—what she was keeping, what she was leaving in the house and what she was giving to St Vincent de Paul's. She explained it all to me, talking about everything else except whatever it was she'd called me about. The kids' flight was due in soon, I didn't want to be late for them.

'What did you want to tell me?'

She wrapped newspaper round the teapot. Slowly. Deliberately. 'I just wanted to make sure, you know, with the wedding coming up and everything. So a couple of days ago I went and checked up. I don't suppose the news will come as a surprise, but I thought I'd better let you know anyway.' She spent some time wedging the lid into the pot so it wouldn't rattle.

'He passed away. Years ago—25th April, 1985. Anzac Day.'

She fussed around looking for a piece of paper the right size to wrap the sugar bowl. The time it took me to realise properly who she was talking about. She rarely referred to him as 'he', it was always 'your father'.

She slid open the glass doors of the sideboard to get the next items for packing. In it was the dinner service that was kept for 'best'. In fact I can't ever remember seeing it in use. It was plain white with a blue and yellow pattern round the edge, all the rage in the fifties. She picked up a cup and saucer, holding them fondly. 'Your father gave this to me for our fifth wedding anniversary. Last present he . . .' Her voice trailed away. She wrapped up the cup and saucer and put them in the box destined for St Vincent de Paul's. 'I don't think I could watch

Brian eating off your father's plates,' she said, as if needing to justify her decision not to take them. 'I never used that set anyway,' she said, too brightly. 'What's the point of keeping it?' She busied herself with wrapping another item, folding and refolding the newspaper. Too many times.

We hadn't heard from Guy in over thirty years. He drank and drank till eventually he couldn't find his way home anymore. I would have been three when he gave Mina the dinner set. 'I'll take it,' I said. 'It'll be nice having a set where all the pieces match.'

It was only a couple of days since I'd flown back from Melbourne and here I was at the airport again. I couldn't help thinking about John and Anna Larossa. And the woman in Melbourne. I still felt ambivalent about not telling Anna what I had discovered about her husband. I'd never even met her husband yet I knew more details about his intimate life than she did. The knowledge weighed heavily on me. She'd have my report by now. And the invoice. It would almost have been a relief if she'd rung up and questioned the expenses. But so far she hadn't. I felt bad about carrying this on my own but I was going to have to wear it.

The arrivals screen indicated that the flight from Brisbane had now landed. I hovered at the gate, looking over the heads of the handful of people who'd come to meet the plane. I immediately spotted David. It wasn't because of the instinct that allows parents to instantly recognise their offspring in a crowd. David was the first person everyone noticed. He was wearing a baseball cap back to front, a pair of lime green sunglasses that almost engulfed his face, grunge shorts and a T-shirt with wording on it I hoped he didn't understand. When he walked, the only parts of him that moved were his legs. My son's attempts to look totally cool. I was almost embarrassed to go and claim him. When he saw me, though, his face broke out into a big wide grin.

Amy sauntered along slightly behind, deliberately not looking at him, as if this kid in the stupid clothes had nothing to do with her. She was two years older but ten centimetres taller.

She seemed to be growing before my very eyes. Prepubescent spurt. The tallness didn't seem to bother her the way it had bothered me at that age. At least she didn't have the tangle of red hair to cope with as well. The blond hair she'd inherited from her father was long, straight and shiny. 'Hi Mum,' she said, flicking it back over her shoulder and giving me a hug. I smelt perfume, one of those you sometimes get as give-aways in glossy magazines.

Though he'd almost broken into a gallop when he'd spotted me, David looked like he'd rather die than embrace in public. Nevertheless, he allowed me a quick hug. 'Let's get the bags, OK?' he said authoritatively, heading off in the wrong direction.

'David! Can't you read?' retaliated Amy. 'Just testing,' he said, and came back into the fold.

We managed to get the luggage, despite David's attempts to dive on anything that remotely resembled his bag, and walked outside. Amy turned her nose up at the smell of the pollution I couldn't smell at all. Still, I suppose she hardly noticed the farm chemicals that left my eyes streaming.

I didn't think they'd be concerned one way or the other, since they'd never met him, but on the drive back from the airport I told them that their grandfather had died. They both went silent for a moment then David, as if commiserating, announced: 'Jesse's grandfather died last week. While we were doing our exams.' No-one said anything, it didn't seem like the kind of thing that required a response.

We drove through Stanmore then across Parramatta Road. 'He had a heart attack and fell off the tractor,' continued David, as if no time had elapsed since his last informative comment. 'But that wasn't what killed him,' he went on, sounding just like one of the blokes in the pub telling a story. 'The tractor rolled backwards and squashed his skull.' Amy looked out the window, having no doubt heard this story before. There wasn't much I felt like saying either.

We were almost home, in the line of traffic waiting to turn into Balmain, when Amy said: 'How did he die?' Mina hadn't gone into the specific cause of death, there was no need. We assumed he'd drunk himself to death. 'How do you drink yourself to death?' enquired David when I told him. 'You drink so much you just swell up and burst?'

'Da-vid!' said Amy with exasperation.

'Well? Do you?' For once he wasn't trying to be funny, his question was genuine.

The lights changed. 'It's drinking alcohol. You drink it long enough and hard enough it affects your insides. Your brain, liver and kidneys,' I gave him all the gory bits he loved so well, 'they all just pack it in, refuse to function.' I followed the stream of traffic down Roberts Street and into Mullens.

'Why didn't he ever come to see us?' asked Amy when we pulled up outside the pub. I'd asked myself the same question a million times. 'Did he know about us?' I heard David say. Guy must have considered the possibility that his daughter had had children of her own. If he ever thought about me at all. How much of his brain, his memories, were there left at the end? Did he ever look into the bottle and see his past? Or was it only the future he saw there.

'I think he knows,' said Amy wisely. 'I think he's watching over us from Heaven.'

Heaven? That jolted me back to the here and now. David was poking his finger up in the air, indicating where Heaven was. I could see that it was time for us all to have a little talk. I didn't know where Heaven was but I was pretty sure it wasn't in the roof of this hire car.

'I've got a surprise for you,' I said to them as we got the luggage out of the boot. I took them into the pub via the side door. Usually it's all I can do to stop David going into the bar and staring at George, our resident derelict, but the promise of a surprise had him racing up the stairs.

My living quarters were looking spick and span; I'd got in flowers, frozen pizzas, a stack of videos. 'Nice, Mum,' said Amy, looking around appreciatively.

'Yeah. Nice, Mum,' repeated David, looking around for the surprise.

'It gets even better,' I said. 'This time you get your own room.' Up till this visit they'd bunked on my floor in sleeping bags. But they were old enough now for their own space. Besides, it was an adventure for them.

I'd been living in the pub for years; my living quarters—a combined bedroom/living room with kitchen and bathroom, were comfortable but small. As I was the only tenant I had almost free range. No-one stayed in pubs anymore when they came to town. Some of our regular drinkers suggested that Jack should open up to backpackers, as had other pubs in Balmain. 'Gawd,' said Jack, 'then I'd be working twenty-four hours a day. I've got to get away from the public sometime.'

'We'd help you look after 'em, wouldn't we, Les?' said one bloke, nudging his friend. 'Some of them nice young German frauleins, eh?' As if a nice young fraulein would be interested for one minute in a man whose only personal growth in the last twenty years was a beer gut that practically rested on his knees. Dream on.

Jack and I had cleaned out the room and let the sun in. The wallpaper left something to be desired but otherwise it was very pleasant. There was an ensuite bathroom so they wouldn't have to make midnight forays across the corridor to mine. No balcony as in my quarters but they'd only be in the room to sleep. They sniffed around the room, like cats coming to a new home, wary but at least staying there. Amy gravitated to the bed near the window, while David did a sideways dive onto the other one.

I showed them the wardrobe, empty except for the ubiquitous wire coathangers. 'You can hang your things up in here.' I looked at the way David was dressed and asked warily, 'You guys got something nice to wear to the wedding?' They pulled clothes out of their respective bags and showed me. I was relieved. At least David wouldn't be going to the wedding dressed like a circus. 'Come across when you're ready, OK?' I left them to their unpacking.

But I'd hardly stepped into my room when I discovered David right behind me. 'There's no TV,' he complained. 'Well, it's not going to kill you, there's one in here.'

'I know.'

15

'What's that?' I asked, indicating the computer game in his hand.

'Nintendo. You'll love it, Mum.'

Hot on his heels came Amy. 'Dad's going to have a fit!' she exclaimed. 'I bet he confiscates it when you get home,' she addressed her brother.

'I want to show Mum, that's all. Dad won't care.'

'He will.'

There was a series of alternating 'he wills' and 'he won'ts'. 'OK,' I said, 'that's enough.' I was tempted to tell them to go to their room now that they had a room to go to.

'But, Mum, it's great,' David insisted. 'You'll love it.'

'I'm sure I will. Later. Did you bring a wedding present?' I said, changing the subject. They looked at each other as if this had also been the cause of dispute. David blurted out, 'Rachel wanted to buy her a present but Amy wouldn't let her.' He looked at her defiantly, waiting for a response.

'It's got nothing to do with Rachel,' came Amy's reply. 'She's not related to Gran.' Amy went quiet, trying to put some calm on choppy waters. I looked at her, but she wasn't inviting any further discussion.

'Well, the wedding's tomorrow, let's go shopping.'

We went into the city by ferry. It was one of those brilliant blue afternoons, the sky so bright it looked like it was about to burst. We sat outside, feet up on the rails. Amy's and mine on the rails anyway. David's didn't reach. I don't know where he gets that short stocky build from. Amy used to tell him he was adopted, using this as 'proof'. But I had the ultimate proof—a birth certificate with Gary's and my name on it. It had come to that. Usually an assurance from the parents is enough but David wanted to see it in print. I don't know why, he could barely read at that stage.

'Why is Gran getting married?' asked David.

My mother was marrying a man who'd been a friend of the family for as long as I can remember. Brian Collier and my father were journos on the same paper. He was the one who stuck around when my father pissed off. I think he'd always had a soft spot for Mina but never once did he behave in a manner that my mother would describe as 'untoward'. When she'd announced the news to me, Mina had explained, 'It seems like the right thing to do, that's all.'

'Why didn't you do it years ago?' I'd asked.

'I didn't feel like it then.'

As if that was as much explanation as anyone would need.

It was Amy who supplied the answer. 'She's getting married because she's in love.'

'But Dad and Rachel are in love and they're not married.'

Amy quickly glanced at me to see whether that unintentional little arrow had done any damage. A slight graze but nothing serious.

'Just look at it this way, David—you get to eat a lot of cake.'

It was David who pointed out the two champagne flutes. I guess he thought the quicker they bought the present, the quicker he could get home to Nintendo. Elegant handblown glass that sounded so fine when you tapped your fingernail against it you could have used it to tune an entire orchestra. I wondered how many tuning forks you could buy for $120. That's what it cost for the glasses.

As soon as we were in the door David hooked the computer game up to the TV. He'd done this before. 'Look, Mum, it's really great.' And then I ceased to exist, he had shifted into another dimension. His expression was one of all-consuming alertness. He operated the controls and moved through that imaginary world with the ease, grace and concentration of a downhill skier. Amy lay on my bed reading till she finally flounced out in exasperation at the irritating little tune coming from the game.

I listened to some irritating little sounds of my own—messages on the answering machine. Most of them were from Gary, wondering whether the kids had arrived safe and sound. Whoops! Negligent parent. I should have got them to ring as soon as they arrived.

'David.'

No response. I went and stood between him and the TV set. 'That's enough virtual reality, it's time for some actual reality.'

He didn't know what I was talking about but he understood the tone of my voice. 'I just want to get to the next stage.'

'Now.' He closed the thing down. 'OK, now call Gary.'

He didn't seem too keen on the idea. 'Amy can do it.'

'No. You can. You've seen the birth certificate. You're his child, too.'

'Do you have Optus or Telecom?' he asked, trying to delay the inevitable.

'David, it doesn't matter. Phone.'

He dialled the number. 'Dad? It's me.' I went into the kitchen and took out one of the frozen pizzas. 'We went to buy Gran a present.' I could hear only David's side of the conversation but that was enough. 'Champagne glasses.' Then there was a longer silence. I poked my head around the corner. David was squirming. 'I wanted to show Mum.' More silence, more squirming then, 'Yes, Dad. Sorry, Dad.' A shorter silence then, 'OK. Mu-m!' As if I were three blocks away instead of three metres. He held the phone out to me.

Gary and I had a short friendly chat. Then we had a 'friendly chat' of another kind. 'We went into town, it slipped my mind . . . If anything happened the police would be in touch with you straightaway, Gary. I've got a friend in the force . . . No, he's not playing at present . . . Yes, I'll monitor it . . . Give me a break, my father died.' It slipped through, bypassing all those border controls between the conscious and subconscious parts of my brain. It stopped him in his tracks. He said he was sorry, really sorry. He asked me how I felt, I told him I was OK.

David was looking at me with big eyes when I hung up. 'Did you get into trouble from Dad too?' he asked sympathetically.

I tousled his hair and grinned at him. 'Go and tell your sister that dinner's ready.'

I whipped up a salad and took the pizza out of the oven. As I was putting it on the plates the phone rang. 'Help yourselves,' I said and went to answer it.

'Claudia Valentine,' I said into the phone.

'Hello. I . . . I want to make an appointment.' A woman's

voice, slight accent, desperate tone, talking in a whisper as if she didn't want to be overheard.

I kept my own voice neutral, not too curious or over-sympathetic. Rock solid. The kind of voice a person in trouble could rely on. 'Certainly. When would you like to see me?' As soon as possible. Daytime. Nights were difficult for her. Tomorrow was the wedding, I had the kids for the weekend. 'Monday?' I suggested. Yes, yes, that would be fine. We settled on a time and place. 'And your name, please?' I said in a businesslike fashion.

'Rosa. My name is Rosa.'

'Do you have a contact telephone number in case . . .' It was pointless continuing, she'd already hung up.

I hadn't been on the phone long but the pizza was almost gone. There was plenty of salad left though. 'Who was that?' asked Amy.

'Someone who wants to talk to me.'

'About murder or something?' David asked, picking out a piece of goat cheese and discarding it.

'I don't know yet. Want to go up the street for dessert?'

We walked up to one of the many cafes in Darling Street and sat outside eating cake. With cream. I wondered if I'd ever be able to eat cake again without thinking about Delightfully French and John Larossa. Probably.

Back at the pub the kids automatically went into their new room. It had been a long day. 'Good night, Mum,' said Amy. 'Sorry about . . . your father.' She reached up and kissed my cheek.

It was odd hearing her call him 'your father'. I guess she'd always heard Mina refer to him like that, plus he'd never really been a grandfather to her. It made me want to curl up beside her and tell her all about it.

I sat on the balcony till long into the night, my children sleeping soundly across the way. The occasional car swished by on roads wet with night cleaning. Behind that was the hum of the city across White Bay, the tiny squares of light in the office buildings, Centrepoint above it all. How many times had I sat here looking out at the city, imagining my father out there somewhere. Which doorway, which park bench, which gutter he might be lying in. I could have gone looking for him. But I never did.

The wedding was a flurry of pink organza, the twittering of Mina's old chorus-girl friends, and an embarrassed-looking groom. It was all over now, Brian and Mina were on their honeymoon, the kids had gone back to Queensland. I was sitting on a wharf in Balmain dangling my legs over the side. Alone.

I looked across to the suspension bridge being built to replace the Glebe Island bridge, one of the last opening bridges in Sydney. Nearby were the silos of the former container terminal, now bearing the distinctive squiggly ribbon of the Olympic Committee and Sydney 2000.

My father would never get to see those Games. I don't know why that should have filled me with a sense of melancholy, he was never overly interested in sport. I have a photo of him as a child, one of those school photos which look the same whether they were taken ten, twenty, thirty years ago. He would have been David's age, and looked a lot like him only more studious, not so cheeky. I stared into the face to see if it revealed anything of the man he would eventually become. But he looked like all the other kids. Big teeth, eyes squinting in the sun. It was a small country school, the whole school assembled for the photo, all fifteen kids, most of them barefoot. A couple of photos and a dinner set which, like my mother, I would probably never use, were the only solid evidence I had that he had ever existed.

21

I sat gloomily looking into the water. Well at least I was sober. Yeah, that was a real comfort.

I would get the death certificate. Perhaps seeing it in print might give me the sense of finality I needed to break the old habits. Like my son, I wanted 'proof'.

I pulled my legs up just in time, narrowly avoiding the wake from one of those stupid little jet skis. Mopeds on water. Only the people who speed along in them wouldn't be seen dead on mopeds. I stood up. Tomorrow I was meeting a prospective client, that was something to look forward to. Sure. As if anyone comes to a private investigator bearing good news.

The Births Deaths and Marriages Registry was in Thomas Street, Haymarket; about five minutes walk from the Hoyts Cinema where I was meeting Rosa, the woman who'd phoned. There were still one or two streets left in Haymarket that were seedy enough to give the area character. Real life went on here, trucks unloaded, shopkeepers took delivery, customers flocked to buy their wares. Most of the shops were Chinese supplies shops which sold herbs and pharmaceuticals, or groceries with fruit and vegetables out front.

On the corner across the road from the Registry Office was the building that housed the Burlington Centre, where you could get any number of household items, most of them Asian in style. There were also lots of restaurants—Indonesian, Thai, Chinese—and a variety of other shops: Sincere Real Estate, PN Productions which explained its wares—sheepskin seat covers and sheepskin products—in Chinese and English, hairdressing salons, Laser Video and a Tax Agent. Chinatown, a little urban ecosystem all of its own.

It was warm inside the Registry, an airless, fuggy kind of warmth, artificially created, supposedly to make life more pleasant. How people could work in here eight hours a day without falling asleep was beyond me.

The quickest you could get a certificate over the counter was three hours. Legally that is. And on this occasion I didn't need to do it any other way. I could fill out the form then come back after meeting the client.

I filled out the yellow Death Certificate Application form. There was a place to queue but hardly anyone was there at that hour so I went straight to the counter and handed over the form, plus the forty dollars required for an urgent application.

Then I made my way up George Street. There were three cinema complexes in a row down this end of town. The closer you got to Town Hall, the flashier the cinemas got. The cinema complexes gave rise to other diversions: fast food outlets, including a Japanese takeaway that, while smaller, had the same sterile atmosphere as McDonalds, and, the main diversion, video arcades. Beside the Japanese restaurant was Galaxy World with a list of House Rules—Proper Behaviour, Clean and Tidy Dress, No Bare Feet, No Food or Drink, No Smoking. Most of the people in here were young and male. A group of Vietnamese dressed in smart casual gear all hovered around the one machine, a few young dudes in suits playing their own individual machines.

Still fifteen minutes to go before I was to meet the client. I went in, just for a look. There were large screens with lots of action happening on them. People were playing the machines as if their lives depended on it. In the world of virtual reality, they probably did. No-one talked to anyone, the machines consumed all the interest. In five years time I'd probably find my son in here.

It was ten to eleven when I walked into the Hoyts Cinema complex. Seven cinemas, a cafe, bar, toilets, icecream counter, more video games—you could practically live in it. I wove through the queues of people lining up to buy tickets to the eleven o'clock movies and went into the cafe. I ordered a cup of coffee and sat down in a position that gave me a good view of what was going on. The clientele was not that much different from those in the video arcades across the road. Unemployed or wagging school—they were of that age when they could have been either. Some were watching previews on the bank of video screens, others playing the games machines. In here it was all virtual reality. At least they weren't out stealing cars.

Eleven o'clock precisely. The people in the queues were in the cinemas now. I casually perused the place. The woman had sounded nervous, anxious. Perhaps she wouldn't come. She hadn't left a number, there was no way I could get in touch with her.

As soon as I saw the dark-haired, dark-eyed woman weave her way through the crowd of kids and enter the cafe, I knew it was her. She looked vaguely familiar but I was sure I'd never met her before. 'Rosa?'

'Yes,' she smiled, relieved.

I offered her a seat and asked if she wanted something. 'Just coffee,' she said. I signalled the man behind the counter to bring two coffees. Usually you went to the counter to get served but as we were the only two in there, I didn't think he would mind the trip. Besides, this was Sydney. In Sydney you can get anything you like. If you wanted sauteed orang-utan the waiter would go out and get it for you. With cream.

There was a cloud of worry behind Rosa's eyes and a darkness beneath them. Her curly hair was cut short, short enough to show the thin gold rings through her pierced ears. She had on a flowered dress in shades of brown and russet, and a beige jacket over the top. Matching beige handbag that she held on her lap.

'You're Claudia Valentine,' she said, to make absolutely sure. The kind of checking and double-checking of a person in an unfamiliar situation.

'Yes,' I smiled assuringly, 'that's right.' I handed her one of my business cards. We made some small talk about the weather, about the movies being a good place to go on hot days because of the airconditioning.

'I'll be out back,' said the waiter as he delivered the coffees. 'Just give me a call if you need anything.'

We were left alone. But still Rosa seemed reluctant to start. She told me instead about the long trip into the city. The bus from Lugarno, where she lived, then the train from Riverwood. Lugarno was a southern suburb of Sydney, on the Georges

River, with water views. On the social map of Sydney, wealth but no status. Once full of fibro fishermen's sheds and week-enders, now there were grandiose houses. I'd been there once but it was a long time ago.

From where I was sitting I was able to look beyond Rosa to the people standing in a loose semicircle around the preview screens. I think a new batch of kids had arrived but they looked the same as the old ones. However, there was one person who hadn't been there before. He had the thick black curls that I usually find attractive but the rest didn't quite make the grade. He was thin as a snake and wearing reflective sunglasses. Something spivvy about the way he was dressed. It wasn't the checked jacket or the black shirt, the cream slacks or woven shoes, rather the way these items were put together. There must have been surroundings he'd look good in but it wasn't here. The way he was standing he could have been looking at the screens. Could be looking this way, too. Hard to tell with the glasses.

I'd started my pocket cassette recorder going the minute Rosa had sat down but I'd run out of tape if she didn't start soon.

'What can I do for you, Rosa?'

It took her a while before she finally said: 'My cousin Anna said I should call you. Anna Larossa.'

I'd now received a cheque from Anna Larossa, no questions asked. The case was over. Except here was her cousin sitting across the table from me. I remained silent. I didn't know what Anna had told her. For all I knew she might have just said she'd seen my name in the Yellow Pages.

'Can you find a missing person?' As if she'd misplaced her wallet or lost an umbrella. But the way she said it, she was talking about someone close—a husband, a child. 'Missing person' made it easier to talk about them without collapsing in a heap. But only just.

'Depends who it is and what leads there are,' I said, sympathetic but businesslike. The guy with the sunglasses had changed position but he was still hanging around.

'It's my daughter. Madalena. I'll show you.' She opened the handbag sitting on her lap. The man was looking this way.

Something told me that the last thing she should do was pull out that photograph.

'Not now,' I said hurriedly. 'Do you have a Kleenex?' I said suddenly. She looked puzzled but reached into her bag and handed me a couple of tissues. I blew my nose and put the tissues in my pocket. 'Thanks.' Then more softly, 'Does anyone know you've come here today?'

'No,' she said.

'We're going to the movies. Don't show any surprise, I'll explain later.'

We stood up and walked to the box office. We got tickets straightaway. It was 11.20, the ads and previews would be over, the movie about to begin. He watched us queue and he watched us enter the cinema. I chose seats right up the back. I leaned close to Rosa and said in a low voice, 'In a minute a man is going to walk in here, black curly hair, checked jacket, sunglasses maybe. Tell me if you recognise him.'

He came in. Stood there for a minute, deciding what to do. The screen throws light on the faces of the people watching the movie. The best way of finding someone is to go right down the front and look back. But then you're visible too.

He wasn't going down the front. He looked this way but I wasn't sure if he'd spotted us or not. The light from the screen starts to peter out back here. A couple came in behind him. He moved forward and sat down in a seat next to the aisle. Not real smart. He now had his back to the exit. He looked around. This time I'm sure he saw us. He turned back to watch the movie.

'No,' said Rosa, 'I don't know this man.'

It was an action movie starring Sylvester Stallone. Not my first choice but then we weren't here to watch the movie. Onscreen explosions momentarily lit up the audience even more. I thought he might look around but he didn't. There were more explosions that seemed to last forever, then Stallone started crawling through the undergrowth. The dark undergrowth. Time for us to go.

We made our way to the end of the row then slipped out the other exit. Maybe he was really enjoying the movie, maybe he'd decided we were just two friends having a cup of coffee then seeing a movie. Maybe I'd noticed the luscious hair and the rest of it was sheer coincidence.

We walked out of the cinema complex, down George Street, then turned into the street where my car was parked. 'I hope I didn't alarm you. I guess I made a mistake. There's no reason why anyone should be following you, is there?'

'No. No . . .' In the second 'no' was a small seed of doubt.

'We can talk and drive,' I said, opening the passenger door for her.

'But I need to buy some material,' she protested, 'in case my husband . . .'

'In case your husband what?'

'In case my husband asks where I was today.'

The domestic situation didn't sound good. 'Well, we can sit in the car and talk.' She got in. I closed the door and came round to the driver's side. First thing I did when I got in was look in the side mirror. Then the rear vision mirror. No-one. He was probably still in there watching Sly save the world.

'You were going to show me a photo of your daughter,' I said, bringing us right back to where we'd left off.

She opened her bag again and took out a photo. She held it between us, not wanting to let go. A pretty, smiling girl. The family resemblance was obvious. In the photo she was wearing a simple dress with lace sleeves, flowers in her dark hair, a bridal bouquet in her hands. She couldn't have been much older than Amy.

'It was taken last year at a family wedding. Madalena caught the bouquet, you can see she is so happy. I made this dress for her. It was a big wedding. So much food, so many people!' The smile died on her face and she fell into silence. I glanced in the mirrors again.

'All the bad things come at once. My husband has worries at work, our house is robbed and Madalena disappears.'

'When did she disappear?'

'Ten days ago now.' She pulled her gaze away from the photograph and looked blankly out the window.

'Have you informed the police?'

'No. No.' She spoke quickly, dismissing the possibility of police involvement.

'Would there be a problem with that?' I asked.

'My husband wouldn't want the police. He wouldn't want people to think there are problems in the family.'

'Are there problems?'

'Not more than any family. Madalena is fifteen, she wants to go out with her friends. He doesn't like that, he doesn't like her friends. No-one is good enough for Madalena. He thinks maybe her friends robbed the house.'

'When was the robbery?'

'The day after she disappeared.'

Maybe it wasn't a robbery at all. 'Did he go to the police about the robbery?'

She shook her head.

'What happened the day she went missing?'

'She went to play netball at another school. She didn't come back.'

'Which school?'

'Concord.'

I didn't like the sound of it. After the game, walking to the station in her sports uniform. Maybe she doesn't know the area very well. Looks lost, someone stops and offers to give her directions, offers her a lift. It only takes a minute.

'The day before that, Madalena and my husband had a big fight.'

'What was that about?'

'The tattoo. I didn't like it either. She said she'd had it done weeks ago. Up here,' Rosa said, indicating her upper arm. 'If she is wearing something with sleeves it's not visible. But with the hot weather she forgot and my husband saw it. He told her to get out of the house but he didn't mean it. He didn't mean it,' she repeated, trying to convince me. Rosa was on the edge, one little breath would be enough to blow her over. 'I want to see her, I want to know she is OK, you know?'

It was getting hot and claustrophobic inside the car. 'You want to buy material?' I said. 'There's a good place not far from here. Brocade, red lace, satin, tulle.' I was once hired by a tango dancer to go shopping, I know these things.

By the time we got to the fabric shop I had quite a bit of the story. I got the impression it was a relief for her to tell someone. She made a few quick purchases then I saw her to Town Hall station. I told her it was important that I come and look at Madalena's room. It would give me a feel for the kind of person Madalena was and maybe provide a clue or two. I assured Rosa I'd be discreet. The neighbours would just think I was a friend dropping in. Her husband need never know at all. It would have been best if I'd been able to talk to them both together, but Rosa didn't want that. She seemed afraid of him. It must have taken quite a bit of courage for her to come and see me. Before she got on the train she finally gave me the photo. I stayed there till the train disappeared around a corner of the tunnel, swallowed up by the darkness.

I walked back down Kent Street, mulling over what Rosa had told me. It might have been as simple as Madalena trying to teach her father a lesson. Pissing off for a while to put the wind up him. Perhaps she'd left for good, hitched up the coast, got on the dole and gone surfing. Perhaps she'd ring home when she was safely out of reach. I was trying to hold those thoughts in my mind to keep the darker, heavier one at bay. Occasionally, in shop windows, on telegraph poles, there are photos of smiling teenaged faces. Underneath is the word MISSING. The photos get tattered and torn, the faces fade into ghosts. No-one ever hears from them again, they simply disappear.

Till one day someone digs up a body.

Birth Death and Marriages. The three major events in a person's life, the beginning, middle and end, reduced to a sheet of paper with a government stamp on it.

```
DEATH CERTIFICATE
DECEASED      Family Name: Valentine
              Christian or Given Name(s): Guy Francis
              Date of Death: 25 April, 1985
              Place of Death: Rushcutters Bay, Sydney
              Sex and Age: Male
              Place of Birth:
              Period of Residence in Australia:
              Place of Residence:
              Usual occupation: Unemployed
MARRIAGE(S)
CHILDREN
PARENTS
MEDICAL       Cause of Death: Immersion
              Name of Certifying Medical Practitioner
              or Coroner: BJ Humphreys, State Coroner,
              Glebe
BURIAL        Date: 3 May, 1985
              Place: Rookwood Cemetery
INFORMANT     Name: Sgt. RW Hindley
              Address: Kings Cross Police Station
                       1a Elizabeth Bay Road
                       Kings Cross
```

31

There were so many gaps, so many of the details of his life unknown.

Immersion. Death by drowning. I had expected cirrhosis, any of the number of ways alcohol can kill you. But he drowned. Anzac Day. Big drinking day. Rushcutters Bay. Got drunk and fell into the water.

Had the police tried to get in touch with Mina or me, his 'next-of-kin'? They knew his name. Valentine. It's not as if it was Smith or Jones. They wouldn't have to go through too many names in the phone book. In 1985 I was in America. But Mina was around. Maybe she was out when they called and they left it at that. With a dero you don't try too hard.

I stared at the death certificate for so long that when I looked away I could still see the lines of print. I put it in a folder where I keep things I don't want to lose. Now, as well as the odd photo and a dinner set that had never been used, I had this piece of paper. It wasn't much to sum up a life.

People who live in the trendy harbourside suburbs, who truck off to Europe every second year, are more likely to be familiar with Lugarno, Italy, than Lugarno, Australia. Greystanes, Bidwill, Toongabbie. Lugarno. These are suburbs of Sydney that people who eat stuffed quail with ragout of fava beans, or lamb's heart on a bed of arugula drizzled with grilled capsicum puree, have never heard of, let alone been to. But Lugarno inhabitants are there for the same reason that trendies hug the harbour. For the waters.

Lugarno is on the Georges River, which empties into Botany Bay and from there into the Pacific Ocean, the same way the Parramatta River empties into Sydney Harbour. A mirror image, the rivers like symmetrical veins running along either side of the body. If Capt. Arthur Phillip, leader of the First Fleet, had founded the settlement where he was supposed to found it, we'd all be living in Lugarno. Which is not the way the present residents would have it. In Lugarno you have peace, quiet, water and wide open spaces. Across the river is a nature reserve. Typical Sydney basin vegetation—eucalypts, bottlebrush, rocks, wildflowers in spring, birds in all seasons. In the water itself are mangroves, oyster leases, pelicans, jellyfish, blackfish, bream, flathead, 'jumping' mullet and plastic bags, depending on what's running.

Down at the water level are fishermen's fibro shacks, some of them permanent dwellings, some weekenders. There are also old timber jetties and new aluminium boats. Up on the road are big houses, some of which look like mansions. Underworld figures such as Peter Farrugia and George Freeman, now both dead, once encased themselves in millionaires' mansions, complete with high security, in similar southern suburbs with water views. Neighbours reported they were quiet and kept to themselves. Of course they did. You don't shit in your own nest, you leave your dirty business uptown.

Not that I was expecting to meet any big crime figures when I pulled up outside Rosa Grimaldi's house. I was coming to see Madalena's room, look around, get a feel for the kind of person she was. See if there were any syringes hidden in geometry sets under the bed. I was wearing jeans, a patterned shirt and runners, nothing too inner city. Like I might have been a friend of Rosa's just dropping by. There weren't any other cars parked in the street. I guess everyone round here has a garage. There weren't any people in the street either, especially not men with reflective sunglasses.

It was a quiet street, the houses almost hidden behind bush and high fences. The Grimaldi abode belonged in the 'modest millionaire' bracket. There was an ornate arched gateway that I presumed would be locked but wasn't. Then you went up steps to a deck, or rather a pergola, dripping with grapevines and wisteria.

Rosa must have been peeping out the window because before I had a chance to press the buzzer, she was at the security door. 'Come in, come in,' she welcomed. She was much brighter and chirpier here on home ground.

'Coffee?' she said, leading me past a stuffed kangaroo, into the living room. There was a black umbrella sticking out of its pouch. I swear its eyes followed me as I passed by.

A marquetry inlaid table in the living room was already set up with coffee and cake. I sat down on the lounge while Rosa poured the coffee. She offered me milk, which I waved away, then started to cut into the cake. She put a slice on a plate decorated with gold leaf and handed it to me.

'Very healthy cake,' began Rosa, 'made with carrots. No butter, no sugar.' Yeah, I could tell that. 'I got the recipe from my cousin, Anna.' For a case that was supposedly closed it had an uncanny knack for popping open again. Now I was eating the woman's cake. 'She said she'd come over later.' Great, that'd be just great. I smiled wanly. 'Perhaps I could see Madalena's room,' I suggested.

'Is it always this tidy?' I asked. The bed was made, there was a shroud-like cover draped over a lounge chair. On the top of the ornate dresser little boxes, ornaments and a hand mirror were neatly arranged. On the back of the door were posters of Johnny Depp, Nirvana and Madonna in one of her more modest garbs.

Rosa looked at the rug on the floor and shook her head. 'When she was a little girl, it was always neat. She liked to make the bed, to sit her pyjama dog on the pillows, but the last months . . .' She held her hands out in a gesture of helplessness. 'The last six months, she doesn't care so much about keeping the room nice. I find food in her room, plates under the bed with sauce stuck so hard it doesn't come off in the dishwasher. She leaves Kleenex in her pockets. It makes a mess in the washing machine.' Rosa went on listing her daughter's peccadilloes without stopping for breath.

The room was presently spick and span. I would like to have seen it exactly the way Madalena had left it. Despite the blaring posters the room felt still and quiet. Nothing stirred. 'Did you notice anything unusual when you cleaned up?' I asked.

'You mean the plate under the bed?'

That wasn't the kind of unusual I meant. I was going to have to start lifting covers up, opening cupboards, unscrewing jars and bottles, looking in drawers. I was going to have to invade this child's privacy. For that reason, I preferred Rosa remain in the room. I'd never worked on a case involving a missing child before but I'd had occasion to look through people's rooms. I worked more quickly, efficiently, on my own but if there was something to be discovered I wanted Rosa to see it being discovered. If I found a syringe, condoms, any of the things that parents would rather not find in their kids' bedrooms, I wanted her to discover it the same time I did. I didn't want her denying it, calling me a liar, telling me her daughter would never do such a thing. Besides, she was the kid's mother, she'd want to stay. If it was someone going through Amy's room I'd be watching like a hawk.

'I'm going to have to look through her things, do you mind?' I asked as a matter of courtesy.

'Please. Go ahead,' invited Rosa. She stood back, out of my way but watching.

I started with the drawers of the dresser, lifting things and replacing them carefully so the disturbance was kept to a minimum. There were mainly socks and underwear in the top left-hand drawer. In the right-hand drawer was an assortment of objects, a kind of 'junk' drawer—the butt end of an eyeliner, a few safety pins one through the other to form a chain, pencils, a packet of photos.

I took the photos out and had a look. They all seemed to have been taken on the one day. Girls leaning into each other, holding up their fingers in peace signs, exaggeratedly posed with hands on hips. Half of them had a background of cliffs, and the other half were taken outside a milk bar. 'A school excursion,' Rosa explained. 'They went to Wollongong to look at rocks for science.'

As well as photos of the group there were a couple of Madalena and another girl by themselves. The others looked like babes in the woods compared to this girl. Though she was dressed in the same school uniform, she'd managed to arrange it in such a fashion that it looked like it was breaking all the school rules. The ear that was visible beneath the dyed red hair was studded with earrings and her eyebrows were plucked to a thin line.

'It's Madalena's "best friend",' said Rosa disparagingly. 'Kerry Wells. She lives at Peakhurst. In the last few months it's Kerry this, Kerry that. She goes out with boys, she goes to parties with no supervision. She is a bad influence on Madalena.'

'Have you spoken to her since Madalena disappeared?'

'I've never spoken to her.' And by Rosa's tone of voice she had no intention of speaking to her.

I kept the packet of photos aside and went back to the

drawer. I examined it thoroughly, lifted up the black wrapping paper with silver stars that was lining it. Nothing hidden under there. I got down to the bottom drawers. One contained T-shirts and the other jumpers. Rosa sat on the bed patting the empty pyjama dog but watching me closely. I looked behind the posters and in the wardrobe. There were three yellow blouses, presumably for school. A couple of formal dresses, an overcoat, jackets. On the floor of the wardrobe were shoes—a shaggy pair of split Reeboks that had done all the walking and running they were ever going to do, school shoes and a couple of pairs of dressy shoes.

'What clothes are missing?'

'The sports uniform, the school uniform, Doc Martens shoes, shorts and denim jacket. The backpack she took to school, jewellery, money. The contents of the coin jar—at least sixty dollars worth of one and two dollar coins. Thirty dollars which was payment for the gardener who comes once a month. Also about five hundred dollars in cash that her father kept in the pages of the bible.'

'She didn't take all that to school the day she disappeared, did she?' As Rosa talked I realised that she'd scrolled over into items stolen during the burglary.

'I'm sorry,' she apologised, 'I am confused. It is so . . . difficult.' She looked like she was on the verge of tears.

I sat down on the bed beside her. It seemed pretty clear to me who had robbed the house. It was pretty clear to Rosa too. 'How can she do this to us? Rob her own house, how can she do it?' She put her hand up to her eyes and wiped the tears away.

It might not necessarily have been Madalena in person, but it certainly looked like an inside job. 'Rosa, look at it this way. If she came back to rob the house at least she is still alive.'

Rosa sighed. It was cold comfort but better than no comfort at all.

I looked through the cassettes and CDs—Pearl Jam, Nirvana, Sonic Youth. But there was nothing to play them on.

'That went too,' sighed Rosa. 'A portable CD player. CD, cassette and radio, all in one. We bought it for her last

Christmas. Three hundred dollars,' she said, shaking her head as if Madalena didn't appreciate it. Madalena appreciated it only too well. She probably wouldn't get the full value of it at the pawnshop but at least it would be something.

Seemed odd though, the sequence of it. If you're going to piss off you take it all with you. You don't leave then come back the next day to rob the place. But then, whoever said that the thought processes of a fifteen year old were logical?

Below the cassettes were two shelves of books. Maths and science, Shakespeare, *Wuthering Heights*, books she was studying at school. On the bottom shelf I found the personal reading material—Stephen King, Ann Rice, a few fantasy novels, a stack of WHO magazines, the standard stuff a teenager reads. A book lay on top of the magazines, as if she'd been reading it, or had set it aside for some reason. I picked it up. *The Lost World of Agharti* by Alec Maclellan. Sounded like pretty standard fantasy stuff too. I opened it up. On the title page was a handprinted name—Rafael Khan. Perhaps she had the book out ready to return it to him.

I showed it to Rosa. 'Do you know him?'

Rosa peered at it. 'No.'

'Did Madalena have a boyfriend?'

'Of course not, she's too young.' She seemed shocked that I'd even suggested it.

I felt the pillows and the pyjama dog, and found nothing. 'I'd like to look under the mattress, would you give me a hand?' I said. She stood up, slightly bewildered.

'What do you need to do that for?'

'Just to see if there's anything there. A plate of pasta, for example,' I said, trying to make light of it. There was nothing under the mattress.

'Did she have a geometry set?'

'You mean compasses, ruler, things like that?'

I nodded. That's precisely what I meant. Compasses, set squares, protractors. It's the last place a parent would go looking for a syringe. And at a cursory glance it would probably look like another measuring instrument.

'Yes, she did,' said Rosa. 'A bag about like this . . .' she held up her hands to form a rectangle about 30 centimetres long, '. . . with a tartan check. Made from heavy fabric. I made it for her myself.'

She looked around, opened drawers, moved the books on the bookshelves. 'It's not here.' Didn't mean anything. It was probably in her schoolbag the day she disappeared. The more I examined the room, the less I felt that any serious drug-taking had gone on in here. The room didn't have the dense, disturbed atmosphere of such places. Mind you, it doesn't take much to get rid of it. A bit of a vacuum and a dusting down of the walls will clear the air. And Rosa would have done that when she cleaned the room up.

I looked out the window. Madalena's bedroom was at the back of the house. I could see the river and the bushland on the other side. You couldn't see right the way to the end of the block of land from here because it sloped steeply down.

'What's down the back?' I asked idly.

'Right down?'

Yes, I nodded.

'The jetty. And the shed.'

'What's in the shed?'

'The boat, just an aluminium dinghy, and a few other things. You want to see?'

I wished she'd told me about the 230 steps. The ones on the way down weren't so bad. I was thinking about the ones on the way up. I keep fit by doing karate but lately, with the wedding and the kids being with me, my daily routine had fallen by the wayside.

Once down there it was like being in another world. 'When Arturo and I first came here,' Rosa started, 'we lived in the shed. We worked hard, we built the house. Then the children came . . .'

'Children?' Plural? I'd assumed Madalena was the only one. There'd been no mention of another child.

Rosa looked at the ground and began to move her foot in a slow circular motion as if trying to smooth out some imperfection in the old timber boards of the jetty. 'Roberto.

He would have been twelve this Christmas Day. He was born on Christmas Day. Twelve years ago this Christmas.'

'What happened?' I softly asked her.

She looked across at the bushland on the far side of the river. 'He drowned,' she said, simply stating the fact.

The word hit me like a gong. The sound widened out and dissolved in the lapping water. 'My father drowned,' I told her.

'I'm sorry.'

'Roberto. Was it . . . here?'

Without moving her head or shifting her gaze she waved her hand in a vague direction off to the right. 'Further up. Madalena was five, Roberto three. It was a big barbecue. All the family was here, Anna and John, uncles and aunts, all the children. With all those people you think someone is always keeping an eye on the children. There was a group down here, there were people at the house. Many people. Roberto must have wandered off.' She paused, still looking across the river.

'Madalena came up to the house and said, "Roberto's lying in the water and he won't get out." Arturo and I flew down those stairs. And there . . .' She stopped again, composing herself for what had to be said, and had been said many times before. 'Roberto was lying face down in the water, very close to the edge. In his little hand he was clutching a blue straw.' She sighed. 'He must have seen the straw in the water and reached out to grab it. We called the ambulance, we tried to revive him but . . .' Rosa's voice drifted away.

She turned abruptly. 'Come. I'll show you the shed.' We walked back a little way from the jetty to the shed. There was a padlock on the door but it wasn't secured. Inside were a couple of aluminium dinghies leaning up against a wall with a couple of pairs of oars nearby. There were some fishing rods, an old pair of gumboots that probably belonged to Arturo.

'Anything in the cupboard?' I asked.

'Nothing much. Have a look.'

It contained a few rusty oarlocks, tools, lengths of wire, and other odds and ends that always seem to end up in sheds but serve no discernible purpose. I moved around, just to be thorough, but there didn't appear to be anything in here that might help me find Madalena.

I wondered how Madalena felt about the river, whether discovering her brother the way she did had left its scars. 'Did Madalena use the boat?'

'Yes. Sometimes. For a long time after Roberto died Arturo wouldn't let her anywhere near the water. When he was home, he wouldn't let her out of his sight. She thought it was because he blamed her for it but it wasn't true. He just didn't want to lose her the same way. I told him he had to stop this. The doctor even told him to relax, get a hobby. Go fishing, that's what the doctor advised,' she said with a touch of irony. 'So, we started to go in the boat again. Madalena got bored quickly with the fishing but she liked the boat. She would sit there, trailing her hand in the water. Dreaming whatever children dream. Sometimes she and I would make up stories about bushes and trees on the other side. You know, if you look hard they make animal shapes. But then Arturo would tell us to be quiet, we were scaring the fish,' Rosa smiled. 'I don't know why it would make a difference, the fish back in those days would practically jump on the line. Now Arturo leaves them alone. He doesn't come home, always at work.' Rosa laughed derisively. 'It's better that way. When he comes home he drinks grappa and gets angry. So I go and see Anna. She likes the company, her husband is away a lot.' Yes, and I knew where.

'What work does your husband do?'

'He has the restaurant, La Giardinera in Leichhardt. And he has other properties.'

The trip down here hadn't yielded any material clues about Madalena but it had told me quite a lot. We came out of the shed and Rosa closed the door behind her.

'Please find my daughter,' she said suddenly. 'If she doesn't want to tell us where she is, if she doesn't want to come home . . . I will accept it. I just want to know she is all right. I just want to know she's . . . alive.'

We walked back up the 230 steps in silence. They were every bit as bad as I thought they'd be.

41

D anny, you're joking. We may as well take it out to a field and shoot it.' My mechanic had phoned, to talk about the Daimler. The more Danny worked on the car the more he found. It wasn't just the gasket anymore, it was going to require a major overhaul. Danny had promised the Daimler would be ready today, I had already returned the hire car. I felt stunned, as if I'd gone to the doctor with a sore throat and been told I had cancer. 'It's going to cost you a packet if you want to get it passed rego. However, if you sell it to me . . .'

Danny had made the offer before. He'd buy it from me for a few thousand dollars, do it up, with all the trims, and bring it back to original condition. Then he'd sell it to a collector for ten times as much.

'I'll think about it, Danny.' Mina was selling the house, maybe it was time for me to sell the car.

'Serious?' I told him I was. 'Great. What are you doing for wheels in the meantime? I can lend you a car if you like.' This was the first time he'd ever offered me a replacement vehicle. All generosity now that I was saying I'd think about it instead of a straight-out no.

'I should be OK for a day or two. You'll at least have the Daimler running by then, won't you?' I hinted. 'I want to take it for one last drive.'

I felt virtuous going to Rookwood Cemetery by train, as if I was on a pilgrimage. The way to the cemetery is lined with businesses making a living from the dead—Andrews Memorial Co; Italian Monuments: All Welcome; Star Memorial: Modern, Traditional and Special Ethnic Designs in all Cemeteries; and one of my personal favourites—Monumental Masons, great name for a rock band. As I walked along I could see the headstones lined up in the yard waiting to be delivered. All the dates were recent, within the last month. Down the street was Pleasant Stay Motor Inn, and Globe Memorial, specialising in Monuments and Lettering, Marble and Granite Work, Kitchen Bench Tops.

I turned the corner, crossed the road and entered the clay-coloured gates. In black letters on a gold plate it said: ROOK-WOOD NECROPOLIS. The city of the dead. From the sandwich shop across the road the smell of onions and beetroot wafted.

The first set of graves along Necropolis Drive were old, nineteenth century graves overgrown with dry weeds. Some of them were caving in, their headstones fallen over, the bricks surrounding them sinking into the ground as rain and scorching sun altered the shape of the landscape. Even though I knew I wouldn't find my father in this part of the cemetery, occasionally I looked at the graves as I passed by. Sarah Vickers, died 11th Dec, 1885. Aged two months. There were a lot of baby graves from that era.

The road curved round to more recent times, affording an overall view of weathered headstones, large and small, in a field of yellow daisies and purple native flowers. Beyond that the trees on the park-like area of the cemetery pushed into a hot, bright blue sky with a smear of vapour too thin to be called cloud. I trudged along in the heat, waving away a halo of flies.

By the time I got to the twentieth century I was forgetting about the joys of public transport and wishing I'd taken up Danny's offer of a car. I didn't even have my mobile phone with me to call a cab. I hadn't thought I'd need a mobile phone in a cemetery. Rookwood covered 312 hectares and by the end of the morning I must have walked over every centimetre of it.

The death certificate told me that Guy was at Rookwood, but not the specific location. The city of the dead divided up according to religion—Catholic, Church of England, Independent, Jewish, Greek Orthodox. It was itself a smaller version of the living city. Old, dilapidated parts of town, trendy inner city areas with rows of graves close to each other like rows of terrace houses, sprawling suburbs with elaborate headstones, neat, uniform black granite with white writing, some structures that looked like miniature castles for the ghost to roam at night, messages and goodbye wishes of every kind engraved into the stone, crucifixes, cherubs, gold roses. There was even a Chinatown with a distinctive green and red pagoda at the entrance and Chinese ideographs etched in gold on the pink–brown artificial marble headstones. Other graves in Chinatown were surrounded by white pillared fences. Chinatown had the best views. From here you could see back to the city—arc of the Harbour Bridge, the cluster of tall buildings, small and insignificant from this distance.

As I made my way to the Catholic information office I passed a row of identical graves—grey stone, crucifixes on top and full-length crucifixes on the tombs themselves. Something about it reminded me of knights and the crusades. These were the graves of Catholic clergy, a community of brothers, together in death as they had been in life.

In the office they looked up the date of burial but they couldn't find my father's name. They looked a few days either side but he did not appear in their records. 'Are you sure he's buried in this section?' they asked. No, I wasn't sure. Sorry, but they couldn't help me. I'd have to try one of the other religions.

'Isn't there a central computer? Don't you guys interface with the other religions?' The heat was making me short-tempered. 'What about the World Council of Churches?'

I trudged off, waving flies from off my face. I tried the Church of England, the Independents, the Greek Orthodox. I was hot, thirsty and sweaty. I wouldn't have minded lying beneath a cooling slab of marble myself. Three-quarters of a million bodies out here. I must have walked by all of them.

It wasn't till I was unsuccessfully walking away from the Jewish section that I came across the sign to the Crematorium. My last resort. I trudged up the road.

There were birds twittering and the opulent, velvety smell of rose bushes. There were curved brick walls with name plaques, highrise dwellings compared to the sprawling suburbs of graves. Past the walls I saw the roses themselves, luscious and pink. Sturdy, handsome plants, the pride of any gardener. Each of them bore a plaque in remembrance of a loved one. Some of the best blood and bone in Sydney fertilised those rose bushes. They formed part of an ordered Mediterranean-style garden with trees, bushes and little paths leading to a central fountain. Squatting on the rim of the fountain, dipping its beak into the water, was a fat black raven.

The Mediterranean theme was continued in the portico, potted plants and flagstones of the crematorium office and chapel complex. There were rest rooms, a Coca-Cola machine and, joy of joys, a water fountain. Outside the west chapel entrance was a party of elderly gents with so many medals and RSL badges on their lapels it made their suits lopsided. Suits, despite the weather. But then they'd probably come in air-conditioned cars. The women in the party wore their best summer dresses.

I noticed the refreshing drop in temperature as soon as I entered the office.

'What can I do for you?' said the pleasant chap at the counter.

'I'm looking for my father. For his remains,' I corrected myself. I gave him the necessary details.

He opened a big register, looking up briefly at the sound of someone coming in the door. Being a person who always wants to know who is standing behind me, I turned to have a look. A sober-looking man in dark glasses and driving gloves, with some paperwork in his hand. The driver of the hearse that had just pulled up in the driveway.

The man behind the counter was turning pages and repeating

softly to himself, 'Third, third.' I was following as best I could. In my job you get pretty good at reading things from all possible angles, even hand-written material as the entries in the register were. But the way he was holding the book, I could only see the first couple of lines. 'Yes, here we are. 3rd May.' I saw his eyes move down one column then the next. He started to shake his head then he stopped. 'Valentine. Guy Valentine?'

I don't know which came first, the rippling feeling in my chest or the tears in my eyes. Hearing this man say his name, like a small dense bubble bursting in my face. The man behind me was getting impatient. He had business to attend to. 'Yes,' I said briskly, 'that's right.' He gave me the relevant coordinate points.

'Thanks.' I walked out into the heat again, crossing in front of a woman and two children who were heading for the RSL party. The boy and girl had identical silky red hair. They were wearing baggy shorts and cool sleeveless tops, the spitting image of the woman. Daughter and grandchildren of the deceased. Everything shifted out of focus for a moment, then I saw the scene with crystal clarity. It was me and my children heading towards that group of people. Guy's funeral. Here, now. Everyone gathered, his buddies, his daughter, grandchildren. Sad occasion, they were murmuring, great bloke. And Brian was making a eulogy. Except . . . these people were complete strangers and my father had been dead for years.

I made my way through the rose garden to the wall. 'In loving memory of Walter, loved husband of Kathleen . . .' I continued along, looking at the bricks.

GUY VALENTINE, 25 APRIL, 1985. It was down low to the ground, I had to bend to read it. There was no loving memory engraved on this one. I put my hand on the plaque, felt the coldness of the metal. I'd walked all over the city of the dead looking for my father. And now I had found him. His ashes in this wall of ashes, of people who in life may have been rich, poor, famous, happy, sad. I pressed my fingers on his name. In loving memory. When I took my hand away my moist fingers had left traces in the film of dust.

I don't know what it was about the Anna Larossa case, but I couldn't seem to get away from it. Here I was back in Strathfield, but not outside the Larossa house. Outside Madalena's school. I was sitting in a borrowed Mazda. After Rookwood I'd decided to take up Danny's offer of a car. I mean, who's ever heard of a PI getting around on public transport? Danny had a range of cars at his disposal. He'd offered me the sleek black 1965 Valiant with purple Gothic trim, but I settled on the more modest Mazda.

I'd only ever run away from home once. The issue was broad beans. I emptied the contents of my sock drawer into my school bag. 'I'm going to find Dad,' I'd shouted at Mina, 'he wouldn't make me eat those beans!' I stormed out of the house, all set for adventure. Imagine what a good omen I took it to be when I espied a bright, shiny five cent piece lying in the middle of the footpath. Decimal currency had only just come in then and all the coins were brand spanking new. I felt like Dick Wittington going to London where the streets were paved with gold.

I didn't get to London, I only got as far as the corner store. I spent ages looking at the big jars of lollies. Then, and I recall this moment as being my first experience of logical reasoning, I considered my situation. I was leaving home, I didn't know where my next meal was coming from, so I'd better spend that money wisely. I would forgo the lollies and buy something more sustaining.

'A packet of chips, please,' I said, holding my five cents up to the counter.

I scoffed the lot, sitting at the bus stop, before Mrs Papadopoulos came by in her car and offered me a lift home. I had to take up the offer, she knew I wasn't allowed to catch the bus by myself.

When I snuck back in, Mina was watching television as if nothing had happened. When the first ad break came on she said, 'Your dinner's in the oven. If you're still interested.'

With a whole bag of chips sitting heavily on my stomach, the last thing I wanted to do was eat dinner. But as she seemed prepared to forget my little temper tantrum, how could I refuse? 'Hmm, thanks Mum, don't mind if I do.'

I could see the plate through the glass in the oven door. The chicken leg was still there, and the carrots and mashed potato. But the broad beans had gone. In my haste to get the door opened I burnt my hand. I stood in the kitchen flicking my hand back and forth, my lips tight, face squeezed up, trying to suppress an outcry of pain.

'Oven's still a bit warm,' my mother's voice wafted in. 'You'll probably need to use the gloves. They're on the bench.' How did she know—could she see through walls?

I turned on the tap and stuck my fingers under the stream of water. 'Just getting a glass of water.'

I came back into the lounge room and forced the dinner down.

It wasn't till we were doing the washing up that she said, 'And where were you going to start looking for your father?' At the same time she handed me a plate to dry.

'Oh. Look in the phone book, I guess.'

'And what if you didn't find him there?' I don't know if it was her tone of voice or the actual questions, but I was beginning to feel distinctly uncomfortable.

'I dunno.' I shrugged my shoulders, hoping she'd take the hint, and spent a lot of time wiping the same plate. But it played on my mind. After, when I'd had a bath and put on my pyjamas and was snuggled up in bed, I asked her: 'Why doesn't he ever come to see us?' And Mina told me.

This is what I was thinking about as I sat outside the school waiting for Kerry to appear. The visit to Madalena's house, the family background, the robbery which looked like Madalena coming back for money and personal items—the more I was convinced that she hadn't been abducted, she'd left of her own accord. And if this was the case, her friends would be more likely to know where she was than her parents or teachers. Whether the friends were prepared to tell an adult what they knew was another matter. Amongst themselves kids share confidences and sometimes break them, but they rarely betray each other to an adult. After all, this was the generation they were going to have to live with in the outside world. I wanted to get to know Kerry, from a distance, before I talked to her.

The school was a stately sandstone building like a huge manor house. It didn't exactly frown, but you did get the feeling it was watching to see that you behaved yourself. Even the fact that this was the last week of term and it would soon be child-free didn't lighten its mood. I looked at my watch—3.20 pm. In five minutes the school day would be over. Some early leavers, for the variety of mysterious reasons kids are let go early, had already started trickling out. I was sitting at the exit closest to the train station. There'd probably be about five hundred girls coming through these gates in a minute, but that didn't bother me. I knew which one I was looking for.

Out they came, the five hundred, all looking like soft little canaries in their grey and yellow uniforms. Twittering like canaries as well. Lebanese girls, Indians, Chinese, Korean, Italian. An Anglo girl with dyed red hair wasn't going to be that difficult to find.

Almost every girl in the school must have passed through that gate before I saw Kerry and her group sauntering across the well-manicured grounds. There were five of them and Kerry was the tallest. She had long bronzed legs, set off by yellow socks, and carried herself well. The other girls were hanging on her every word, but she didn't give a shit.

49

The group got closer to the gate, walking along, suddenly bursting into laughter and putting their hands up to their faces. They came out and turned in the direction of the station, oblivious to everything around them. They were in Year 10, they'd had four years of walking this exact same path. They looked like they could have done it blindfolded.

I didn't really want to cruise down the street following a group of schoolgirls in my car, so I got out and continued on foot. I followed them into Strathfield Plaza. There were lots of schoolkids in here, boys and girls licking recently purchased icecreams and chomping into battered saveloys, doing wonders for their pimples.

One of Kerry's group broke off and lined up in the icecream shop. The rest of them hung around looking idly in the window of a boutique. It was all there again, all that stuff from the seventies we laughed so much about in the eighties. The crocheted vests, the platform shoes and even, God forbid, the flared trousers. 'That's cute,' said a girl with a pudgy face and well-shaped eyebrows. Kerry stuck out her bottom lip as she considered the black crocheted vest.

'Nothing special,' she said, delivering her verdict in a blasé tone of voice. They kept moving, slowly, waiting for their friend buying the icecream. They looked in other windows. They weren't serious buyers, they were just using the Plaza as a more interesting way of getting to the station.

They were almost out the other side when the pudgy-faced girl looked over her shoulder in the direction of the icecream shop. 'Tamara's going to miss the train if she doesn't hurry.'

'She'll catch up,' said Kerry. 'C'mon, let's go, Gula.' The girl hesitated, torn between Tamara and Kerry. She followed Kerry. Into the station and down the ramp to the platform.

The few adults waiting for the train were far outnumbered by schoolkids. Not that that made me feel conspicuous. As far as the kids were concerned, adults were just part of the scenery. Like the benches, or the waiting rooms. They were there but completely outside the intrigues of the kids' world.

There was a bunch of pimply-faced boys in maroon jackets talking to the girls. Standing there in their long trousers, five foot tall trying to look six foot. The hand on the hip holding the blazer open, developing the swaggering kind of gait that would serve them well at the bar, the pub kind as well as the court kind. The pudgy-faced Gula suddenly went all giggly in the presence of these budding representatives of the opposite sex. The girls and boys bantered friendly insults back and forth. But Kerry showed little concern or interest. In fact, she appeared downright bored. The boys seemed wary of her, as if they instinctively knew she had it all over them.

There was a whoosh of breeze—a train approaching. Kerry looked down the line towards the city, the direction the train was coming from, then asked casually: 'Where's Tamara?' The other girls stopped flirting with the boys. Kerry had spoken. They looked around, at the entrance to the platform, anxious expressions on their faces. If Kerry was even the slightest bit worried, then they were too. The train was pulling in, slowing to a pneumatic halt. I folded my newspaper under my arm, a natural enough gesture if you're catching the train, and watched Kerry's face. She was still looking back towards the ramp. The doors of the train had parted now and people were getting off, trying to push their way past the throng of schoolkids crowding through. 'Honestly!' exclaimed a frustrated older woman, shoving her shopping past the kids who threatened to engulf her.

Except for Kerry, the others had forgotten all about Tamara. Their consuming interest at the moment was storming their way onto the train. My eyes flicked between Kerry's face and the entrance to the platform, saw real anxiety as she searched for the stray member of her flock. Is this the way it had been with Madalena? She stopped for an icecream then simply disappeared?

Kerry's face relaxed as Tamara came running down the ramp, icecream in hand, ponytail flying behind her. 'Jesus, Tamara,' said an exasperated Kerry. 'There was a queue,' Tamara explained feebly. She looked at Kerry, wondering what the big deal was. 'Go on,' said Kerry, closing off the conversation, 'get on the train.'

It wasn't necessary for me to stay on the train with her, I knew where she'd be getting off. Riverwood, the end of the line. I went back for the car and drove to Riverwood station. It was getting busier but it was still a little early for the full force of peak hour.

A bus pulled into Riverwood station and shuddered to a halt. The driver spread his newspaper out over the steering wheel and began to read, seemingly oblivious to a small grey-haired lady tapping on the door. No way he was going to open that door. He was off-duty, even if it was for only a few minutes.

I got out of the car and sat in the bus shelter, next to an enormously fat man who took up half of the bench that was built to accommodate four people. Despite the grey-haired lady's insistent tapping, the bus driver remained mute. Eventually she stopped and approached the bench. Usually when someone goes to sit on a public bench, those already on it move along to make room. I squeezed up beside the man but this man's mass remained immutable. I vacated the space altogether. Prolonged body contact with an unattractive stranger is not my favourite way of passing time.

The lady sat down, smiling in recognition of my good deed. The bus driver glanced at his watch then went back to the paper.

The lady dug into her voluminous bag and pulled out a book, *The Principles of Russian Formalism*. She'd only just opened the book when we heard the rumble that heralded the imminent arrival of the train. The bus driver folded the paper up and put it away. As the train pulled into the station he started the bus up and wheezed open the door. Quick as a flash the grey-haired lady sprung up.

I watched the people getting off the train. Hardly any schoolkids alighted, only Kerry and one of the boys in the maroon blazers. She gave him a cursory wave and he lurched off in the opposite direction. Kerry sauntered to the bus. She was in no hurry. The school hat was now perched right back on her head, her gloves were off and so was her belt. It was as grungy as you could get a uniform that was designed to be neat and 'ladylike'. She showed the driver her school pass and went up the back of the bus.

The fat man was in front of me, fiddling in his pockets.

Eventually he produced a stream of coins and the driver processed the ticket. I asked for a $2.50 fare. Peakhurst, where Kerry lived, couldn't be any more than that. I went up to the very back seat. Kerry was sitting, feet propped up, gazing out the open window. She didn't even give me a second look. The seat beside her was empty, as was most of this section of the bus. She was on her own now, no school, no group of admirers. No Madalena.

I watched Kerry the whole way to Peakhurst. She chewed her fingernails, gazing out the window, looking at nothing in particular. Then she pressed the button, indicating she wanted the next stop, and stood up. I did too.

I watched her open the gate and walk up a path either side of which grew weeds and a few stalky geraniums gasping for water. There was a verandah of weathered floorboards with a couple of black garbage bags sitting near the front door. The house looked like no-one lived there. She turned the key in the lock and went in.

I, **William Kirby**, a registered medical practitioner, carrying out my profession at the New South Wales Institute of Forensic Medicine in the State of New South Wales do hereby certify as follows:
At 8.00 hours, on the 26th day of April, 1985 at Sydney in the said State, I made a postmortem examination of **Guy Francis VALENTINE**.

   The body was identified to Mr P. Kennedy of the New South Wales Institute of Forensic Medicine by Sergeant Hindley of Kings Cross Station as that of Guy Francis VALENTINE aged about 55 years.

   The body was identified to me by the wristband marked D45197.

   The forensic assistant in this case was Miss S Theodourou.

I had in front of me more information about my father now he was dead than I ever had when he was alive. Or at least, information about his body, in microscopic and macroscopic detail.

   'EXTERNAL EXAMINATION' gave the body weight and length, body mass index and stated that 'the body was that of a middle-aged male of approximately stated age. Postmortem lividity was present on the front.' Lividity. After a person dies, the blood pools in those areas in touch with the surface on which the body is lying. He died lying face down.

   The description of injuries included minor cuts, abrasions,

contusions, an old surgical scar on the abdomen. And a skull fracture.

'INTERNAL EXAMINATION'—head and neck, cardio-vascular system, respiratory system, gastro-intestinal, hepato-biliary, haemopoietic, genito-urinary and finally the endocrine system. Specimens of tissue were retained for histology and blood for storage.

Facts. More chilling in their clinical objectivity than a lurid description.

I thought that visiting my father's grave would be enough to lay the ghost to rest but it wasn't. First of all, there wasn't a grave to visit, just a plaque on a brick in a wall. Second, you could know everything there is to know about a person's life but it's still not enough to bring them back from the dead. I was gathering documentation, visiting places. Somehow the attempt to lay the ghost to rest was becoming a case. A case in which I was both detective and client.

If I'd peeled back the layers of reasoning I might have found the real reason I was doing this—my own guilt and regret at never making serious attempts to find him while he was alive, despite the lip service I paid to that search. But peeling back the layers didn't happen till later, till events took the turn they did.

The deaths I come across in my line of work are rarely natural causes or accidental. Even taking into account my propensity to jump to the most suspicious conclusion, by the third time I'd read this postmortem document I didn't like it any better than the first time I read it.

I invited Lucy to lunch and brought with me the documents I'd obtained from the Institute of Forensic Medicine. I gave Lucy the postmortem report to read, minus the cover sheet which identified the body.

Lucy Lau wasn't a specialist in forensic medicine, she was a doctor with the Allergy Centre at Royal Prince Alfred Hospital, but she would at least know the meaning of the words. I kept having to go to a dictionary and then half the words weren't there. We went to a tiny down-market restaurant in Dixon Street, one of those places that have faded photos of the dishes pasted to the inside of the window. It was mostly noodle soup in various guises, with the solid meals all resembling crumbed pork chops.

While I fished around in my soup sorting the solids into known and unknown, Lucy managed to read the report, turning the pages with one hand and scooping pieces of fish and vegetable into her mouth with the other. Lucy was a busy person. Even when she wasn't busy she ate like a busy person. She had a quick metabolism, the food hardly touched the sides before it was being converted into the energy that fuelled this little fireball.

Once I'd put aside those rounds of white rubber edged in bright pink, the seafood equivalent of Spam, I watched Lucy's face. Quite frankly, I didn't think I could have eaten while reading this kind of material, but Lucy didn't miss a beat. When she got to the last page, she briefly referred to something in an earlier page then pushed the report aside. She frowned as she noticed that the only thing left in her bowl was a single bean sprout in a sea of chicken consomme. She exchanged her chopsticks for a spoon. 'Looks like the guy hit his head, fell in the water and drowned,' she announced. She put the ceramic spoon to her mouth and delicately drank the broth. 'Of course, there is always the possibility that he was pushed. Is it murder you're looking for?'

'Not particularly. I just want to get a general feel for the circumstances surrounding the death.'

Lucy had finished her soup now and was looking around for an ashtray. The woman who served us placed an anodised metal ashtray on the table. She lit her cigarette and drew back deeply. 'Only at mealtimes now,' she pointed out to me. 'They make it so difficult, I feel like a leper.' She looked at me quizzically. 'Is my smoking bothering you?'

'No.'

'What then?'

'The subject was presumed to be an alcoholic. I expected the body to show more signs of damage.'

'Well, I certainly wouldn't have said so on a superficial reading. Normal brain. Nothing remarkable about the liver.

Those are the places where alcohol damage usually shows up.'
She flipped over pages of the report and quoted. 'The liver
weighed 2850 grams. Some congestion.'
   'What's the "some congestion"?' I asked.
   'Mucus, fat, alcohol, pollution, whatever. With any guy that
age you'd expect some congestion. If you or I died tomorrow
they would probably find "some congestion", but with an
alcoholic there's normally more extensive damage than what's
reported here. Maybe he was lucky, or perhaps he was reformed
and the liver had repaired itself.' She flipped over to the
pathology sheet, and pointed out the blood alcohol level to me.
'If he was reformed, he busted the night he died. That blood
alcohol level wouldn't have passed the Random Breath Test.'
She stubbed out the cigarette and moved the ashtray to a
neighbouring empty table.
   He was over the limit but not a lot over. Not so bad that
he'd fall unconscious into the harbour and not be able to get
out again. The skull fracture. Maybe somehow he'd fallen and
hit his head in such a way that it knocked him unconscious.
But he'd just fall to the ground. To fall into the harbour he'd
have to have been walking along the seawall. A fifty-five year
old man walking along the seawall like a kid doing a balancing
act. It didn't ring true to me, even a drunk fifty-five year old
man.
   But there was much much more to it than that. I felt as if
I had pulled a loose thread and everything had started unrav-
elling. The whole fabric was coming undone. The whole story
that had been woven about my father. Maybe all that stuff
about my father being a dero was a myth, a fabrication, a story
Mina had told herself and I told myself, a blanket to soften
the impact of the hard truth. Because if he wasn't a dero, if
he wasn't an alcoholic, if he was alive and well and living in
Sydney, why had he never tried to contact us? To contact me.
Whenever my mother told me the story about him, which
wasn't often, it always ended with 'and we never heard from
him again'. Then she'd shut her mind as firmly as one shuts a
book when the story is finished.
   I replaced the missing top page of the report. Lucy gave it

a cursory glance then looked at it hard. 'Your father? I'm so sorry, Claudia.'

The woman serving us came and asked if we wanted anything else. 'Just the bill,' I said.

'Claudia,' said Lucy, 'one of my uncles, when he died, this woman and a teenage boy turned up at the funeral. She was married to my uncle and the boy was his son. But this uncle was married to my mother's sister, they had five daughters. No-one knew about this other wife and the boy. You can imagine the family's surprise. Sometimes it's not till someone dies that we find out the truth about their life.'

William Kirby, a registered medical practitioner, carrying out his profession at the New South Wales Institute of Forensic Medicine in the State of New South Wales, had now retired but he'd agreed to see me at his home.

His home, on Sydney's North Shore, was quite large. There was a lawn out front so green and immaculate it looked like artificial turf. Along the driveway was a stand of roses as brilliant as any you'd see in the Royal Botanic Gardens. He was watering them as I pulled up outside. He didn't look up till I closed the car door behind me. He was neatly dressed: cream slacks, white long-sleeved shirt, and a big garden hat. By the look of the skin cancer scars around his nose, he should have started wearing the protective clothing years ago.

I stood at the top of the driveway. Inhaling in long slow draughts, letting the scent of roses swish around whatever the smell equivalent of tastebuds are. I felt almost drunk. No wonder bees dive madly from flower to flower. How could he stand there idly watering? I allowed myself one more inhalation.

'Dr Kirby?'

'Come in,' he invited me down the garden path. The path was edged with low-growing flowers in shades of pink and red. If they had a perfume at all it was overwhelmed by the roses. He turned the tap off and rolled up the hose. 'I could get one of those sprinklers,' he said, 'but it wastes water. Besides, I like watering by hand, the spray is invigorating. Negative ions, you know.' I knew but I let him tell me anyway. He seemed to be one of those distinguished elderly gents who like to spout knowledge. Which is just what I wanted him to do. 'Come around the back,' he said, 'we can sit down there.'

The back garden was full of roses as well. The man was obsessed.

'Cleopatra had her bedroom knee-deep in rose petals. Any movement in the room, a light breeze through a window, the idle play of her hand, and more exquisite perfume would be released. She and Antony copulated, drowning in the ecstacy of bruised rose petals. Coffee?'

I wondered what he talked about when he really got to know you. I accepted the offer of coffee and sat down at a wooden table on the back verandah. He went inside. There was a rattling of cups. He came back out again with a tray of coffee and little crescent-shaped biscuits covered in icing sugar.

'We just don't have a vocabulary of smell as vast and intricate as the vocabulary for the other senses,' he said. 'The appreciation of smell occurs in the limbic brain, not the intellect. I have spent a lifetime dissecting, analysing and naming. I find the fact that smell eludes our attempts to define it enormously satisfying, don't you?'

'Mmm,' I murmured. Sure, doctor.

He poured the coffee with a steady hand and offered me the plate of biscuits. 'Kourabedes,' he explained. 'My wife makes them.' I accepted one. It was delicious, much better than the ones you buy in the shops. He was very sociable, as if he was used to people dropping in.

I made a few complimentary comments about the roses, took a sip of coffee, then placed the folder containing the postmortem report on the table. He took the cue.

'This is what you wanted to see me about?'

'Yes.' I flicked my thumb along my fingers to get rid of the powdery film of icing sugar, opened the folder and turned it around for him to read.

'A relative, Ms Valentine?'

'My father.'

'I see.' He read through the report, refamiliarising himself with it. When he finished he placed his hands on it and leaned forward slightly. 'This *was* a number of years ago. I hope I can still be of service.'

I didn't want to start with the possibility of murder. After all, he was the one who had examined the body and there was nothing in the report itself to indicate that the death wasn't accidental.

'I have only recently discovered that my father died. I wouldn't say there's a problem, it's just . . . '

'The need to know, is that it?'

I nodded.

'A common enough reaction. Even those who are present at a death go over and over it in their minds, wondering if there was anything they could have done to prevent it. They are the lucky ones. At least seeing the dead body gives a sense of finality.'

'How well do you recall the bodies you examine?'

'Examined,' he corrected me. 'I have been retired for a number of years.' He paused for a moment and inhaled the scent of his roses, distinguishing different varieties like a conductor distinguishing instruments in his orchestra. 'I'm sorry to say nothing immediately springs to mind with this one but let's have a closer look at what the report tells us.' He studied it in a little more detail then came to some sort of conclusion. 'Yes,' he said. 'I would have had to examine this body in some detail to ascertain the *exact* cause of death. Whether it was the blow to the head or immersion in water. Forensic medicine is a most precise science, Ms Valentine.'

'Is it possible that he might have been killed first then the body dumped in the water?' I voiced my suspicions.

'No, no, nothing like that,' he hastened to assure me, smile on his face as if I was a child who'd inadvertently said something amusing. 'It's obvious from the postmortem evidence that he drowned. Look,' he turned the report around so we could both read it. 'Oedema fluid in the pharynx, larynx, trachea and bronchi. Both lungs were oedematous. Oedema fluid noted in the nose.

'If he had been dead *before* immersion there would be no

oedema fluid. Oedema is excessive accumulation of serous fluid in the intercellular spaces of tissue. It occurs when the drowning person breathes in water. Even if he were unconscious he would breathe in water. If he had stopped breathing beforehand, if he had died as a result of the head wound, we would find small amounts of water that trickle in through the nose and mouth, but not enough to cause oedema.' He sat back, as if he'd just wound up a lecture.

Then the expression of satisfaction on his face changed to one of acute interest. A slow memory that had begun its journey while he was reading the report had now arrived at its destination.

'Actually . . . yes, that's right. Of course. Anzac Day, 1985. The floods. Do you remember?'

Not till he reminded me and not through personal experience. I was in America then and didn't hear about the floods till I returned. Like recalling exactly what you were doing when you heard that President Kennedy had been assassinated, everyone had their story about those floods.

'The city was in chaos,' he began, 'some of the main roads were virtual rivers. Parking was impossible, I was late for work. My first wife was a school teacher. She hated those times when it rained for days on end. The children would get . . . "ratty" was the word she used. So it was with everyone during the floods. We like to believe we are so civilised, that we are immune to the weather. But every so often Nature imposes her presence on us and suddenly all our logical thought processes become unhinged.' His gaze wandered over the beds of rose bushes, the neat clipped lawn in between, this little patch of nature he so carefully controlled.

'I remember the coat. I'm sure this was the body. It was worn and threadbare, a couple of sizes too small for him, but it was a Burberry.'

'A Burberry?'

'Yes. It's an expensive English make. I had one just like it. A present from my son the previous Christmas.'

That was all very jolly, my father and Dr Kirby having the same sort of coat. I wondered where my father came across his 'Burberry'. Probably wandered into a St Vincent de Paul's shop and got lucky.

'Dr Kirby, the man wearing that coat—was he a derelict?'

He put his hand to his chin and rubbed it thoughtfully. 'Difficult to say, really. He wasn't clean-shaven, but that doesn't necessarily make him a derelict. Hair and nails keep growing after death.'

'I was thinking that for a derelict there appeared to be little alcohol-related damage to the internal organs.'

'My discipline has taught me never to rely on assumptions. Being a derelict doesn't necessarily mean being an alcoholic. Granted, many homeless men are alcohol or drug dependent, but not all.'

A car pulled into the drive. The engine was turned off and a few seconds later a car door slammed.

'Sofia? I'm round the back,' he called. He turned his attention back to me. 'I'm sorry I can't be more specific. Perhaps the person who identified the body might be able to help.' He looked at the report to find the name. 'Sergeant Hindley.' I politely thanked Kirby for the suggestion. I'd already made enquiries in that direction. Hindley, now Detective Senior Sergeant at Parramatta, was out of the office for a few days. 'He would have completed the Report of Death to Coroner, the P79A form. They must have sent it to you, along with all the rest of this.' There was no such form in the material Forensic had sent. 'Oh well, it probably got lost in the translation. As I mentioned earlier, with the floods and everything, there was so much chaos. Hello, darling. Did you have a good game?'

Around the corner came a woman in a sleeveless tennis dress, a yellow sweatband keeping her shiny dark hair in place. She was a good twenty years younger than Kirby. When she saw me she gave Kirby a subtle look of enquiry that didn't escape my notice. They embraced, then he took her tennis racquet as if helping her with her luggage. 'Claudia Valentine, may I present my wife, Sofia Theodourou.' Even though he was retired he was not out of touch. Not only did he have a wife twenty years younger than himself, he had a wife with her own surname. I bet his first wife didn't have her own surname.

She relaxed, and extended her hand to me. 'I think we spoke on the phone,' she reminded me. The woman who'd answered when I first rang Kirby's home. Kirby handed the report back to me. 'If there's anything else we can do, don't hesitate to call.'

'Thanks for the coffee. And kourabedes,' I smiled at his wife. 'They were delicious.' She smiled back graciously. 'Must be heaven living with all these roses,' I commented.

'Close,' agreed Sofia.

It wasn't till I was in the car and back on the highway that I thought of the roses in another garden—the crematorium at Rookwood. Rose bushes fed with human blood and bone. Such luxuriant growth from our mortal remains.

And it wasn't till I was on the Harbour Bridge heading back to the city that I realised why the name of Kirby's second wife sounded familiar to me. Sounded wasn't the right word, because I'd never heard her name before today. But I had seen it written down. Miss S Theodourou. Kirby's second wife was the forensic assistant on my father's postmortem.

Rushcutters Bay is a harbourside suburb, a quiet residential area next to Kings Cross. It has views of blue water edged in emerald green, the Opera House and the Harbour Bridge and you pay a lot of money for them. But it has a nice big park where even deros can enjoy the million-dollar views. I drove along New Beach Road and found a parking spot just beyond the Cruising Yacht Club. I bought a bottle of spring water from the canteen outside the club and proceeded to stroll along. Near the children's playground, I watched a tall elegant woman in a big floppy hat trying to persuade a two year old to get back in the stroller. But the child didn't want to know about it. He was standing on top of the jungle gym, king of the castle, master of his world. A world just out of mother's reach. She had to sweet-talk him back to the ground and she wasn't having a very good time of it. Ah, it took me back—all that cajoling and bribery, all that waiting around. I was certainly glad that bit was over.

I left her to it. Apart from the mother and child the only

other person I encountered was a man walking his dog. Probably a procrastinating writer. People were staying out of the sun, and rightly so. Another hot day, so many of them in a row they seemed to melt together into the one long, hot day. It was too late and too early for the joggers who would inevitably be running the path around the bay, before or after work. There was a seawall a metre or so high with a two-metre drop to the water. OK, so it was the time of the floods and it was raining. Easy to slip. Hit the side of your head, lose balance, over the wall and into the harbour.

I was more than halfway round the park before I came across the stormwater canal. There was barely a trickle of water in it. It was hard to tell whether it was drain water or backwash from the harbour. I wasn't about to bend down and taste it. There was a fair amount of rubbish where the canal met the sea—plastic bags, drink cans etc. They may have travelled kilometres down the canal to finally end up here.

The canal had a slightly deeper trench running down the middle of it. I climbed down from the footbridge into the canal. It was not unlike a river bed, with a layer of sandy soil having washed into the canal and the trickle of water. If you held a close-up camera on it, it could be a major river system. I walked gingerly along, towards Bayswater Road where the canal curved and became a tunnel under the road. It was slippery in places, the darker wet patches being silt rather than sand. Along the walls of the canal you could see the high-water mark stained mossy green. Above that grew the ubiquitous asthma weed, other scrubby weeds, then the civilised, manicured grass of the park. I walked under a second bridge.

I was closer to the road now and could hear the muted sound of traffic. See the tube of darkness as the canal disappeared under the road. At the edge of the road was a small brick building, possibly a pumping station, with a series of pipes running out of or into it. About three metres from the tunnel a bright pink and white beach ball sat grounded on a sandbank, unmoved by the trickle of water continuing inexorably to the sea. Innocent and forlorn, as if a child had abandoned the ball for more exciting pursuits.

There was a flick of movement as a cockroach scurried along the wall. On a foraging expedition to the world of light, the aboveground. Our six-legged neighbours, eternally with us. In stormwater canals, in the subterranean passages of the city, under our floorboards, in the cracks and crevices of our houses they also dwell. The human population of Sydney is almost four million. How many hundreds of millions of cockroaches are there? The cockroaches would know—they're getting so smart they're probably collecting their own census information.

The closer to the road I walked, the higher the walls of the canal became, higher than my head. I couldn't be seen now from the park unless someone was specifically looking. A wire fence, rusted but still sturdy, ran alongside the canal. But you could climb over it if you wanted to. Or fall.

There wasn't enough water at the moment to drown in but the high-water mark was at least a metre up the wall of the canal. During those floods the water level would have been even higher. You could drown then. The body float down to the harbour. It could have happened even further up, across the road and beyond, where the stormwater canal started.

I was approaching the mouth of the tunnel. From the road there was a steep little path worn into the growth of weeds and the wire fence was bent over to the ground. Then I saw where the path led. To a ledge just inside the tunnel. The ledge was deep enough and wide enough to accommodate two full-length single mattresses. Because that's what was on the ledge. Tucked away under the road, higher than the water level, it would be safe and dry. You would get cockroaches, but the rats wouldn't climb up here.

Anzac Day. A national holiday. Drunk and playing two-up. Maybe he'd won enough to buy an extra flagon. Coming back to the mattress. He slipped on the steep slope, lost his footing. Flying through the rain, skidding, knocking his head on the side, drowning in the water.

They say death by drowning is pleasant, as pleasant as death gets. Breathing the water in and out. Oedema fluid in pharynx, larynx, trachea and bronchi, but that wouldn't have started yet. After the screaming, burning sensation as the unfamiliar element enters your lungs, you become briefly a water creature. The water from the streets of the city swims in you as you swim in it. Perhaps you have lost consciousness already, perhaps not. You hallucinate, dream, till finally the dreams float out of you and dissolve in the ocean.

This could have been the place where my father died but those mattresses weren't his. They were more likely now to belong to street kids than deros. I climbed up the side, wedging the edge of my foot into one of the crevices that didn't have weeds growing out of it. I pulled myself up and looked around before I trespassed.

It was daytime—hopefully the occupants of those two mattresses were out on a foraging expedition, or sitting in a doorway or on a park bench somewhere. I didn't think they'd take too kindly to an intruder. You find a place like this, you don't give it up easily. They'd probably have knives or at least broken bottles, the sharp edge of glass every bit as effective as a steel blade.

I stepped across to the ledge. On the mattresses were a couple of crumpled, dirty blankets. No pillows. Around the area a few Coke cans, other scraps of rubbish, no personal items. I crouched down. From here there was a pretty good view of the length of the canal right down to the bay. This was a place for light sleepers who didn't toss and turn. You wouldn't want to roll too far or you'd end up in the drink. Across the road was a highrise of luxury apartments. The tenants were paying around $700 a week for the view. The occupants of the mattresses were paying nothing. I crouched there, elbows resting on my knees. Looking at the windows across the way, the mattresses, the walls, looking at the darkness of the tunnel under the road. Waiting for the place to whisper to me the things it had seen. But the place remained still and silent. All I could hear was the eternal hum of traffic heading into the city.

Friday night. The third night in a row I'd watched Kerry's house. Exams finished, all that freedom, she'd have to go out sometime. I'd changed cars. Another one of Danny's. This time it was a dark green Monaro. I preferred not to ask how it was he had access to all these cars. Parts for the Daimler were taking longer to arrive than expected, he said. I had the feeling Danny was deliberately holding back to wean me off it. Three nights, three different cars, three different parking spots. First two nights no-one came to the house and no-one left; the lights went out at eleven. But on Friday nights in Sydney everyone goes out.

Kerry came out wearing a black bomber jacket, Blundstone boots and a short gold-flecked skirt. She walked the short distance to the bus stop and leaned against a fence, waiting. To pass time she took a small gold compact out of her pocket, flipped it open and checked her face in the mirror. There appeared to be a small skin blemish under her chin. She rubbed her finger over it a couple of times but before any permanent damage could be done the bus came along.

I followed the bus to Riverwood station where everyone alighted. I grabbed my leather jacket and made it to the platform just as the train arrived. It had only gone two stops when Kerry got up and went to the door. But instead of getting out when the train came to a halt she waved to someone waiting on the station platform. It was her friend from school,

Tamara, but I barely recognised her. The hair that had been neatly held back in a ponytail was now running rampant. If you lost something in that hair you'd spend a week looking for it.

When the train started up again, Tamara took out a pair of big gold earrings and put them on. 'What did you tell her?' I heard Kerry ask.

'The movies. That was cool, but guess what?' Tamara grimaced. 'Midnight curfew.'

'Bummer,' sympathised Kerry.

'She gave me money for a cab home but.'

'Great,' said Kerry, 'maybe we can buy our own drinks for a change.'

'Come off it,' retorted Tamara. 'It's only for a cab from Strathfield.'

Fifteen years old trying to look eighteen. Acting tough and being cool. I hoped that's the way it would be if they got into any trouble.

They alighted at Kings Cross, where trouble is easy to find, even for those not looking for it. I followed them up the escalators and out past a shoe shop. Tamara was briefly diverted by a pair of red patent-leather platform shoes but when she saw Kerry striding so purposefully along, she quickened her step. They stood at the traffic lights, waiting for the WALK sign.

This was the hour when the Cross was at its best. The night was young by nightlife standards, some of the clubs were just getting going. There were bright lights, pleasant rich garlicky smells emanating from restaurants. The people up here for a night out wore an air of hope and expectancy for what the night could bring. The touts and hustlers hadn't yet started working the street with that quiet whispering desperation.

Kings Cross drew street kids and deros like a magnet. It was the place you came when you no longer had a home to go to. The public space that people who have homes only ever visit. In a way it was the village green, the kind of village green you might find in hell. A sick and seedy place that only really looked good when all the lights were on. In the glare of bright lights the tourists, partygoers, couldn't see the homeless. They were invisible, blending into the shadows of side streets and darker areas off the main drag. Once the partygoers went home, they would reclaim the streets.

When you become homeless you develop cockroach habits. Scavenging, hunting for food in bins, wherever you can find it. You enter a parallel universe, living in the buffer zone of the drugs you take to numb the damage caused by the hard edges. You become the truest citizen of the city, inhabiting its streets and public spaces, its parks, its doorways and recesses, the cracks in the wall. Its stormwater canals.

Kerry and Tamara walked a little way down Bayswater Road and went into a large terrace house converted into a club, from which music was faintly emanating. A neon sign above the doorway—Horn of Africa—pulsated red light. I hung back and made a few adjustments to my person. I mussed my hair up, letting the front section drift over one eye. Then pulled the collar of my leather jacket up and walked in.

Horn of Africa was a serious music venue with a live band, tables to sit at down the front for the people who wanted to listen rather than talk. Mostly though, everyone hung around the bar area. I made my way to the bar and held out a ten-dollar note. Being tall, I got served almost straightaway.

I spotted Kerry and Tamara with a couple of guys. They were leaning up against a side wall. Not the best place to listen to the music but it was a nice safe corner in the dark, where they didn't look as underage as they would have in the light. They were all chatting away but in between sips of what appeared to be rum and Coke, Kerry would look around, as if expecting someone. When she finished her drink she excused herself and went to the rest rooms. She came back amidst applause—the band had just finished a number.

As the applause died down I became aware of the smell of patchouli oil. 'There's a better place down the road, R 'n' B, funk, great dance music. Like to give it a try?' I looked at the guy who'd just sidled up to me. No, I did not want to give it a try.

Kerry and Tamara were saying their goodbyes and leaving.

'That sounds great. Can you hold this?' I handed him my beer. 'Thanks. Won't be a minute.'

I followed Kerry and Tamara back to the entrance to Kings Cross station. They were having a discussion, Kerry pointing up the road and Tamara hovering. Kerry trying to convince Tamara to go somewhere with her, Tamara hesitating and looking at her watch. Tamara had forty minutes to make the midnight curfew. She'd be late, but not by much.

A bit more discussion then the two girls waved goodbye and went their separate ways. Tamara down the steep escalator into the bowels of the earth, and Kerry into the heart of the Cross. I followed Kerry.

She turned off the main drag and cut through to a back alley. Suddenly all the noise and bright lights stopped. There was nothing but the backs of buildings here, very few windows. It was a short alley that crooked around and disappeared into the backs of more buildings. It looked like a great place for a mugging. There was no-one else in the street. I stayed where I was and waited to see where she was going. Kerry walked briskly, with purpose. Just before the bend, she disappeared.

I walked on down to The Squeeze. A facade painted matt black, Gothic lettering in silver. If it hadn't been for the sign it would have been hard to tell the black door from the black wall. Behind me I heard a car pull up. A cab. Out of it got a group of adults dressed like schoolkids. Thirty year old women in short short tunics, hair in plaits, a smattering of fake freckles across the noses and cheeks. Men in short pants and dinky little caps. I pushed the door and went in, wondering just what sort of place The Squeeze was.

But I wasn't inside yet. There was another door to get through with three bouncers guarding it. Black trousers, white short-sleeved shirts on the tight side to make the biceps bulge just that little bit extra. We had guys like this at karate class. Martial artists. Tuning their bodies to be perfect fighting machines. Then looking for fights to put the whole thing in motion.

The outer door opened behind me and in came the

'schoolkids'. The bouncers stood aside and we all went in together.

There was lots of chrome and flashing coloured lights inside but it still managed to look dark and mysterious. The club was divided into two sections, a bar in each. In the bigger, more 'public' section was a dance area where the lights were flashing. Circling this entirely was a counter with bar stools. If you wanted to sit you could watch the dancers; if you wanted to dance there was somewhere to rest your drink. An arc of the far wall was entirely enclosed by glass, for use by private parties. This is where the schoolkids headed.

I don't know if it was because the night was wearing thin or if it was simply the venue, but the atmosphere here seemed more dissipated than at the previous club. Darker, smokier, lots of black clothes. The sort of place you wouldn't have to look far to find whatever it was you develop a taste for in the wee small hours. A few groovers danced, some alone, some glued to each other. Most of the patrons stood in clusters around the walls, outside the range of the flashes of light. I couldn't see Kerry. It was hard to see anyone. People were in either darkness or distorted light. Gradually though, my eyes got accustomed to it. I made out the rest rooms which were designated M and W, presumably Men and Women. I bet as the night wore on those M's and W's got confused.

'Well, here you are. I thought I'd lost you.' I didn't even have to turn around to know who it was. The sweet stale smell of patchouli. Good grief. Even as he talked he was moving in time to the music. I gave him a tired smile and started dancing. After a minute or two he was completely self-absorbed and I was able to lose myself in the crowd.

I spotted Kerry at the pay phone near the M and W. She said something then she waited. And waited. Finally she slammed the phone down and left.

Outside, the early hopefulness of the night had worn off and the desperation was showing. Kerry seemed oblivious to the drunks making lunges at her, the streetgirls watching her pass. She waited for the lights at William Street to change. Further down this road, outside the car showrooms displaying Ferraris,

Porsches and Jaguars, HIV-positive transvestites did business in cars with blokes from the suburbs too drunk to know or care.

She crossed to Darlinghurst on the other side. So did I. Though we were only a road's width from Kings Cross, everything felt different. We had left behind the prickly garden of delights and were back in the city again. Shit happened here but there was less of it. There were no neon signs winking lecherously at you, you didn't feel as if the whole place was lying back, legs open.

She walked past the fire station and the row of little Italian cafes, converted terrace houses with seats out on the street so you could see and, more importantly, be seen. Andiamo's, Morgan's, Nicolina's, the Coluzzi bar. Breakfast, any time of. the day or night, for high profile lawyers, bankrupted property developers, boxers, film producers, and the people who want to be seen with them. Kerry walked straight past without giving them a second look.

A minute later the ambience changed abruptly. We were in the part of Darlinghurst where street gangs fought, gays got bashed and low-rent prostitutes plied their trade to cruising cars. Kerry knocked on a door, a pink door with graffiti and street art sprawled all over it. A brass number 9, or maybe it was a 6, was dangling by one screw. Two steps was all that separated the house from the street. Music was thumping away inside, you could almost see the door vibrating. From somewhere in the vicinity wafted the slow pungent smell of dope. No-one came to the door.

Kerry then tried tapping on the window. 'Maddy,' she called out over the music. No response. 'Ralph? Simon?' Still no response. Kerry spread her fingertips out on the glass, pushed the window up and climbed in, disappearing into the darkness of the house.

She'd called out her name. Maddy. She was here, in this house. Madalena was here.

The window remained open. When Kerry didn't reappear I assumed she'd found her friends and joined the party. I was just about to climb in and join it myself when the door opened, letting out an even louder blast of music. A wispy young man was there, seeing Kerry out. 'Well call me if you hear anything,' I heard Kerry say.

'Sure you won't stay?' invited the young man. 'No, I'm going home. Mum's there by herself. See ya, Simon.'

'See ya, Kerry.' The door closed.

Kerry sat down on the steps; back hunched, elbows on knees, chin cupped in her hands. The confident young woman who had strode through the streets of Kings Cross was gone now and a worried child took her place. Something was weighing her down, something she didn't understand. Reluctantly she stood up and started meandering back to the Cross, lost in thought.

Before I'd taken two paces, someone stepped out of the shadows and barred Kerry's path. He was dressed differently and it was dark, but I was positive it was the man I'd seen at the Hoyts cinema. He said something to her. She may have replied, I don't know, with her back to me I couldn't tell. She tried to get past but he blocked the way. She took a few steps back, but he grabbed her by the shoulder. Suddenly in the darkness I saw the glint of a blade.

'Hey!' I started running towards her. The guy saw me coming. He pushed her to the ground and ran off into the darkness.

I bent down and helped Kerry up. 'Bastard,' she swore. 'Look at my tights.' She couldn't be too badly hurt if all she was worried about were her tights.

'What did he want?' I asked.

'He was asking questions about a friend of mine.'

'About Madalena,' I said.

She looked at me curiously, wondering who I was.

'Her mother is worried,' I went on. 'If you are in touch with her, ask her to call home.'

Kerry looked away, biting her lip. I thought she may have been deciding whether I was an adult she could trust but there was more to it than that. 'She's disappeared,' she finally blurted out.

'I know,' I spoke softly, 'that's why her mother is worried.'

'No,' Kerry said, 'you don't understand. She left home. But now she's disappeared.'

'Perhaps I can help,' I suggested.

'I was on my way home,' Kerry said.

'I'll see you get there safely.'

'It's OK, I can manage. It's a long way. Peakhurst.'

'It's no trouble. I'm going there anyway. My car's parked near your house.' She looked at me, completely stunned. 'My name's Claudia Valentine, I'm a private investigator. Mrs Grimaldi hired me to find Madalena. You're her best friend, I thought you might know.'

'Have you been following me all night?' I told her I had. 'You mean, right from my house?' I said yes, right from her house. 'Far out.'

We got the train from the Cross then a cab from Riverwood. By the time we got to Peakhurst I had Kerry's version of events. There'd been the fight with Madalena's father over the tattoo. The next day—the day, according to Rosa, that Madalena had disappeared—Madalena, Kerry and the rest of the netball team had played at Concord. But Madalena hadn't come home with everyone else, she'd decided to go to Leichhardt. To see her father. Kerry didn't know exactly why but she thought it was to apologise about the fight. Leichhardt's not far away from Concord and she figured she could maybe get a lift home with him. That was the last time Kerry saw Madalena.

But she had a phone call from Madalena a few days later. To say she'd left home and was never going back. She was OK, she was staying at Darlinghurst but she made Kerry promise she wouldn't tell anyone, especially her parents, where she was. Something had happened that afternoon when she went to see her father but she wouldn't talk about it.

She had arranged to meet Kerry tonight at Horn of Africa, just to hang out, listen to the music. The things they used to do. But Maddy hadn't shown up. Kerry thought maybe she'd be at The Squeeze but she wasn't there either. When Kerry phoned the Darlinghurst house someone had answered the phone then just gone away and forgotten about it. So Kerry came round. They were having a party and couldn't hear her knocking on the door so she went in the window. 'I guess you saw that bit,' she said to me. But Madalena had disappeared. Completely disappeared. She went out to buy some milk and didn't come back. I suggested to Kerry that perhaps Madalena had decided to get out of town altogether, maybe hitch up the coast.

'She'd never hitch, not after those backpacker murders.'

'Perhaps she got a lift with someone.'

'She would have let me know,' said Kerry. 'It's not as if they don't have phones up the coast, is it?'

I asked Kerry what Madalena's father was like. She said she'd never met him but he sounded like a bit of an arsehole. 'Totally freaked by the tattoo. I mean, it's not like she had a nipple ring or anything.'

'What was the tattoo like?'

'Like this.' Kerry pulled her jacket off her shoulder and showed me. It looked like a keyhole with ornamentation around the top of it.

'Madalena's was the same?'

She readjusted her clothes. 'Yeah. We had them done together.'

'What did *your* mother say?'

'Couldn't say much, could she? She's got a tattoo herself.'

We'd arrived at Kerry's house. I gave her my card. 'If you want to call me anytime, here's the number.'

'Thanks,' she said. 'See you later.'

I watched till she went in the door and turned the light on. I waited a few more minutes, just to be sure.

Arturo Grimaldi's restaurant, La Giardinera, was on Parramatta Road, Leichhardt. It wasn't one of the trendy restaurants. They're on Norton Street, a good few blocks away from the grime of Parramatta Road. Parramatta Road is the major artery to the west—not a place where you sit and have a quiet meal. Further down the road are car yards bristling with plastic flags and blokes with blow-waved hair ready to take your money off you. Leichhardt is the heart of the Italian community. There are fruit and vegetable shops, delis, discount clothing stores, places you can buy christening presents and religious statues. I couldn't help noticing the signs in shop windows as I walked towards the restaurant—CLOSING DOWN SALE . . . TO LET. There are still remnants of what life must have been like in the village, but the massive supermarket complex is the business that's booming.

La Giardinera was on a corner block with an alley behind it leading to an area where a couple of cars were parked. The doorway, on the Parramatta Road side, was arched. The theme was continued with the arched windows. A few faded plastic flowers adorned them, lipservice to the garden this restaurant was supposed to be.

I'd picked one o'clock to pay a visit because that was peak lunchtime. I'd be eating alone and I didn't want to be too conspicuous. I had on a pair of glasses with round rims, my hair pulled back. The studious type, always reads a book when she's eating, a little vague. Someone who might get lost looking for the toilet.

But at one o'clock there was hardly anyone else there—one couple. The restaurant was pretty dark, with a well-equipped bar. Perhaps it did more nighttime trade. Nevertheless, the tables were set for lunch and I sat down at one of them. The only other person apart from the couple was a short thin woman with neat grey hair and no make-up. She handed me a menu. It had the usual pasta and lots of veal dishes. There was a specials blackboard, but it was blank.

I settled on a small spaghetti marinara with side salad. It wasn't an enormous amount to get through if I had to leave in a hurry and if I didn't, I could stretch it out as long as necessary.

The marinara, when it arrived, was chock-full of fresh seafood, king prawns, mussels in the shell. The salad too was fresh with a classic Italian dressing. The food was great. How come there were so few people in here? I propped my book up beside the food and began reading.

A door at the back opened and I heard a man's voice. I looked up casually. Arturo. I recognised him from the photo in the lounge room at Lugarno. Tanned skin, grey hair receding at the temples, tension in the neck and shoulders. He squeezed in behind the bar, into a little alcove, almost but not quite out of sight from the dining room. He asked the waitress something in Italian, I didn't catch all of it. 'Giovedi,' she answered. Thursday. 'Va bene.' Then he poured himself some grappa. Before he replaced the top he turned his back and took a swig straight from the bottle. Then he went out again.

I wondered if drinking like that was something he always did or whether it was a recently acquired habit. I'd seen it before—the alcoholic who gets tanked up in private while sitting on one drink all night. I let a few minutes pass then I asked the woman where the toilets were. 'In the back,' she said, pointing to the door. I left my book on the table and went out there.

I was in an asphalt yard. The toilets were to the right.

Between the toilets and the restaurant was a set of stairs. I walked past the toilets, turned round the corner and came to the two cars I'd seen before. A grey Mercedes about eight years old and a beige Toyota. I went to the entrance of the yard. The alley continued up to the next street. There were a few bins outside. When it came time for garbage collection they would have to move them up to the street. The alley was too narrow for a garbage truck to drive through.

From over here I had a better view of the upstairs part of the building. There was a small window that looked as if it hadn't been cleaned in years. Guttering needed fixing too. No customers in the restaurant, repairs needed doing, where did the money come from for that big house in Lugarno?

I ventured up the stairs. There was a closed door at the top. I pushed it open and came into a big room, sparsely furnished with tables and chairs. To the left four men sat playing cards. Money in the middle of the table, twenties and fifties. At the other end of the room sat Arturo with another man, a well-dressed man. They were drinking coffee and seemed to be in the middle of a discussion. Both the conversation and the card game stopped when I appeared in the doorway. I stood there peering through my glasses. Arturo looked my way but didn't come forward, didn't make any movement that would distinguish him from anyone else in the room. No-one said anything but everyone was looking expectantly at me.

'Ah, excuse me, I was looking for the toilets.'

'Down there. Outside,' said one of the card players.

'Thanks.' I started to back out. Arturo watched, trying to work out whether my mistake was genuine. I closed the door behind me and went into the toilets. I should at least let him hear the sound of flushing. If that's what he was listening for.

Perhaps he heard a car pull up, because that is what I heard as I flushed the toilet. Then footsteps going up the stairs. I came out quietly, walked up to where the stairs turned at a right angle and caught sight of someone going in through the door. I saw only the back of him but it was enough. It was the same man. The lush curly hair that I noticed the first time at Hoyts. The same man who'd attacked Kerry in Darlinghurst.

There was now a third car beside the Merc and the Toyota. A big American Chrysler with a personalised number plate, FABIO. I strolled over and had a look. Sheepskin seatcovers, a St Christopher medal dangling from the rear vision mirror, a Gregory's Street Guide sitting on the passenger's seat.

So maybe Arturo had hired a private eye of his own. He didn't look like any of the private investigators I knew, even the cowboy type.

I went back inside. The woman had cleared away the spaghetti plate but left the salad. My book remained in the same place I'd left it. The couple who were there before had now gone.

'You want dessert?' she asked me.

'No thanks. Just the bill.'

She brought it over to me on a saucer. 'Is there another part of the restaurant upstairs?' I asked.

'No,' she said, 'just here.'

'I saw someone go up there. Just thought I'd let you know.' As if I was being a good Neighbourhood Watch citizen.

'That's OK. Old men play cards up there sometimes. Nothing to worry about.'

She seemed to believe it but I wasn't convinced. I paid the bill and left.

I finally had the Daimler back. I'd made the decision to sell it to Danny and I wanted to take it on one long last drive to explain to it what was happening, to say goodbye. Parramatta was a nice long drive. It used to be the limits of suburban Sydney but now Sydney had sprawled so much that Parramatta was the geographical centre. The geographical centre, not the heart.

Parramatta wasn't a destination chosen at random. I was going there to see Sergeant Hindley, now Detective Senior Sergeant Hindley. I had been in touch with Forensic Medicine again, to see if they'd simply overlooked the P79A form when they'd sent me the other material, but the form couldn't be found. Despite the kind of work I do, despite the fact that I have a good friend in the Force, I don't enjoy visiting police stations. The bureaucracy, the paperwork, the uniforms, it's too much like prison for my liking. I always imagine they're going to find some pretext for keeping me there. Run my name through the computer and discover unpaid parking fines from fifteen years ago.

Today wasn't one of my lucky PI days, the kind of day when, just like in the movies, there's a parking spot right outside the door. I had to leave the Daimler three streets away and walk back to the station. There may have been a lot of space out west but there wasn't much parking.

Sitting on a bench in Parramatta Police Station was a woman

with blotchy skin wearing a thin summer dress. Through the ample armholes I could see a safety pin holding the bra strap to the bra. She was smoking a cigarette, sucking in as if it was a respirator. Beside her sat a lad, presumably her son. He had tatts and earrings, a skinhead look that had gone a little past its use-by date. He sat staring at the space between his thongs. Maybe he couldn't afford Doc Martens. But I don't think that's what was troubling him in this particular instance. He looked as though the world was pressing very heavily on the back of his head.

'What can I do for you?' said the guy at the desk. He was young, fresh-faced and eager to please. Just the way I like them. It wasn't so much what he could do for me as what I could do for him. Take him away from this nasty world of crime, tuck him up in my bed, handfeed him chocolates.

'Hi, my name's Claudia,' I said, friendly but professional. 'I'm here to see Detective Hindley.'

'Sure,' he said. 'Trace? Can you tell Detective Hindley there's someone here to see him?'

'Trace' smiled pleasantly then disappeared around a corner. 'Won't be a minute,' the guy said to me, 'have a seat.'

Any other place you walk into off the street, any big corporation, they'd want to know your name, the company you're representing. They make you sign a book and give you a special visitor's pass. Police stations you can just walk in and see whoever you want to. I guess if things got dicey they could always shoot you.

Hindley had a receding hairline, and distinctive black eyebrows separated by a single vertical frown mark. His nose was flat, chin dimpled and no matter how hard he tried he was a guy who'd never look tidy. Shortish for a cop but he made up for it in width. Late fifties, early sixties, and showing it.

'Lady here to see you, sir,' said my nice young man.

He could hardly conceal his pleasure when I stepped forward. A long-legged redhead asking for him. Boy, was this going to be good for his image at the station.

'Good morning,' I greeted him, 'can we talk?' What I meant was somewhere private.

'Come up to my office,' said the spider to the fly. He let me in behind the counter and took me upstairs. 'Have a seat,' he said, dragging a chair over in front of his desk. He sat behind the desk, leant his chair back against the wall and looked me up and down. I was glad to have the desk between us. I imagined a wall of glass with him on one side and me on the other so that his leery look didn't get on my person.

'It's—?'

'Claudia,' I said, 'Claudia Valentine.'

I watched his reaction. There was a flicker, then a slight narrowing of the eyes. With eyebrows like his, even this slight movement was noticeable. If there was a Richter scale of reaction it would probably register 3 or 4. A slight tremor but not enough to damage the furniture.

'News reporter?' he said, as if he'd heard the name but couldn't quite place it.

'No. I'm Guy Valentine's daughter.' Even less on the scale this time. I expected it to be more. I prompted. 'You identified my father's body when he died.'

Still it meant nothing to him.

'Rushcutters Bay, 25 April, 1985. Anzac Day. The floods.'

I didn't know whether it was the time, place or mention of the floods, but suddenly the furniture was rattling. A strange look in his eye as if he'd seen a ghost risen from the dead. It lasted for one second, then it was over and he became a cop again.

'My sincere condolences.' He didn't mean a word of it. 'I'm sure your father would be pleased you've grown into such a strong, strapping girl.' Oh spare me!

'You knew him personally?'

'Well . . .' he seemed to be considering which had more mileage in it, a yes or a no answer. '1985 is a long time ago.'

What was he playing at? You either know someone or you don't. There was a game of cat and mouse going on here. A game for two players and each took a turn. Sometimes you can corner a mouse with a few bluffs so that it has no alternative but to tell the truth.

'How come you guys didn't get in touch with his next of kin?'

He was on guard now and had his answers ready. 'They would have tried,' he explained, 'but unsuccessfully. The floods . . .' as if that was the explanation for everything. 'Water leaking into the Telecom tunnels, phone lines were going down. Everything was in chaos.'

He could have been right. They could have phoned a few Valentines without striking Mina. But I still didn't like it. 'On the death certificate it says you were the one who identified him. How did you know who he was?' I asked Hindley.

He looked at me, taking his time, rubbing his chin. I'd struck bureaucrats, petty bureaucrats, who won't even tell you the time of day in case they're infringing some regulation. But Hindley wasn't one of those. He was playing as if all the cards were in his hand and if he were to flip one over and show me, he'd be doing me a big favour.

'By the Social Security form in his pocket.'

'And that was enough?'

Was I in some way implying he was lax in his duties? He must have thought about it for no longer than half a second. He was well-protected. All that flood water under the bridge flushing away any slackness, all the time that had passed making it harder to check on things, this nice big desk jutting out in front of him like a giant beer gut.

'All procedure was carried out. He had formal identification on him. This was further verified by one of his cohorts.' He leaned forward now, friendly but with a glint in his eye, relishing what he was about to say. 'You look like a girl who's big enough to hear the truth, Claudia. Your father was a dero. A pisspot.'

Oh boy, I hated that big girl stuff. I swung my legs up onto the desk and gave Hindley a view of the soles of my shoes. In some cultures that is considered a heinous insult. 'I hope you don't mind, when you're tall it's always difficult to know what to do with them. But I guess you wouldn't know about that.' I was probably the first person on this side of the desk to ever put their feet on it. He looked at me, not quite knowing how to take it. I smiled at him, as if it was a bit of a joke and he was such a good sport.

So my father was a drunk. This sounded more like it.

The phone rang. He picked it up and identified himself. He listened to the person on the other end for a while, then he looked at his watch and said, 'Yeah, OK. I'll be down in five.' He'd be shooing me out of there before long.

'Look, Sergeant,' I started. With all those bits to his rank I wasn't sure what to call him. 'I've only recently become aware of my father's death. He left home a long time ago, I never really knew him. I just want to know how it was, I just want to . . .'

He reached over and patted my shoe, the way you do with someone's hand. 'I understand,' he said condescendingly. Bereaved family member, he probably dealt with them all the time.

'The P79A form is missing. You were the one who filled that in, right?'

Again a slight seismic tremor. Bereaved family members don't usually go into this sort of detail. 'That's right,' he said warily.

'What did you say in the Narrative?'

Whatever charm I had was wearing thin. 'Give us a break, it's nearly ten years ago. How can I remember what I wrote ten years ago?'

'Believe it or not, Sergeant, you're the closest link I have to my father. Otherwise I wouldn't be bothering you.'

His tone softened a little. 'We found the body floating face down in the water, near the entrance to the stormwater canal. When I turned him over I realised it was one of the deros that hung around the place. I was stationed at Kings Cross then, the park was part of my beat.'

'Did you know him well?'

He laughed derisively. 'Getting acquainted with the occupants of the park was not high on my list of priorities. I knew him by sight. That's all. When we searched through his pockets we found the Social Security form.'

'Anything else?'

'Just the form.'

'No wallet, no little personal items? Didn't that strike you as odd?' I asked.

'Well, maybe the coat with his gold AMEX card was at the drycleaners,' his voice heavy with sarcasm. 'Maybe he was rolled, how would I know?'

'So he might have been murdered then? Bashed unconscious, then pushed into the stormwater canal.'

Hindley stiffened and his face got uglier. 'I don't like your implication, missy. We thoroughly investigated the matter, as we would for anyone. It was raining, he was drunk, he fell and hit his head and couldn't get out again. He drowned. That's all there is to it. Now if you don't mind, I've got police work to do.'

I could tell by his tone of voice that he wasn't going to be asking me out on a date. I stood up, made departure movements. He didn't budge. Wasn't he going to see me out? 'Thank you for your time,' I said. 'You seem to have a nice crew here. Very pleasant desk staff downstairs.'

'Yes,' he grunted. 'One big happy family.'

I noticed now the dartboard hanging on the back of the door. 'Just straight down the stairs, is it?'

'Same way you came up,' he said, as if I was the world's biggest fool and he didn't suffer me gladly.

'One more thing and I'll be on my way.'

'What is it?' an expression of pain on his face.

'What did he look like, my father?'

'What do you think he bloody looked like? He looked like someone who'd drowned.'

'Did he look relatively . . . healthy? For the sort of life he led, I mean.'

He was really fed up now. 'What do you do for a living? Train pig dogs?'

'I'm a private investigator.' I thought about giving him my card but it would more than likely end up in his waste paper bin.

He looked at me as if I was the scum of the earth. 'He looked like they all do—grey, unshaven, grisly. I'm surprised he didn't fall in sooner, the state of him. I can tell you, it's no skin off my nose. One less bludger the taxpayer has to support.'

'Thanks for your concern and sympathy. Goodbye, Sergeant.'

'People usually call me sir,' he shouted after me.

I banged the door hard behind me and heard a satisfying clunk as the dartboard hit the floor.

Downstairs the woman who had been sitting on the bench was now standing at the counter signing a piece of paper. The boy remained in the same position, still staring at the space on the floor. I waited till she'd finished before I let myself out. 'C'mon, Shaun,' she said to the boy. 'Thanks, Sergeant,' she said to the lovely young man. I doubted he was a sergeant but what did it matter. I also thanked him. 'No worries,' he said, opening the door so I could get through. If I'd had a chocolate on me I would have offered him one. Still, I'd always know where to find him later.

I stepped out of the station just in time to see the woman give the kid a hefty slap across the back of the neck. He went to hit her back but let his hand fall away before it made contact. 'Don't you fuckin' dare,' she growled. 'You wait till your father gets home,' she warned him.

'Yeah, sure,' he smirked. 'He's coming home, is he? You know something I don't?'

I walked the three streets back to where the Daimler was parked. I didn't particularly like Hindley, his smart-arse comments or his leery style, but the description he gave me of my father did verify the impression I'd always had. So why didn't I feel satisfied with that? The more I tried to fill in the gaps, the more holes appeared.

Shit. When I got back to the Daimler I discovered a scratch down the entire length of one side, as if someone had dragged their car keys along it. Why do people do things like that? I got in the car and sat there without going anywhere. We'd had a lot of good years together, the Daimler and I, I couldn't let her go quite yet. Not with a scratch on her.

When I got back to Balmain there was a message from my

mother on the answering machine. Just ringing to let me know they were back from their honeymoon.

'Hello?' I heard Mina's tentative voice. She always answered the phone as if she expected bad news.

'Hi, it's Claudia. How was the south coast?'

It was wonderful. The place was just what they wanted, they lay out on the sundeck, went to nice restaurants and guess what? 'We've taken up golf.'

Maybe that's what I should do—take up a hobby. Put the past behind me as Mina and Brian appeared to have done. I couldn't even give up my car, let alone allow my father to rest in peace.

'When are you coming over to see the photos?' Mina asked. I forgot there would be photos. Lots of shots of the sky, if I knew Mina. 'Come over for dinner,' she burbled. I accepted the invitation. 'Brian wants to say hello,' she said. 'See you next week, dear.'

'G'day,' Brian greeted me.

'That golf's going to interfere with your sedentary way of life, isn't it?' I suggested.

'Well, a dog is never too old to learn new tricks. It's not weight-lifting or anything. All you do is walk around and hit the ball occasionally. You meet some very interesting people that way.'

'So is this the new career path?' Brian was old enough to retire but it had always been impossible to imagine that he would. 'No fear. I still want to be in amongst it. I'm married, not dead.'

'What's Mina doing?'

'Unpacking. Why?' he said warily.

'Nothing serious,' I assured him. I explained that I'd been thinking a lot about Guy, now that we knew he was dead. That I wanted to speak to people who knew him, to have something to make up for all those years of absence.

'Claudia . . .' I could tell by the way he said my name that he didn't think I should be keeping this wound open. He was in a sensitive position himself. Guy's best friend, now married to his wife. He couldn't very well say forget about it, leave it alone. Guy was what brought us together, the common thread.

If I wanted to know about my father, Brian would tell me. He wouldn't like going over it all again but he'd do it. As many times as I asked.

Brian and Guy had been colleagues, crime reporters. Young, brash and ready to change the world. But the world had got to Guy, the underworld in particular. They'd threatened him. He had a wife and young child, he backed off. He found it difficult to live with himself, he started drinking.

I told Brian that Guy had been found in Rushcutters Bay and asked if he knew any of his cronies, someone I could talk to. Brian said he'd lost contact with him long before that. 'After he left your mother, when he really hit the turps, he started drinking in a pub in Chippendale. Pub near that alley where The Fish got shot, remember it? Early eighties.'

I remember Brian telling me about The Fish. His memory for crime facts and figures was formidable. Googly-eyed Frank 'The Fish' Hashem, a heroin dealer who ripped off other dealers, was shot in an alleyway by a cowboy cop, Richard Harrington, in what was probably a set-up. Harrington went on to bigger and better things for a while then he was shoved sideways, then out all together.

The pub was frequented by what Collier would describe in his newspaper reports as 'colourful characters' on both sides of the law. Or at least that's the way he described them then.

'Guy hung out in that pub?'

'After he stopped drinking at the journos' pub near work he went to the other side of Parramatta Road. When you're on the way down, you don't want to be reminded of what you're leaving behind. I'm telling you because you want to know, but it's not a pleasant story.'

I pressed on. 'You think Guy could have been involved in something?'

'What are you getting at?' he said, already with an inkling.

'Well, you know, if that's the kind of pub he drank at, maybe he unwittingly came across someone who harboured a grudge, someone he may have written about, who caught him at a vulnerable moment and killed him.'

'Why bother killing someone who's already dead.' The way

he said it, it wasn't really a question. 'Do you really want to put yourself through this?'

'I can handle it.'

'And the views were breathtaking,' his voice got louder and jollier. Mina was back in the room. 'You could see for miles up and down the coast.'

'Thanks, Brian.' I paused. 'There is something else, an entirely unrelated matter.'

'Fire away,' he invited.

'You know La Giardinera restaurant in Leichhardt?'

'Not particularly. Should I?'

'What about Arturo Grimaldi? And a guy who drives a Chrysler with FABIO plates?'

'No. You want me to check them out?'

'Maybe. I'll let you know. What goes on in the back rooms of restaurants in Leichhardt?'

'A lot used to. But the action's practically died out now. Times change. The kids get an education, they become lawyers or stockbrokers and learn more sophisticated scams. They invest in the short-term money market—$30 000 to an unknown party. Money back in ten days with interest, no questions asked.'

I hung up then rang Carol. 'Detective Sergeant Rawlins, please.' I could feel myself getting sucked along the police phone lines, through hierarchies and subdivisions. Almost as bad as actually going to police premises. I felt that way about hospitals too. You know you're not sick but you can't help feeling you might catch something. Maybe it's the airconditioning. I always suspect that in hospitals they use the airconditioning to take out the oxygen and replace it with something that saps your strength so you lie down and meekly take whatever they mete out to you.

Carol wasn't there. But they were expecting her back in the office tomorrow, would I like to leave a message?

I'd barely put the phone down when it started ringing. It was Jack. 'You can talk, can't you? I've been trying to get through to you for the last half hour. There's someone here to see you. Want to come down or will I send her up?'

A duck can't stick its bill up its arse.'

I couldn't believe it. Was this my old friend Carol, who sits outside in her car rather than wait for me in the bar where she might actually have to talk to someone, telling lawyer jokes to a group of suits?

She twiddled the olive in her martini, waiting for the laughter to die down before starting on the next one: 'What's the difference between a spermatazoan and a lawyer? At least the spermatazoan has one chance in a million of becoming a human being.'

She wasn't even drunk, it was only 6 pm. After work and before dinner, a busy time for the pub. For the full-time locals it could have been any time of the day. They were sitting on stools, elbows squarely on the bar, minding their own business, thinking about Life and Death, reviewing their pasts, thinking about something they said to someone in 1953 and wished they hadn't.

I nodded to a few of them as I came into the bar and managed to slip by without George noticing me. He was the fullest-time local. He sat here day and night. Every pub has a patron like George. Like the verandah and the beach, the pub is an intermediate zone, the place between the inside and outside. Before he stepped outside altogether, my father would have been a patron like George. Despite the obvious similarities I felt no overwhelming urge to make a father figure of him.

He was amiable enough but I didn't want him sidling up to me any more than he did already, whispering confidentialities that sprayed all over your cheek.

'Claudia!' Carol seemed pleased to see me. 'Excuse me,' she said to her audience. 'Game of pool?' she suggested to me.

Did she see my eyebrows raise or not? Telling jokes in pubs, playing pool, what had come over her? Carol never played pool, she didn't even like watching. She'd never learnt and wasn't about to, even though lots of her buddies, including me, played.

'Why not?' I grinned. I got a Tooheys Lite from Jack and we installed ourselves up at the pool area.

Those satisfying preliminary sounds—the coin going in, the clunk, the balls tumbling along and coming out into the catchment area.

'Mugs away, is it?'

I was choosing my cue from the rack. Mugs away? Just what had Carol been doing the last few days? She'd suggested a game of pool, she was using the jargon. Not appropriately, but at least she knew the words.

'When there's no-one holding the table we have to decide who the mug is. Heads or tails?'

'Heads,' she said. It came up heads.

'So how's life?' I asked.

'Good,' she said. 'Very good.'

The balls were ready for the break. She came to the table and methodically chalked her cue. Then spent a long time placing the white ball directly over the dot and measuring up the angle. The break was OK, nothing went in but the balls were spread around the table nicely.

'Have you been away?'

'In Melbourne,' she said, leaning against the wall.

'Anything exciting?'

'A matter related to Sweetie's Icecream Parlours. A member of state parliament has been pushing for an investigation for years. It's finally happening.'

I'd read about the planned investigation on the plane back from Melbourne. Sweetie's went bust in the mid-eighties amid allegations of 'drugs, murder and corruption'. Allegedly, the franchise was a front for an elaborate network that involved most of the big names of the time—crims, cops, businessmen, many of whom were now dead, discredited, in jail or living in countries with lax extradition laws.

'So I've been gathering information. Asking questions, getting bullshit answers. Asking the questions again. And again.'

I'd been present when Carol asked questions. She has a mind like a steel trap. One little anomaly, one little flaw in your argument and she feeds it back to you with a 'please explain' note. But that's just the technique for the smaller skirmishes. When Carol's on the job she goes into a different frame of mind. She looks at you, sits completely still. Interested but neutral, like a cat watching a skink. You get the feeling that anything you say to her will never be repeated or have reper-cussions. That her compassion and understanding are infinite. You could be talking to a therapist or a priest. Except that when it's over, Carol becomes once again Detective Inspector Rawlins.

'I was in Melbourne myself recently,' I said, hearing the satisfying sound of the ball making its way into the inner recesses of the table.

'Business or pleasure?'

'Oh, you know, I always try and combine the two.'

I missed my next shot. Carol came to the table. She walked around it like a teacher inspecting a classroom, placed the cue between the white ball and hers, measured angles. For a moment there I thought she was going to construct a bridge.

'Parking's good in Melbourne compared to Sydney,' I said, making conversation.

Carol came round behind the white and brought her eye down to table level. 'So you park. Then what do you do?'

'Play pool for a start. Looks like that's what you've been doing.'

'I had to frequent some unsavoury places. I thought I'd take a few lessons.'

When Carol says take a few lessons she doesn't mean hanging around the table and watching what's going on, or having some local stand behind her positioning her arm, breathing over her shoulder or, more to the point, breathing down her designer jacket. She means professional lessons. I don't know what they taught her but her shot seemed to take forever. And she still hadn't taken a poke at the ball.

'Didn't think Melbourne had unsavoury places.'

'Sure they do, they just keep them out of sight. One of the three most liveable cities in the world.'

'So I heard,' I said.

Finally, finally she did it. And unfortunately for me, the ball went in. Which meant a repeat of the long slow process of bridge building. To compensate for her lack of speed, when my turn came I took a run up to the table and shot, without taking aim. Eventually I lost, worn down by Carol's slow hand.

We'd taken so long to play the one game that there were three sets of initials chalked up on the board—players waiting for a game.

'Doubles?' one of the blokes invited us.

'It's all yours, Darren,' I said. 'We're drinking.'

Back in the bar we found a quiet table to sit at and I bought Carol a winning martini.

'I met someone in Melbourne,' Carol said.

'A pool player?' I ventured.

'As a matter of fact, yes.'

'Good for you. I hope that doesn't mean you're going to move down there.'

I'd said it jokingly but it looked as though Carol was seriously considering the possibility. 'It's early days yet, we'll see how it goes.'

What was happening? My mother, my best friend, everyone I knew was coupling. The closest personal contact I'd had lately was getting my car scratched.

'Heard from Steve?' she asked casually.

'No.'

Carol sat there, not saying anything. She was doing it to me, the interrogation technique, the tone of voice, the look, the silence going on forever. Underneath that casual comment she wanted to know why, how I felt, what had happened.

Resisting the urge to confess to Carol was relatively easy because I didn't have anything to tell her. I'd stuck the whole break-up with Steve in the too-hard basket. It wasn't a break-up as such, just a slow dwindling away. 'I saw Russell Hindley today.'

'Now that's a name I've heard recently. He's just started at Parramatta, hasn't he?'

'That's where I saw him,' I told Carol.

'I wonder how he's liking it?' Carol mused. 'He used to be with the Drug Enforcement Agency. Those boys don't like being shifted back. Bit of a glamour job the DEA—big cars, big money, high profile.'

'Plus anything they make on the side.'

Carol gave me a withering look. She hated it whenever I brought up the subject of police corruption. The DEA was the agency that confiscated and evaluated the worth of drug hauls. Seemed an opportunity too good to pass up by someone with connections.

'So why did they move him?'

'It wasn't him in particular. New policy. To avoid the kind of corruption you're implying, Claudia. Restructuring, decentralising, breaking the power bases up. No more than five years in the same position. Based on the idea that flowing water does not stagnate, become a cesspool. Less opportunity to build up contacts. It has its down side—what does it mean for your career if you're moved every five years? That's how some people are viewing it anyhow.'

'You, Carol?'

She slid the olive off the stick and closed her mouth around it. 'We'll see,' she said philosophically. 'Another drink?'

'Sure,' I said.

She got Jack's attention and indicated another round. 'What did you go and see Hindley about?'

Instead of answering directly, I asked her a question. 'Have you ever taken charge of a dead body?'

'You mean, fill in the forms, get in touch with the relatives? Lots of times.'

'How much detail do you remember?'

'It varies. You might remember if there's something unusual.'

'If I gave you a name, would you remember a body from eight, ten years ago?'

Carol looked doubtful. 'If I had the paperwork to prompt me, perhaps. Or, as I said, if there was a particular reason to remember. Where's all this leading?'

I told her.

'Maybe old Russo's got a photographic memory,' Carol suggested. She said she was sorry to hear about my father and expressed surprise at the fact that he drowned.

'It was during the 1985 floods. Apparently he hit his head and fell into a stormwater channel. He drowned in the middle of the city.'

'Well, maybe that's why Hindley remembers it. Simple.'

'I think he remembers because he stuffed up in some way. He didn't seem too fond of "dole bludgers" as he called them. Guy had a fractured skull, he could have been bashed. Maybe Hindley saved himself the trouble of investigating that possibility because Guy was a dero and who cares? The only thing that concerned Hindley was getting in out of the rain and keeping the paperwork to a minimum.'

'Nearly ten years ago, Claudia. You're going to have a hard time proving it. Believe me, I know what it's like trying to get the facts straight on events that happened years ago. Everyone's memory suddenly gets very selective. Why don't we go and get something to eat? Winning always gives me a healthy appetite.'

We didn't have to go far, there's a restaurant attached to the pub which is where I get most of my sustenance. It changes hands every year or so, partly because Jack likes to give battlers a break, people just out of prison, others who've just arrived in the country, rehabilitating drunks. He reckons the way things are going, someone has to remind people that Balmain was once a community-minded suburb.

At the moment it was being managed by a young couple who'd met at a drug rehab place up the country. They were still getting used to things—service was sometimes slow, even when it wasn't busy; things they ordered didn't arrive in time, or they got to the market too late. But they were excellent cooks. They could make a meal taste good even without balsamic vinegar and shaved Parmesan all over it.

The male half of the couple was called Luis. He had black hair tied back in a long ponytail. Arms skinny as poles and a face like an Aztec. Nicole, the female partner, had tight skin and an expression in her eyes as if she'd been on a long journey somewhere and didn't like the scenery.

We'd been sitting there five minutes and still hadn't received a menu. Though Carol didn't say anything, you could see she was having a hard time restraining herself from going into the kitchen and telling them how they should run the place. When Luis finally brought the menu over, she ordered antipasto. For two.

'A side salad? Garlic bread?' said Luis pleasantly.

'Yes, OK. Green salad and plain bread.' Talking quickly as if that would make them hurry up. The way she plays pool I didn't think she'd care how slow it was. 'The antipasto in Melbourne is so wonderful,' Carol said, suddenly an authority on the matter.

Thing is with Carol, she was usually just one step behind the fashion. She didn't have a nose for it like the trendsetters, she had to read about it like the trend followers. She did know her wines though. And fortunately here the selection was fine.

Luis came back with the bottle she ordered, showed it to her, uncorked it and poured a taste portion in her glass. Carol went through the ritual of tasting. It passed the test. 'Carry on,' she instructed him.

The antipasto was huge—marinated artichokes, bocconcini, grilled red peppers, salami, raw ham, eggplant, olives, the lot. Carol tucked heartily into the vegetarian portions of the meal. She didn't even refer to me as a carnivore when I ate the salami and raw ham. Which was just as well because actually I'm an omnivore. Like most humans, I have the teeth to prove it.

Carol used the fresh crusty bread to soak up the oil left on the plate. 'The best part,' she explained, dipping the bread. 'A meal in itself—good bread, fresh-pressed olive oil. Delicious!' For someone who'd spent only a few days in Melbourne she'd certainly gone a long way.

'You're running yourself round in circles, you realise that?' she said suddenly. 'This thing with your father,' she gestured, waving a piece of bread, 'you've got to get some perspective on it.' She stopped eating and looked at me with concern. 'Is that really the problem? Is everything else OK with you?'

'Sure. Why shouldn't it be?'

'I just thought, you know, breaking up with Steve and all . . .'

She was getting to me. 'Look,' I said defensively, 'will people stop calling it a break-up? Nothing cracked, nothing needs mending, it just fizzled out. End of story.'

She was gazing at me steadily. I felt the need to push on. 'What's your perspective on it then?'

She took a sip of wine. 'Well, I don't know. He was great looking but he seemed a bit, you know, boring.'

'Carol, I meant perspective on this business with my father. How do I stop going round in circles?'

She put the glass back down on the table. 'There are several options,' she began in the businesslike voice I knew and loved so well. 'Some of them you can do something about, some of them you can't. One,' she counted on her fingers, 'you can accept that your father's dead and get on with the rest of your life. But by the look on your face, I'd say that's out of the question. Let's review what we have here. You haven't seen your father since you were five. No attempt at contact has been made by either party.' I started to protest. 'No *contact* has been made,' she corrected herself. 'The assumption is that Guy Valentine spent the greater part of his life as a derelict. This has been confirmed by street sightings of him by ex-colleague Brian Collier. Also, the circumstances of his death seem to suggest same.' Again I started to protest. 'But the postmortem report . . .' she went on, reminding me she hadn't forgotten, 'the postmortem report, while revealing alcohol content in the blood shows little or no damage to organs characteristically associated with long-term alcoholism. And that's the rub, is it not?'

'That, plus Hindley's attitude.'

'Let's leave Hindley out of it for the moment, shall we? You can't prove attitude in court. Although, yes, I agree, he's not one of the finer examples of the species,' she confirmed. A rare acknowledgement from Carol. She never openly criticised her colleagues, whatever she thought of them. She may have met someone in Melbourne but she was married to the New South Wales Police Force. 'He tried one on, did he?' she added casually.

'For a while it looked like he might but I think I talked him out of it.'

The dead rarely leave deliberate clues but clues are left nevertheless. It seemed to me what we had with my father's death was anomalies. What the police call 'suspicious circumstances'. 'OK', I went on, 'let's assume Guy was a reformed alcoholic. But he had been drinking the night of his death. Perhaps someone with a long-term grudge set him up then took advantage of his state, bashed him unconscious and pushed him into the storm-water canal.'

Carol was shaking her head. 'It's just the business you're in. *We're* in,' she said. 'No-one ever dies "accidentally", they're always murdered. No-one crosses the road because they want to get to the other side, they're going over there to do a drug deal.' She finished off the wine in her glass. 'You don't know any of that. And besides,' she said darkly, 'if on the remote chance any of it were true, how are you going to prove it?'

'Cases can always be reopened. At any time,' I reminded her. 'Yes,' she sighed, 'technically they can. But it's a long time ago. Memories and bloodstains fade. He was cremated, wasn't he?'

'Yes.'

'You haven't even got a body to exhume.'

The bottle of wine was empty and Carol didn't want another. She was going home to do boring things like iron some shirts for the office. I signalled Luis to bring the bill. Carol said to give her a ring, if I wanted to talk. About anything. She meant about Steve, I could tell. I'm sure she thought I was pursuing this matter with my father to take my mind off other things. She was wrong. When I want to take my mind off my personal problems I drink.

I walked her to the door, waved her goodbye and watched

her drive off in her smart red car. Then I went to the bar and ordered a bottle of Scotch from Jack. The one I keep under my bed for special occasions was almost empty.

Back in my room I got out a red marker pen and drew a horizontal line about a third of the way down the new bottle. Enough to let my mind deviate from its usual pathways but still able to think productively.

There's nothing so pleasing as breaking the seal of a new bottle, seeing the glow of honey-coloured liquid. The first shot I had neat so I could feel the fire. In my mouth, down my throat, all the way down to the intestines. Then I poured a modest amount in a glass and topped it up with soda and a slice of lime. I opened the French doors to let in some air and lay there on the floor, propped up on my elbows. Laughter wafted up from downstairs, crickets pulsed out the sound of summer.

I had the door open but no messages were coming through. I took out the postmortem report and leafed through it. I'd read it so many times I almost knew the thing off by heart. It was a pity there were no photos. When a body comes into the morgue now it is videoed, so you have three-dimensional shots of it. But they weren't doing that back in 1985.

Cremated, nothing left. A box of ashes at Rookwood and some specimens in the morgue. I couldn't really stick that on the mantelpiece. This was morbid. I put the drink aside and went out onto the balcony. Maybe a pet would take my mind off things. A low-maintenance pet such as a bird or a fish. I didn't like being cooped up, what made me think a fish would enjoy swimming round and round in circles? That's what Carol thought I was doing—swimming round and round in circles, not even recognising my own reflection in the glass.

I could hear a car horn honking. It was Mrs Fields from across the road. Someone was parked outside her house, in the place she considered her parking spot. It happened at fairly regular intervals, not surprising seeing she lived opposite a pub. She slammed the car door and marched into the bar. I couldn't see it or hear it but I knew what was happening. She'd give Jack the rego number and make him get the owner to move the car. 'And next time I'll call the police!' she'd announce with a menacing twirl of her umbrella. From somewhere or other she'd managed to obtain a No Parking sign which usually stood outside her house, but someone must have moved it. One of these days she was going to get really fed up and smash a window with that umbrella, do some real damage.

Damage. Maybe the damage had repaired itself . . . the liver is one of the few organs in the body that can regenerate itself. I sifted back through my conversations with everyone involved. With Lucy, with Kirby, with Brian, Hindley and Carol.

Mrs Fields marched down the street. There was her No Parking sign, in front of someone else's house, doing what it was supposed to do. The whole street was parked out except for this space. She picked up the sign and moved it back outside her house. As far as anyone else was concerned, if the sign said No Parking then it was no parking. But the sign had been moved, and though it had been short-lived, a different place had become the No Parking zone.

I sifted through all the conversations to come back to the thing that had caught my attention in the first place. The state of the body. Too healthy for the life my father was supposed to have led. I had gone from that anomaly to thinking there were suspicious circumstances. Then it struck me. As I watched Mrs Fields moving the parking sign it all fell into place.

The only ID was a Social Security form in the name of Guy Francis Valentine. There was nothing else—no wallet, no personal items, nothing. All the time I'd taken it for granted. Like the No Parking sign. Because a piece of paper found on the body had Guy Francis Valentine printed on it, I assumed that the body was Guy Francis Valentine. But what if it wasn't? Like the No Parking sign, that piece of paper could be moved. Perhaps for some reason my father couldn't return the form that day and a friend was doing it for him. Perhaps my father had lent the deceased his coat and the form happened to be in it.

Mistaken identity. If only the morgue had kept photographic records back in 1985 the problem could be solved instantly.

But they *had* kept something. They had kept something. I went to the report and flipped through the pages.

```
Specimens retained: Tissue for histology. Blood
retained for storage.
```

They'd kept blood. And some of that blood ran through my veins.

I dialled Dr Kirby's number so quickly the first time that I misdialled and had to do it again. I told him what I wanted to try. He said he was sure it could be done but perhaps I should speak to his wife. He called her to the phone. I asked her how long specimens were retained.

'Indefinitely.'

'Even ones taken in 1985?'

'Yes,' she said. I told her what I wanted to do. She said there was no problem with that. All I needed to do was to bring a sample of my blood. She offered to take the sample for me if I wanted. Could I come to the morgue tomorrow morning? The earlier the better, the more the day wore on the busier she got. I said yes, that would be fine. I would be there when the doors opened.

I stopped drinking, put the bottle of Scotch away for the night. Tomorrow my blood was going to be scrutinised and I wanted it to look as good as possible.

Vince Reynolds was someone I'd met through Steve. Once we were all happy couples—Vince and Judy, Claudia and Steve. We'd go out for dinner, play pool, maybe go to the movies. I'd seen Vince once or twice since he and Judy split up but not recently. Steve and Vince had known each other for years, they used to go abseiling and caving with the university Speleological Society. But I hadn't called him up to discuss outdoor pursuits. At the time I met him he worked at the Youth Crisis Centre at Kings Cross. He knew as much about runaway children as anybody. We were meeting near the El Alamein Fountain in the heart of the Cross. There were places we could sit and talk and it was about five minutes walk from the Crisis Centre itself.

I got there first. I was up early anyway. I'd been to see Sofia Theodourou at the morgue and now had a small Bandaid over the place near the crook of my elbow where she'd taken blood. I didn't mind the short wait, in Kings Cross there was always plenty to look at. In the daytime all kinds of people hung out at the Cross, from film makers to street people. But they didn't hang out together. Unless one was using the other as their subject. Each group seemed to have their own map of the area. One group's main thoroughfares were the other group's back alleys.

I saw Vince walking towards me. White T-shirt with big sleeves, blue jeans, shiny, shoulder-length hair. He looked so clean he almost glowed. He broke into a broad grin when he saw me. 'How're you doing?' he greeted me.

'Great. Couldn't be better,' I lied. 'See that guy over there, the one all the others are listening to? It's Bruce Malone, isn't it?'

Vince turned to see where I was looking. 'Yeah. I've seen him round here before.'

Bruce Malone was one of the high fliers of the eighties, one that managed to avoid going to jail. Old developers never die, they just go quiet for a while then turn up somewhere else. Not that Malone was old. In fact, he looked in pretty good shape. He was surrounded by a bevy of male beauties. Too casually but carefully dressed to be real estate agents, no suits so they weren't businessmen, a little too healthy to be drug dealers.

'How's life in the education system?' Vince had done his time at the Youth Crisis Centre in the Cross and was now working three days a week as a school counsellor.

'Calmer. Flatter,' he said after a while. 'More successes but less rewarding, if you know what I mean.'

'Who do you reckon those blokes are?' I said. One of the male beauties was now standing out in the middle of the street holding a mobile phone up to his ear as if it were a comforter. The thumb of the other hand was casually hooked into the pocket of his pleated trousers. Must get better reception that way. Not that I have anything against mobile phones, I have one myself. But at least I turn mine off when I'm out in company.

'They don't look like social workers,' commented Vince. 'Film Industry?'

'Not enough beards. Well, not for feature films. Maybe it's Advertising.'

A big pink Thunderbird convertible came shimmering down the street. The driver had long blond hair, a headband and wrap-around sunglasses. He stopped in front of the group and let off a guy in a billowing white shirt, slim black trousers and with a video camera. In the end we were both right. They were in Advertising and they were making a video.

Further down the street was a tall brown-skinned girl who couldn't have been much more than fifteen, the same age as Madalena. Her face was still plump and smooth. A recent arrival.

I told Vince that I had a case involving a runaway girl and that I wanted to pick his brain.

'What exactly do you want to know?' he asked.

'Nothing exactly. Everything in general. Give me an idea of the terrain.'

'First of all, is it a runaway or a throwaway?'

'What do you mean?'

'Runaways are the kids whose parents—one or both—want them back. Throwaways, the parents don't want them. Mum and Dad split up, Mum gets a new boyfriend. She's spending time with the new man, she doesn't want the kid hanging round. Or the new man doesn't want the kid around. Kid feels insecure, gets a bit difficult, things get rough and it just snowballs.'

A man was standing in front of the girl now. A man wearing jeans and a windcheater. He asked her something, she answered. But she didn't look at him.

Vince continued, 'I had a client at the Centre, a guy fifteen or sixteen. He had a few problems but not radical. He comes home from school one day and all the locks are changed. He can't get into his own house. So that night he sleeps in the park. The next day he rings his mother at work and tells her about the locks. The mother says, "So?" The kid says, "I'm going to commit suicide if you don't let me come home." "Do it," says the mother, and hangs up. So he came to the Crisis Centre.'

The girl got up and walked down the street with the man.

'*He* did. They don't all do that straightaway. The Crisis Centre is just that. We deal with crises, not the long term. It's temporary accommodation only. Three nights maximum while we try to find them somewhere else—long or medium term refuges in the suburbs. Some kids come to us as the last resort, they can't take life on the streets anymore, they want to come back in.'

Vince was talking in the present tense, as if he was still there. 'You never really left, did you?' I said softly.

He'd been doing it without realising it. 'You see stuff there you never forget,' he explained. 'There are kids that I . . .' his voice trailed off. 'Your whole value system changes, the way you measure success. You might think that you have succeeded when the child is restored to her family and they're all living happily ever after. No. Up here success is when you get them to practise safe sex, to use the needle exchange.'

She was back, the girl on the street. Licking an Icy Pole, getting the bad taste out of her mouth.

Vince was launched now, talking animatedly. 'Think of it as a holiday camp. Friendships are formed but they're transient. The kids get close to each other quickly because for many of them, they only have each other. They've been abused by parents, uncles, figures of authority. They don't trust adults. We'd get guys coming in there, middle-aged men. Well dressed, respectable. They'd say they'd seen a kid on the street, that they could provide a good home. Their motives are far from philanthropic. But sometimes the kid chooses that option. Shacks up with the older man for three or four months. Sex for shelter. At least it's with the devil you know. Then the kid loses his fresh-faced look, his innocence, and the man chucks him out and looks for sweeter meat.

'The kids make friends with each other because in one way or another they share the same predicament. Then the person you thought was your best buddy vanishes into thin air. They get busted, they go missing. Even from the streets.'

The girl on the street could have been Madalena. She could have been my own daughter. 'It couldn't happen to any kid, could it?' I asked. 'I mean, if the kid is resourceful, strong; it couldn't happen.'

'At the Crisis Centre we'd get kids from all different backgrounds, from the North Shore, from Blacktown, different ethnic backgrounds. There'd usually be some disruption in the family, abuse of some kind. The kids have low self-esteem, the people who should love them the most abuse them, the people who should be their strength are unreliable. They're like baby birds pushed out of the nest before they can fly. So they flounder around on the streets. They have no skills, the girls go into prostitution to get the money to survive and it's so unbearable, they take drugs to dull the pain—marijuana, pills. Heroin eventually. Then they're caught in the vicious circle. They need the money from prostitution to buy the drugs to make the prostitution bearable. Sometimes the payment for sex is in drugs.'

The girl on the street had disappeared again. In my mind I was making up a life for her. She wouldn't get caught in that vicious cycle, despite the faraway look in her eyes. She was dreaming of the country from where she came, of Lismore, Moree. She was only down here temporarily. She was writing home every week telling her folks she'd be home soon. She had a really good job. And she'd be home soon.

I looked further down the street, to a girl sitting with her head bent, eyelashes black in her stark white face. She was wearing shorts, socks and Doc Martens, bruises on the legs. Everything on the outside of her shouted, I'm here for the taking. Everything on the inside of her shouted desperation. But the shouts coming from the insides of a person are rarely heard.

'The street kids are easy prey. Low self-esteem, abuse. They become victims, if they're not victims already. It's not just sexual abuse. When kids go missing, sometimes they're found alive, sometimes they're found dead. And sometimes they're never found.'

There were young girls, and boys, on the street who were prostitutes—drug users, many of them with only a few years left to live. There were old men lying in the park too drunk to brush away the flies settling on their weeping sores. There were ex-property developers producing corporate videos. There were people meeting each other for coffee in the trendy cafes, going shopping, doing deals. Sunny Sydney, most beautiful harbour in the world.

Nothing that Rosa had told me led me to believe that Madalena was an abused child. There'd been a fight with her father and she'd left. She wasn't on the streets, she was living in shared accommodation. Kerry told me she was smart enough not to hitch. If she was anything like Kerry she'd walk confidently around these streets.

But even a streetwise kid like Kerry had been attacked. And Madalena had disappeared. It was one thing that she was missing as far as her parents were concerned. It was another matter entirely that now even her friends didn't know where she was. One day she simply didn't come home. If a runaway child suspects someone's on her trail she runs even further. But it was different now. 'I think it's time we visited the Crisis Centre,' I said to Vince.

We walked. There was a dero sitting on a milk crate at the corner of the street, the best place in the world to watch the comings and goings of the street. He had a can of beer in one hand and an empty on the ground in front of him.

'G'day, mate. 'Ow're ya goin'?' he said to Vince. ''Aven't seen you around for a while.'

'How are you, Marius?' Vince took the hand that Marius offered.

'Can't complain, mate, can't complain.' They talked on. The words weren't always comprehensible, but you didn't need to hear every word to have a conversation.

'This is my mate Claudia,' Vince introduced me.

As he had with Vince, Marius offered me his hand. I took it. The hand was sticky, hopefully only from the beer he was drinking.

'You pretty much know what goes on around here, don't you, Marius?' Marius nodded wisely. 'You see the kids come and go, you hear the whispers.' Vince was giving me the opportunity to ask Marius about Madalena. 'Claudia here, she's looking for someone.' He could trust me, I was a mate of Vince's. I thought of giving him money. I often pay for information in my job, but I had a feeling Marius would be insulted if I offered him money.

I brought out the photo of Madalena and showed it to him. He studied it for a while then shook his head. He hadn't seen a girl like that. 'Thanks, mate,' said Vince.

'You been here long?' I asked Marius.

'Sometimes it feels like I've been here all my bloody life,' he joked. 'Four, maybe five years. I been lots of places. I like it here. I got mates. Good people.'

I wanted to ask about Guy, but it was too long ago.

The Crisis Centre looked like every other terrace house in the quiet street except it had bars on the windows and the door. They must have seen us walk in the gate because by the time we got to the door there was a woman with a strong handsome face, a big wide smile and perky short black hair opening it for us.

'Hey, Vince, how're ya doin'?' Vince gave her a hug.

There was a long hallway down one wall. The front room had been converted into an office. Half a wall had been knocked out to provide a counter. On the counter were cards and pamphlets explaining what the Crisis Centre did. 'The purpose of this centre is to provide homeless young people with accommodation, support, information and access to resources that enable them to take control of their lives and make informed decisions about their futures.' There were other pamphlets with advice on safe sex and needle use, in language kids could relate to.

Vince introduced me to everyone—to Paula, Ed and Michael. Handshakes all round. The general mood of bonhomie was interrupted by the appearance of a young guy about fourteen with blond curly hair flopping down into his face. He looked a little agitated but was doing his best to hold himself together. 'Ed? Can I see you, Ed?'

'Sure, mate, what's the problem?'

Whatever it was, he didn't want to discuss it in front of everyone. Ed got up and walked down the corridor with the guy. 'Madonna up in your room again, is she, Troy?' I heard Ed say as they disappeared up the stairs.

'Claudia's looking for someone. I know the drill but this is different,' Vince explained to the others.

I produced the photo of Madalena and briefly explained the story. 'If you know this girl, if you know where she is, you don't have to tell me. Just ask her to ring home.'

Paula studied the photo then passed it on to Michael. Neither of them recognised her. 'We can make a photocopy and put it on the wall,' Paula suggested. I looked at the wall. There were photos on the wall already under the general heading 'Have you seen this person?' Some of them had details—name, date of birth, last seen etc. Young faces, young hopeful faces in photos taken on birthdays, at graduations, the happy joyous occasions when photos are taken. I looked at the dates these kids were last seen. None of the dates were recent. These kids had been missing for years and none of them had been found. I didn't want to put Madalena up there on the wall with them.

'No,' I said, 'it's OK. Just, now you know what she looks like, if she turns up . . .' I gave them my card. 'Thanks for your help.'

I was just about to move out of the office when Ed returned, having placated whatever monsters Troy was grappling with. It was worth a shot. The three of them probably weren't all here all of the time. I didn't hold much hope but I showed Ed the photo anyway.

He studied it thoughtfully. 'Yeah,' he said, as if he recognised her.

'You've seen her?' I asked, wanting to know everything.

'Not in person. Seen a photo of her, not this photo but I'm almost sure it's the same girl.'

'Where did you see the other photo?'

'Bloke came in sometime last week. Paula, what day was it you and Michael had that meeting with the woman from Youth and Community Services?'

'Thursday,' said Paula.

'Yeah, Thursday. Reckons he was her uncle but I thought he looked a bit suss, eh? Thought maybe he was a pimp looking for one of his girls.'

'Did he have black curly hair? About thirty years old, reflective sunglasses maybe?'

'That's him. Is he really the uncle then?'

'I doubt it. He didn't by any chance leave a calling card, did he?'

'No. He started to back off then, when I asked for a name and address.'

'Vince, I'll give you a call. I'm sure you have a lot to catch up on with your buddies. Thanks for your help,' I said, addressing them all.

I walked back out to the street. Up on the corner Marius was deep in conversation with one of his cronies. It was early afternoon now and the beer cans were piling up. No doubt they were discussing the meaning of life. It was sunny and bright, the kind of day you felt good to be alive. If you were alive to feel it.

All the smart people were eating their sticky date puddings, fruit salads and risotti marinari when I went by the row of cafes with Italian names in Darlinghurst. That bit was easy. Finding the street took more time. I'd only been there once before, and that was at night. In the inner city things look quite different in the bright light of day.

Once I found the street the actual house was no problem. The '9' house number was still hanging by one screw and the distinctive artwork on the door was the same. Actually, it was better. At night, it had simply looked garish, but in the daylight I could see that it was quite skilful. A stylised Buddha in the middle of the door, with ornate patterning around the edges, which made it look as if the Buddha was guarding an entrance.

Maddy, Ralph, Simon. These were the names Kerry had called out that night. And later, when she came out again, she'd said, 'See ya, Simon.' A wispy young man as I recalled. I hoped I'd recognise him again.

The house still had music snaking out of it but at a much more bearable level. Certainly low enough for anyone inside to hear me knocking on the door.

The Buddha swung inwards and was replaced by the young man.

'Hi. Simon?'

'Yes,' he said warily.

'My name's Claudia. I'm a friend of Kerry's.'

He looked me up and down, wondering whether Kerry would have someone like me for a friend. For a start, I was old enough to be her mother. But you couldn't tell that just by looking.

'What do you want?'

'Can I come in? It won't take long,' I assured him.

He took a minute to think about it, then let me in. Into a time warp. There was incense burning, the walls were painted either blue or pink and the dark blue ceiling of the hallway had silver stars painted on it. As I walked by the bedrooms I saw mattresses on the floor with bright-coloured Indian spreads. There was even a girl sitting in the kitchen wearing a long diaphanous top and skirt. The anomaly in all this was her workboots and thick socks. That wasn't part of the seventies wardrobe. For most of the seventies she hadn't even been born. If you were old enough to remember what it was like the first time, you were too old to wear it the second time around.

'Hi,' she said, a friend to all. 'I'm Melissa.'

'Hi, Melissa. I'm Claudia.'

We were now all seated at the kitchen table. They each had a half-finished cup of tea in front of them but neither of them offered me a cup. Maybe the pot was empty.

As far as Melissa was concerned there was no need to ask questions of me. I'd simply come in and joined the camaraderie of the house. But Simon didn't have the same trust and faith in his fellow beings. He was waiting for me to state my business.

'We have a mutual friend. Madalena.' I watched for their reactions. Melissa's expression changed only slightly. It was as if the rosy hue emanating from her filtered out any harshness in the world. Perhaps it was just the reflection off the pink walls. Simon, on the other hand, took the full impact of it.

'She's not here,' he said.

'But she *was* here, wasn't she?'

He didn't say anything. I thought perhaps I should help him out.

'Look, I know what she said,' I took a guess. 'Not to say anything if anyone came looking for her, right?'

He shrugged a shoulder noncommittally.

'Madalena disappeared. If she's in any danger I want to help her. Don't you want to help?'

He started fiddling with the teacup in front of him, avoiding my eyes.

'Did a man come here? A dark-haired man who maybe said he was Madalena's uncle? Is that why you're afraid to talk?'

'I'm not afraid,' said Simon, 'I've got nothing to say, that's all.'

'Hey, I remember him,' said Melissa. 'Simon? You remember, he had those really cool sunglasses. When he moved his face they were like . . . rainbow colours.'

Far out. 'What happened that night?' I now turned my attention to Melissa.

'He came during the day.'

'Not at night?' I said, thinking it might have been the night of the party.

'No, it was the day. He said he was Maddy's uncle and he had a message for her. He must have found her because she didn't come back. I think she went back home because her sleeping bag and everything's gone, hasn't it, Simon?'

Simon was staring daggers at Melissa. He wanted her to shut up but at the same time he didn't want to make a big deal of it in front of me.

'Is that what happened, Simon, she moved back home?'

He shifted uncomfortably. He knew it wasn't true as much as I did. 'Yeah, I guess that's what happened.'

'Can I have a look at her room?'

'Sure,' said the ever-friendly Melissa. Simon shrugged again— if all her things were gone, there was no harm in me looking.

She showed me to a blue room, a mattress on the floor, some fold-up chairs stacked against the wall. Apart from that the room was bare. I had a good look around but could see no sign of anything.

'It's a spare room,' Melissa explained. 'You know, when we have parties and things, people can crash here.'

'Well, thanks for showing me, I hope I didn't take up too much of your time. Simon?' Like the gentleman I expected him to be, Simon showed me to the door. When we got there I said, 'What really happened?'

I must have been in the house a good twenty minutes. Enough time for him to decide whether to trust me. I had been courteous and polite, I hoped he had a good impression of me.

Melissa was out of earshot but he looked around anyway. 'I . . . I don't know.'

'You didn't think it was strange that she just upped and left?'

'I thought she'd gone back home. When she first came here, she was really upset, she wouldn't say why. Kerry said she'd had a fight with her old man the day before so we just assumed it was that. Then when she left, I assumed she'd gone back home. But she hasn't been in touch with anyone. You'd think she would have let someone know. I mean, she didn't even call Kerry.'

'So when she left she took her things with her.'

He frowned. 'No. They went missing later. I thought, maybe she'd come back for them when everyone was out.'

The same pattern as when she'd left Lugarno. She disappears then her belongings disappear. 'Who lives here?'

'Melissa, me. Alex, but he's away.'

'Does anyone else have a key?'

'Raf does.'

'Raf?'

'He did all the painting,' said Andrew. 'On the door here, on the ceiling in the hallway.'

'Does he live here?'

'He comes and goes.'

'Where might I find him?'

Simon gave me one of his shrugs, but this time without the surliness. 'He just turns up. You never know when.'

I walked back past the trendy cafes and waited at the main intersection that separates Darlinghurst from Kings Cross. Raf. I kept saying it over and over in my mind. When I'd heard Kerry call it out the night I'd followed her, I thought she'd said 'Ralph'. But it was Raf. An abbreviation. Raffia. Raffish. Rafael. Not a very common name but one that rang a bell with me. I'd seen it in Gothic lettering in a book in Madalena's room, a fantasy book about a lost world. Rafael Khan. Maybe there was a phone number in the book as well. Has a key to the house but 'comes and goes'. A mystery man. An artist who has books about lost worlds. I wondered if he knew anything about lost girls.

Raf wasn't the only mystery man. There was also the one who drove the car with the FABIO plates. Wherever I went he had also been. Always one step ahead. Maybe that's because he'd started sooner. And knew something I didn't.

I descended the escalator into Kings Cross station. Was it possible that Madalena's father had hired someone, and not told his wife? Just as she was not telling him about hiring me. I didn't like his tactics with Kerry but then he wouldn't be the first private investigator to bend the rules. Perhaps he wasn't a professional, just someone who worked for Grimaldi.

I had to talk to Madalena's mother. I looked at the posters on the wall on the other side of the track, Speed Kills. I could imagine Rosa sitting at home waiting for the phone to ring. Hoping it was Madalena. I told her I would let her know how things were going. How could I tell her the story so far and make it sound hopeful rather than alarming?

There was a rumbling and a whoosh of cold steely air heralding the approach of the train back to the city. The headlights appeared out of the darkness of the tunnel, people stirred. Got themselves ready for when the train stopped and the doors opened. One or two people alighted, then those waiting on the platform got on. The automatic doors closed behind us and the train started up. We travelled briefly underground then the train burst out into the open, the roofs and buildings of Woolloomooloo visible below us.

It was then that I saw the two young boys outside the carriage, standing on the bit that joins one carriage to the other. Joyriding, scared shitless but trying to look nonchalant, getting a buzz out of flirting with death. The train went into the tunnel again and down under the city. Down and down it went, all the way to Town Hall.

Naturally, the first thing Rosa did when I phoned her was ask about Madalena. I said there'd been some developments but I'd prefer to discuss them with her in person. She said yes, all right, there was still time this afternoon before her husband came home. That was one of the things I wanted to discuss with her, this skirting around her husband. If he had hired someone, perhaps we should all sit down and pool our resources, I thought wryly.

The next phone call I made was to Danny. He was patching up the Daimler's scratch and I needed another car. Despite my refusal to sell just yet, Danny was still working on me. If I'd asked him for a whole fleet of cars he wouldn't have objected.

This time it was a panel van, a blue iridescent number with portholes in the sides. Love machines, I think we used to call them. It wasn't exactly the most inconspicuous car but at least it wasn't registered in my name. The van was airconditioned so the long drive to Lugarno was bearable. It had a CD player installed as well, and some good country music.

But good music wasn't the reason I drove right by the Grimaldi house instead of stopping. He was there. Watching the house. When you do surveillance for a living you recognise someone else doing it straightaway. He wasn't in the Chrysler with the FABIO plates but it was him just the same. So I drove right on by. He'd had a good look at me at Hoyts, he may have recognised me that night in Darlinghurst, but he hadn't yet worked out how to follow me. I wasn't going to give him the chance this time either. I turned the corner and kept driving. When I'd worked out what to do I rang Rosa.

I was on my way to Strathfield, to Anna Larossa's place. I was surprised to find I was looking forward to the visit. Anna was Rosa's cousin, she knew what was going on. And Rosa saw her frequently so that when Fabio followed her to Anna's place he would think it was just a routine visit.

But there were other reasons I was looking forward to the visit. It would give Anna a chance to ask questions. If she had any. Her silence was making me curious. The travel expenses had been pretty hefty. If it had been me, I would have queried them. But maybe she'd just taken it at face value. If you had nothing to compare it to, how would you know? I walked up to the house. Anna was expecting me. Rosa had phoned her and Anna was on the lookout. 'Nice to see you again,' she said.

The house was pleasant, a polished timber hallway, white walls. 'I'm making coffee. Will you come into the kitchen?'

The kitchen had black and white vinyl tiles that looked like a chessboard. The theme was continued in the black and white check curtains, now closed, at the window. On the stove sat a coffee percolator making noises. Anna reached up to a cupboard and got out a packet of muesli biscuits.

'John's doctor is pleased with the progress he is making. There are not so many restrictions with the diet now.' She arranged the biscuits on a plate and turned off the heat under the percolator, which appeared to have reached its climax. 'Come, we will wait for Rosa in the living room.'

The living room had the same polished timber as the hall. Grey leather lounge suite around a smoky glass coffee table. Beneath it was a fluffy white rug that looked like it might once have been a dog.

'John will be home later,' said Anna, as if I'd be really pleased to hear this news.

'He's not on the road, then?'

'You remembered,' beamed Anna. 'No, he has a different run

now. He does the libraries around Liverpool. He doesn't go away at all now.'

'How nice for you.'

'Well, I've had to make some adjustments,' she hinted.

I didn't get to find out what those adjustments were because the doorbell rang. Rosa. Anna sprang up and went to the door. They exchanged greetings, I could hear the voices getting louder the further they came down the hall. Anna went into the kitchen to get the coffee and Rosa came down and sat beside me on the lounge. She seemed flushed from the journey.

'Here is the book you asked me to bring.' She handed it to me, *The Lost World of Agharti*. I put it in my bag. 'The car followed me here,' she announced. 'I did like you said and didn't look at it but when I got to the last traffic lights, I saw the car in the mirror.'

'Did you recognise the man?'

'I couldn't see the driver too well. It was too far away.'

Anna came in with the coffee on a silver tray. She deposited the tray on the coffee table then left us in peace.

'It's the same man we saw at the cinema that first day,' I told her. 'I think he's working for your husband.'

'To find Madalena?'

'Yes.'

'Why is he watching my house instead of looking for her?'

'Perhaps your husband thinks Madalena might try to contact you. Rosa,' I said, lightly touching her on the arm, 'you and your husband have to talk about this. It's stupid you both having someone look for her.' And it wasn't making my job any easier having this guy putting Madalena's friends, the people who usually know something, offside.

Rosa looked down at her hands in her lap. 'You don't understand. It's very difficult to talk to my husband. I can't even mention her name to him. Besides, when would I have the opportunity? He hardly comes home anymore. You know, I would come and stay here with Anna and John except . . . except I keep hoping . . .' She put her hand up to cover her face. 'I have to be there in case she rings. She's not dead,' she burst out, 'my little girl is not dead.'

'Rosa,' I said softly, 'there's a good chance that Madalena is alive.' I tried to keep my darker fears at bay. There *was* a chance she was alive. Somebody had come back to the house in Darlinghurst for her things, it could have been Madalena herself. I told Rosa that I had been in touch with friends who'd seen Madalena since she left Lugarno.

'Why didn't she call and tell me she was all right?' Rosa implored.

'That's what we don't know. Rosa, she went to see her father the day she disappeared, did he tell you that?'

'She went to see Arturo? No, it's not possible.'

'Why not?'

'He would have told me this. Why didn't he tell me?'

'They may have had a fight, perhaps he hit her. He was ashamed to tell you. I don't know. You have to speak to your husband. If he hardly comes home anymore, go and see him at work.'

From somewhere in the house I could hear the little electronic jingle of a computer game. Rosa closed her eyes, her face tense. It was a hard thing I was asking her to do. 'He doesn't like me going there. He doesn't like me to be involved with the business.'

I was sure he didn't. 'For Madalena's sake,' I reminded her. 'Speak to him. Ask him about the man in the car. I think his name is Fabio.'

She thought about it. It had to be easier than what they were both separately going through now. Couldn't they at least share their grief? 'I will speak to him. I will ask him what happened that day, I will ask him about the man. I will ask him if he will consent to a meeting with you.' She spoke with resolution, as if swearing on a bible; the words becoming a pledge to herself. She stood up. 'Now. I will drive to his work and do it now. Anna?'

No doubt Fabio would follow her. I wondered how he'd enjoy the trip back to his employer. And what he'd do when he got there.

We left the living room, went down the hallway and came into a small alcove where Anna sat glued to a computer screen, playing a game. 'She likes to ride the super airwave,' explained Rosa. 'But only when John is not here. He thinks it's bad for her brain.' I thought it was super highway but what would I know?

Rosa tapped Anna on the shoulder. 'I'll see you tomorrow,' she said. Loudly, as if Anna was behind glass. Anna put her mouse down. 'I'll come to the door with you.'

'Is there a way out the back?' I asked.

'Not really,' said Anna. 'It's the neighbour's house at the back.'

I waited for Rosa to leave. Through the window in the front room I saw her car drive up and disappear round the corner. Then Fabio's car did the same. If Anna wanted to ask me anything now was the time. But she didn't ask. She smiled politely and showed me to the door.

The Lost World of Agharti. The rays of the late afternoon sun shone through the windscreen of the panel van as I sat in a quiet backstreet of Strathfield leafing through the book. On the front page where Rafael Khan's name was written in stylish Gothic calligraphy was a map of the world with the North Pole near its centre. Naturally the map did not feature that great southern continent, Australia. A dotted line was drawn in a roughly circular shape through North Africa, Tibet, Mongolia, the rim of North and Central America. This dotted line marked the boundaries of Agharti, a world hidden beneath the surface of the earth. As I leafed through the book I learned that though the kingdom of Agharti was a Tibetan Buddhist utopia, most cultures had myths and legends of an underground world that could be accessed by a labyrinth of subterranean tunnels and passageways. Could be but very rarely was. Although the underground world had intrigued people throughout history, Bulwer Lytton, Madame Blavatsky, even Adolf Hitler who sent soldiers and scientists off on expeditions, those who had purportedly gained access either didn't come back, were sworn to silence, got lost and couldn't remember exactly where they'd gone underground or had some other convenient reason why the many entrances to this world were never precisely pinpointed.

It wasn't the kind of thing I took to like a duck to water but I could see how it might appeal to the imagination of a fifteen year old on the brink of discovery of self, others and the world in general. I wasn't exactly cynical—I realised that the human species had sheltered in caves under the ground for eons longer than we'd lived in houses—I just didn't think there was a better world elsewhere. This was it, for better or worse. The text was mildly intriguing, but when I got to the photos I was absolutely riveted.

Not only was there a photo of a Buddha statue, obviously the inspiration for Raf's artwork on the door of the Darlinghurst house, there was also another one that showed the peculiar keyhole-like entrance to a tunnel system in India. This was a dead ringer for the tattoo on Kerry's arm. The one that Madalena had as well.

When I pulled up outside Kerry's place I saw a woman sitting on the front step in a dressing gown, smoking a cigarette. She looked about fifty but could have been as young as thirty. Kerry was coming up the street. She'd been to the supermarket.

The front gate creaked as Kerry pushed it open with her foot. In either hand she had a plastic carry bag, a bunch of spinach poking out the top of one of them. The bags were heavy, judging by the way her arm muscles tensed. The woman looked up with vacant eyes and smiled a thin smile at Kerry. Kerry, on the other hand, wasn't looking too pleased to see her mother sitting there in a dressing gown, hair dishevelled, at this hour of the day.

But as she got closer to the front step her expression softened. She bent down as if bending down to a child with a sore knee. Some words were exchanged, words I couldn't hear. Then the mother took on the look of a chastised child. Reluctantly she got up and went into the darkness of the house. Kerry picked up the shopping and followed her mother in. I gave them a few moments to settle then walked up to the front door.

When Kerry opened the door I was assailed by the odour of

rancid fat. Lightly in the background I could hear the shower going. Kerry looked for a minute then rememberd who I was. 'Hi.' She wasn't displeased to see me.

She didn't invite me in, rather she closed the door behind her and sat down in an old canvas director's chair on the narrow verandah. I sat down in the other one, gingerly at first. One false move and the whole thing would collapse on the ground.

'Is Raf Maddy's boyfriend?' I asked.

She gave a little laugh, as if she found the idea amusing. 'No, not really. He's just a guy we used to hang out with.'

A small ginger cat appeared from out of the tangle of tall weeds and jumped into Kerry's lap. Absentmindedly she began stroking it.

'What do you mean hang out with?'

The cat was obviously having a soothing effect on her. 'Oh, you know, we used to do stuff together,' she said dreamily, as if it had all happened in some distant past.

'Like what?'

'Explore the tunnels.'

'You mean train tunnels?'

'Whatever. Train tunnels, Telecom tunnels, stormwater tunnels, old coalmines. As long as it was underground, it didn't matter which.'

I thought of the two kids I'd seen earlier today riding on the outside of the train. As long as it was dangerous, as long as it got the adrenalin going.

'You still do it?'

'It got a bit weird. Not Raf, he's really cool, but some of the others.'

'There was a group of you did this tunnel thing?'

She idly played with the cat's ears, running her fingers to the tips of them, watching the cat flick away the tickle.

'Well, Maddy and I weren't really in the group, we just liked going into the tunnels. Like, they were all into this thing about some lost kingdom under the earth, you know, Atlantis or something.'

'Agharti.'

'Yeah. Anyway, there's this tunnel in Glebe, a disused railway tunnel. The group would meet there and light candles and chant about the King of the World, like he was Jesus or something.'

'So you don't see Raf anymore?'

'Yeah, I see him occasionally. You know that house in Darlinghurst? Raf painted that beautiful door. He is such a good painter. He does other stuff as well. He does huge paintings in chalk on the street. You know Hyde Park, opposite David Jones in town? He does street art there. Such beautiful colours, and the people look really real. It takes him weeks to do one.'

'Raf did your tattoo?'

'Not the tattoo. Raf did the drawing then a tattooist up the Cross went over it. We were a bit pissed,' she explained.

'Have you seen Raf since Maddy disappeared?'

'No.'

'Do you know where he lives?'

She laughed, as if the question had no meaning. 'He has a couple of places he stays but he doesn't actually have an address. He could make a lot of money if he went into advertising or graphic design, but he doesn't want to do that.' Integrity and the artistic spirit. I wondered how long that would last.

The door opened. 'Kes, I've made some cheese on toast if you want some.' It was Kerry's mother, freshly showered and holding a cigarette in her hand. 'Oh sorry, I didn't know you had company.'

'Hi, I'm Claudia,' I introduced myself.

'Want some cheese on toast?' she asked me. 'I can easy fling another slice of bread under the griller.'

'No thanks,' I said, getting up. 'Maybe some other time.' Over the cigarette smoke I could smell something burning. I didn't like to say anything, she'd probably put a lot of effort into making what seemed to be their dinner.

'I better get back to it. You coming in, Kes?'

'Yeah, Mum, rightaway.' She gently put the cat down on the ground and picked a couple of its hairs off her black jeans.

'That guy hasn't bothered you again?' I asked.

'What guy?' He mustn't have bothered her too much if she had to be reminded of it. I reminded her, all the same. 'No. I haven't been to the Darlinghurst house recently. Mum's been . . . sick.'

It seemed futile but I had to ask. 'Have you heard from Maddy?'

All the brightness in her face disappeared. 'No.' Then she pulled herself back from the yawning chasm that had momentarily opened up before her. 'She's OK, though, I just know she is. I guess one day there'll be this postcard from Byron or somewhere. That'll be Maddy.'

The breath caught in my throat at her optimism. Inexplicably I felt my eyes prick with tears. I stepped down onto what was probably once a path to the gate. 'Enjoy your cheese on toast.'

'Yeah, thanks.'

'Kerry,' I said suddenly, as she was about to go into the house, 'if ever you need anything, anything at all, give me a call.'

She looked at me oddly, wondering what I was making all the fuss was about.

I t was after six but I knew Brian would still be at work. The honeymoon was over now and he was back in the thick of it. Traffic was heavy but at least I was going the other way—towards the city rather than away from it like everyone else, returning home to the suburbs after a hard day at the office. I waited till I got to the first big intersection, then I phoned.

'Brian? It's Claudia . . . No, not Brazil. Hurstville. I'm in the car.'

Brian made some comment to the effect that he never thought he'd live to see the day I'd make a phone call sitting in my car at traffic lights. I told him I'd gotten over that glitch as soon as I realised how practical a mobile phone was in my line of work.

'You know we were talking about Grimaldi the other day? Well, if it's not too much bother, can you check him out?' He asked me what in particular. 'Companies, business records, tax returns if your intelligence stretches to that.' I could almost see him grinning, appreciating the joke. The Tax Office knew everything about everyone but getting information out of them was worse than getting blood out of a stone. 'Also, if he has an employee called Fabio—sorry I don't have the surname—or if there are any records of payment to such a person. That'd be the best Christmas present I could hope for.' He said he'd see what he could do. Maybe he'd have something for me when I came over for dinner. With perfect timing I hung up at the exact moment the lights changed.

It was just on 6.30 when I got back into town. Peak hour parking restrictions were finished and I had no trouble finding a parking spot outside David Jones. But that turned out to be my ration of luck for the day. Across the road I could see the painting but the artist had gone.

The painting was alongside Hyde Park, close to the entrance of St James station. There was a florist on one side of the entrance and a newsstand on the other. They were both packing up for the day. I asked the woman in the florist if she knew where the street artist was. She just shrugged and continued bringing the buckets of flowers inside. I tried the same thing with the guy selling newspapers. 'He's gone. Probably be back tomorrow,' he assured me. 'He comes most days.'

I went back and examined the painting. It was The Last Supper. Kerry was right—the colours were beautiful. The cobalt blue of Christ's robes was reflected in the blue of his eyes. His fair hair framed his face like a halo. Strange that a Sephardic Jew like Jesus would have blue eyes and fair hair. Artistic licence I suppose. I stood back to admire the painting as a whole but soon my view was obscured by people walking along the street heading for the station. Some of them skirted around the painting but most walked straight over it, thinking of nothing else but getting home for the night.

Our hair colour, our clothes, our names, even our facial features can be altered, but our genes don't change. Deoxyribonucleic acid is the stuff genes are made of. In the biochemistry of a person's chromosomes are features unique to that individual. Blood, semen and other body fluids present at the scene of a crime can be analysed and matched with a suspect's unique DNA patterning.

DNA analysis was first used to establish paternity. Some of an individual's unique features are shared by family members and are passed from one generation to the next. It was paternity I was thinking about as I drove to the morgue. There'd been a message from Sofia Theodourou. She had a result on the bood tests. Could I come and see her at my earliest convenience?

The Glebe morgue, as well as housing the Institute of Forensic Medicine also houses the Coroner's Court. The brown brick complex is on Parramatta Road opposite Sydney University. You can get a degree in medicine or law then pop across the road for a job.

When I walked in off the street, however, I wondered if I'd come to the the wrong place. It was chaos. The foyer was filled with people whose average age was eighteen, milling around, dressed to kill, chattering on to each other like long-lost friends. Disregarding the policeperson who was endeavouring to get everyone's name and address. She was fighting a losing battle.

I made my way through the throng. 'Why the big crowd?' I asked one of the sheriffs. 'It's a drive-by matter,' she said tersely, as if she'd told me too much already.

The inquest into a drive-by killing. I remembered it now, happened about six months ago. A drive-by shooting outside an all-night cafe in Marrickville. It had to be the same one. Drive-bys are rare in Australia.

I left the Coroner's Court section, walked through the door to Forensic Medicine and told the woman in the office I was there to see Dr Theodourou. She asked for my name then picked up the phone. 'A Claudia Valentine to see Dr Theodourou,' she said. 'Won't be a minute,' she said, putting down the phone.

Less than a minute later a door opened and a man wearing glasses over a lean tanned face appeared. 'You're looking for Dr Theodourou?' he asked.

'Yes.'

'Come this way,' he invited.

I went that way. He led me down a maze of corridors and left me in a room with a tea urn, fridge, chairs, a table and magazines. It must have been some sort of common room but there was no-one else there at the moment. I flicked through a couple of the magazines. Still no-one came. I went for a little walk, wondering what was behind all those closed doors I had passed. I pushed a set of double doors, which let out a draught of cold air, and found myself looking in a storeroom with rows and rows of bodies in bags on shelves.

'Looking for anyone in particular?' I heard a voice behind me. It was a woman with steely grey hair and a steely grey face. She wore nurses' shoes and a watch pinned to her ample bosom. If she wasn't a matron she had a strong desire to be one.

'It's OK,' I assured her, 'I'm waiting for Dr Theodourou.'

'You can wait at reception,' she went on in her authoritative yet matronising tone.

I'd already got this far, I wasn't going back to reception. I started to head towards the common room. She came with me.

Then parked herself in the doorway so I couldn't get through. 'This is for staff only.'

What was wrong with the woman? 'A member of staff showed me to this room,' I glared, starting to lose patience with her behaviour. 'If you don't mind.'

We stood there glaring at each other. The stalemate was broken by the sound of another voice. 'Hi. Sorry you had to wait.' It was Sofia Theodourou. 'Beryl?' she said to the matron. 'What are you doing up here, is everything all right?'

'Yes, doctor, perfectly all right.' Beryl skulked away down the corridor.

'What a morning! I've got to get a cup of coffee, do you mind?' I thought Sofia would open a cupboard, drag out a jar of Nescafe, but no. She meant a takeaway coffee from up the street. She led me out the back way, past the delivery dock. 'Beryl wasn't annoying you, was she?' Sofia asked when we were outside.

'Only mildly. What does she do?'

'She does the laundry.'

Sofia took me up to a tiny cafe on a corner. There were hessian sacks on the floor opened to reveal their cargo of coffee beans. There was coffee from Eastern Europe, from Italy, from Brazil and Nicaragua. The place smelled like heaven.

'Cappuccino to go,' she told the woman behind the counter. 'I'll have the same,' I said.

We were on our way back when Carol walked round the corner. 'Well, well,' Carol greeted us. We looked at each other quizzically, each wondering what the other was doing there but, in the presence of a third person, too cool to ask. I was about to introduce her to Sofia but they seemed to know each other already.

'You haven't brought me more bad news, have you?' Sofia said to Carol.

'Not today. I've got business in the other half of the building. See you later.'

'You know Inspector Rawlins?' Sofia sounded surprised.

'Quite well,' I said.

Sofia dropped me at the common room then disappeared.

She came back with a folder under her arm, and a moustache of foam from the cappuccino, which she deftly licked away. She laid the folder down on the table and took out something that looked like an X-ray.

'This is an autoradiograph,' she announced. 'DNA analysis. People call it genetic fingerprinting but it's more akin to blood grouping, a highly specific and individualised blood grouping. Do you know how it works?'

I had the feeling she was going to tell me anyway, whether I knew or not.

'The testing involves a polymerase chain reaction. The polymers show up like this,' she said, holding the autoradiograph up for me to see. I saw vertical blotches of varying length, similar to the barcode on goods at the supermarket. 'This is your DNA patterning.'

She took a second autoradiograph from the folder. 'And this is . . . well, analysis of the blood sample from the body identified as Guy Francis Valentine.' She superimposed one DNA patterning on the other. 'You can see for yourself, not the remotest resemblance. To check, we also tested the histology sample.' Yet another autoradiograph came out of the folder. 'These two are identical—the tissue and the blood specimen from 1985. They're definitely from the same body. But neither of them remotely resembles your patterning. I don't know who that person was, but he's not your father. There's no way the two of you are related by blood.'

Even though I had gone over this possibility in my mind, told myself this was the only logical explanation, it was still a shock to actually hear someone say 'He's not your father.' The sentence seemed to echo like a sonic boom.

'I'm sorry,' said Sofia sympathetically. 'I hope I haven't upset you.'

'To tell you the truth, I'm not sure how I feel. It's not as if I wasn't anticipating this result. I wouldn't have asked you to do all this otherwise. Thanks,' I said.

'Not a problem. If there's anything else, just let me know. I'll take you out the back way,' said Sofia. 'It's quicker.'

She accompanied me as far as the delivery bay. There was

now an ambulance in the dock. Two men were lifting out a body on a stretcher. There was a sheet running the length of the stretcher but the corpse beneath it was small. A child.

'Sofia, there is something else.' I showed her the photo of Madalena. 'Her name's Madalena Grimaldi.' I didn't have to explain any further.

'No,' Sofia shook her head. 'In fact in the last few weeks there've been no unidentifieds at all.' She handed me back the photo. 'Good luck.'

'Claudia!'

It was Carol. I must have walked straight past her car without realising it.

'He's not my father.' I explained about the DNA testing. 'Not even a remote connection.'

'Claudia,' Carol said with gravity, 'I know this is really an outside chance but it's something you should at least consider.' She paused, as if it was something she didn't even want to consider herself. 'Is it possible that Mina . . . I mean, perhaps the person she was married to wasn't your father. These things happen.'

I knew the answer to it without even thinking.

'No. Definitely no.' If there was any way she could have disavowed him she would have. 'Are you sure you're not just denying the possibility? I've seen that photo you have of him, there's no family resemblance.'

'So?' I didn't look like Guy but David did. The short robust build, the freckles.

'You all right?'

'Yeah, thanks Carol.'

'I'm off to Melbourne for a couple of days. We'll have a game of pool when I come back, OK?'

I watched her drive off then continued on to my own car.

But I didn't go home. At the Darling Street–Victoria Road intersection, instead of turning right into Balmain I went straight ahead. Before the Iron Cove Bridge I turned left and drove down one of the quiet backstreets. Then I got out and walked. Across the oval to the waterline of Iron Cove. Not fast enough to call it power walking but briskly. My intention wasn't to exercise, it was to think. The left–right movement, the coordination of limbs. Walking balances the brain.

The body found at Rushcutters Bay on Anzac Day, 1985, was not my father. I would probably never know who that body belonged to. The chances of it being someone else with the name Guy Francis Valentine were one in a million. I was almost sure that the man who died that night had somehow ended up with my father's Social Security form. Hindley had botched it. Either he'd not checked it out thoroughly or he'd somehow got hold of the form and planted it on the body. To save himself the paperwork. I'm sure he'd even managed to justify it to himself. One dero is the same as the next, why not save the taxpayer some money? Conveniently, the Report of Death to the Coroner was missing, the body was cremated. No way of checking this little misdemeanour.

So if my father wasn't in the wall at Rookwood Crematorium, where was he? Was he buried somewhere else, under someone else's name? Or was he still alive?

I had passed through the quiet gardens of Rozelle Hospital and was walking beside the traffic roaring along Henley Marine Drive. There were a few other walkers and joggers around, even though it was now midday and the day was hot.

Off the road now and on the Drummoyne side of the cove. All I had to do was cross over the Iron Cove Bridge and I'd be back at the car, the circle completed. I climbed up to the walkway. It was windy on the bridge and the traffic was even louder. Through the gaps in the safety railing I could see the murky blue water below, flowing all the way in to the city. Somewhere along the way was an invisible line where the water stopped being the Parramatta River and became the harbour. Only real estate agents knew exactly where that demarcation lay.

I had come this far, I couldn't back off now. I was going to look for him. All these years and all these streets I'd walked, I'd never made a concerted effort to seek him out. Because always in the back of my mind lurked the fear that I might not like what I found. But now I was determined to find him.

I turned off the bridge and into the street where the car was parked. There was a car parked behind it now, a Holden Commodore with tinted windows, the owner no doubt down here for his lunchtime jog around the bay. Suddenly the door opened and in this quiet street I felt a small round pressure in the middle of my back.

'Get in the car.'

It was Hindley. I was trapped in a square of footpath. The open door blocked my way ahead, a brick wall on one side, the length of the car on the other. Behind me stood Hindley with a gun in my back. I thought it best under the circumstances to get in the car. I was dismayed to see who was sitting in the driver's seat. The lovely young cop from Parramatta, hands gripping the steering wheel, looking straight ahead.

The small round pressure was gone from my back but had now found a new home near my left ear. Without moving my head I glanced sideways and saw Hindley's hairy hand holding a Smith & Wesson .38 Special. Police issue. Carol had one just like it. Despite the heat of the day the metal was knife-edge cold, as was the interior of the car. They were running the airconditioning. Despite the coolness of the air I could smell Hindley's stale sweat as he leaned forward.

'So maybe we didn't try as hard as we could have but that matter is now dead and buried.' His hot wet breath turned to ice on my neck. 'I'm looking at retirement in a couple of months and I intend going out with a clean slate. I'm not having some dero from ten years ago stuffing it up for me. There'll be no further enquiries made, understand? You keep pursuing this matter, it'll be more than just a friendly little chat, missy.'

The lovely young cop was still looking ahead, face rigid. Like he'd rather be anywhere else than here.

'This giving you a hard-on, Hindley?' I enquired.

The answer to that was a whack across the back of the head. The door was flung open. 'I've said all I've got to say to you. Get out of the car.'

'But I was just beginning to enjoy the conversation.'

'Start the car,' he ordered the driver.

The lovely young man did as he was told.

'You can get out while the car is stationary or we can drop you off on the bridge. Literally. Take your pick.'

I took my pick. The car drove off, leaving me standing on the footpath. A jogger came by and crossed to the other side of the street, looking at me strangely.

How could Hindley do that? Bring that kid out here and make him take part in this? Job training, I suppose he'd call it. I guess that's the way the corruption starts.

I returned to the van. I went to put the key in the door but my hand was shaking like a leaf. I tried to calm myself. Hindley was showing me his muscle, that was all. I got the door open. I sat sweating in the hot stifling air of the van. But it was better than the cold sweats I had in the police car. With the DNA results I had good grounds to get the coroner to reopen the case if I wanted. Under other circumstances I might have done it. But right now I wasn't interested in having slack cops like Hindley get wrapped over the knuckles. I just wanted to find my father.

When I got back to the pub the answering machine was blinking with messages. Including messages from Danny and from Rosa. Danny's had to do with the never-ending saga of the Daimler and Rosa wanted me to ring as soon as possible.

'Rosa? It's Claudia.' She was so pleased I'd called. Her voice sounded different—stronger, more purposeful. 'I went to see my husband,' she announced ominously. There was no stopping her. I got the whole story from beginning to end.

'I went to the restaurant. I said to the woman there that I want to see Arturo. She tells me he is upstairs, she'll get him for me. I told her I am Mrs Grimaldi, I can go upstairs myself. It is years since I have been to the restaurant but I still know where the upstairs is. Besides, she has customers in the restaurant, she shouldn't leave them.

'So I go up, thinking the stairs look dirty. It doesn't matter they're at the back, they should be kept clean. I try to turn the door handle but it is locked. I can hear voices in there, men's voices, so I knock loudly. Then I notice the door has one of those little spyholes in it. Before I have time to think about why there needs to be a spyhole in this door, it opens—just a little—and a man asks what I want. "To speak to Arturo." "Arturo who?" he says. "Arturo Grimaldi," I say. "Tell him it's his wife." "Uno momento." He means me to wait at the door but I step in. I can't believe it. The room is full of smoke and men playing cards. For money. I saw lots of money on the tables.

'Arturo comes to the door very quick. "What you doing here?" he demands. I could ask him the same thing! Anyway, I tell him it's about Madalena. "Deviamo parlare, Arturo." We gotta talk. He looks back in the room, he doesn't want to bring me in there. "Let's go to the restaurant," I say, thinking Arturo won't get too angry if there are other people present.

'Downstairs he pours himself a drink and asks if I want one. I think yes, a drink is a good idea. He sits down. Then he says, "Did Madalena come home? You've heard from her?" He seems different. Not since she left has he spoken her name. Perhaps because we are in the restaurant, not in the house that he built for the children that has no children in it now.

'I told him no, Madalena has not come home. I asked him why he didn't tell me Madalena came to see him the day she disappeared. He looked very surprised and said she didn't come that day. Then I took a big breath and told him about you, Claudia. I waited. I thought he would get very angry but he seemed almost relieved. He sat there slowly nodding his head and said, "Yes . . . yes. It's the best thing."

'And then when I finish being surprised that he's not angry I think it's a bit strange he didn't tell me he already has an investigator. He said no, why do I think that? I asked him if he knows someone called Fabio. "Fabio?" he repeats, like he knows the name. "Who is he?" I ask. Fabio is the nephew of one of his business associates. From Italy, but he stayed three years in America before coming to Australia. He's doing odd jobs for Arturo, running errands. "Do odd jobs mean watching your house?" I asked. "Following your wife?" Arturo doesn't understand a thing. "Where is he now?" Arturo told me he is not here all the time, he does jobs for the uncle as well. "So how do you keep in touch with him?"

'Arturo was getting annoyed with all the questions. Perhaps it's time for me to go home now. I said, "Why don't you come home with me?" He tells me he'll come as soon as he can. He's playing cards with some friends, he can't leave right away. I say, "Arturo, you sure have a lot of friends. How come I never meet all these friends?" He just shrugs.'

I could almost hear Rosa taking a deep breath at the other end of the line. It sounded as if the confrontation had given her newfound strength. At the very least she and her husband were talking to each other.

I thought about the phone conversation as I drove to Danny's garage in Lilyfield. Lilyfield is the suburb next to Leichhardt where Arturo had his restaurant. Apparently Madalena hadn't shown up there that day. I didn't get the impression from Rosa that Arturo was lying about it. Nor did he seem to know about Fabio's extracurricular activities. Why was Fabio so interested in Madalena's whereabouts? Perhaps it was Fabio she saw that day, not her father.

'Hi Danny, how's it going?'

'You like the van?' he asked.

'I like the Daimler better but then maybe I'm biased. You got bad news to tell me?'

Danny wiped a hand across his forehead. 'Yeah, mate, I have.'

'What is it?' I asked with a sinking feeling.

'Can't get that colour anymore. It'll have to be specially mixed.'

'Look, Danny, I don't care. Near enough is good enough.'

Danny didn't seem too keen on the idea. 'It'll ruin the resale value,' he pointed out.

I smiled. 'But, Danny, I'm going to sell it to you. Eventually. Then you can paint it any colour you like.'

'OK, suit yourself,' he said reluctantly. 'I'll try to get as close as I can but you'll be able to tell it's not the same.'

I looked around at the array of cars parked in the garage. Danny could service anything. His personal favourites were classic cars. Didn't have to be European, he liked the Americans too.

'You ever get a Chrysler in here, light blue, mid-sixties vintage? Personalised plates—FABIO.'

Danny pulled a face. 'Yeah,' he said, not relishing the memory, 'once. What a dipstick that guy was.'

'Oh?'

'He brought the car in for something minor, grease and oil change I think. Anyway, when he comes to pick it up he notices this smudge on the duco. The guy grabs hold of my T-shirt. Honest, I thought he was going to knife me. He tells me he brought the car all the way from America without a mark on it. I says to him, "Listen, mate, maybe that's how they get service over there but it's not the way we do things round here." Cheryl must have seen what was going on because next minute she comes out of the workshop with a monkey wrench in her hand. "Everything OK, Danny?" she says. The guy backs off. I wiped the smudge off with one of those Chux things and he's never been back since.'

'You don't have an address for him, do you?'

'No. He brought the car in. I told him it would be ready in a couple of days, he came back in a couple of days. Paid cash.'

I didn't particularly want to visit Fabio. While I was still looking for Madalena I didn't want to go anywhere near him. More importantly, I didn't want him anywhere near me. There wasn't any need for it at the moment but having his address up my sleeve might have proved useful.

'Give me a call when the paint job's done, OK?'

'You want to change cars?' Danny offered me the pick of the garage.

'No, the van's fine. For the moment.'

Fabio was after her for some reason and she was scared. So scared she couldn't go back home. So scared she couldn't even tell her friends where she was. But if she was alive she had to be somewhere. Where does a kid go when she's so scared she's got nowhere else to go?

'Vince? G'day, it's Claudia . . . Yes, I know it seems like only yesterday. What are you doing?' He was at home, waiting for the sun to be over the yardarm so he could crack a few cold ones.

'What are you doing indoors on a beautiful afternoon like this? Why don't we crack a few cold ones at Bondi?'

We parked the van in the parking area on the beach front. It would feel right at home on this spot. Later at night, especially Sunday nights, people the papers describe as 'youths' gathered down here to show off hotted-up cars like this van. Hanging out, mucking around. Easy pickings for the cops who cruise by. But they weren't here yet.

It was what the film industry calls magic hour. When they can give the illusion of night. Street lights are on but it's not yet dark. Enough natural light to shoot by but not enough to make it look like bright harsh daylight. There was a gathering of clouds over the southern extremity of the beach but they didn't look like they'd cause any problems to the people still enjoying the surroundings. It all looked like happy families as Vince and I walked along the beach front. Surfers on boards far out on the darkening water, small and toylike at this distance, as were the men, women and children splashing about in the white foam that spilled onto the sand. The wave at the end of its journey, before the molecules of water were sucked back out to sea to start the process all over again.

We walked past a man under the public shower rubbing his hands over his prominent stomach to wash off the salt. As if the spray of water couldn't do the job on its own. Beside him a sandy, sunburnt child waited patiently. The man appeared to ignore her.

At the north end of the beach, near the rock pool, was a mosaic mural with an appropriately marine theme. On the grassy verge beside the footpath, groups of people dressed in shorts and summery clothes were having barbecues. The smell of steaks and grilled calamari hung on the air. Guaranteed to make anyone within smelling range feel hungry. I wondered if I was starting to get obsessed with food. Seemed to me, everywhere I went lately there was food. I was either eating it or watching whether other people were eating it. The textbooks say it's a substitute for sex. Yeah, well.

Shafts of golden light were coming down through the clouds as if God had left the door of heaven open. It certainly was magic light. Everyone full of bonhomie, goodwill towards their fellow humans, how could there be suffering, pain or evil in a tableau like this? We didn't know it then but this was to be the last barbecue of summer. The next day a total fire ban was declared. Ironic really, because in less than ten days the city would be ablaze.

Vince stopped and looked silently at the shafts of light. Even a rational mind like his could not help be moved by it, I thought. He gazed at it a while longer then said, 'Just proves light travels in straight lines, doesn't it? It'd be a great idea for science teachers to bring a bunch of kids out here to see this.'

'Yes, it would be a great idea for a bunch of kids to see this,' I agreed.

We continued walking, the path now starting to rise. Below us was the rock platform, the waves splashing over it, filling the honeycomb weathering with foam. There was the rock that once had a bronze version of 'The Little Mermaid' sitting on it, but the mermaid had long since been ripped off.

When we got to the crest of the cliff there was a bench at the most scenic point. The bench was occupied by a couple of teenagers gazing out to sea. Well actually, she was gazing and he was trying to talk to her. 'Seduction in progress, stage one,' announced Vince. It sure was a nice place for it—all that crashing surf, the setting sun, no-one up here but seagulls—and a PI and a social worker doing a commentary.

On we went, further around the north end. There was a group of kids sitting in a car. They looked like they were waiting for us to leave. Maybe I was just being suspicious. I looked down at the rock platform. There were good places to take shelter down there, out of reach of the sea's long watery fingers. Under ledges, in crevices between rocks. You'd have to climb down there, or walk the long way round from the beach but it was safe, at least from the elements, once you were there. I couldn't help thinking that all that climbing and walking would be good exercise, the sun and the sea a healthy environment. Like a holiday resort for homeless people.

We ignored the kids in the car and walked on. 'Homeless kids shelter down here sometimes,' Vince said, putting words to my thoughts. There were signs—some crumpled-up navy blue material. It could have been a shirt, part of a sleeping bag, some old rags. Something to put between your soft body and the hard rock.

'Where else do they shelter?'

'Anywhere they can. Caves, clothing bins, under railway bridges. In tunnels.' Vince stopped. He turned away and mumbled something but the words were carried away with the wind.

I touched him lightly on the arm. 'Vince?'

'I found a kid in a tunnel once. Or what remained of her. Rats don't seem to care what they gnaw on. It's all protein to them.'

We were almost at the end of the walkway now. The streets of North Bondi—Ramsgate Avenue, Brighton Boulevarde, Hastings Parade—all came down to the cliff edge. Blocks of flats sitting right on the cliff edge. They weren't too extravagant, given the breathtaking location. Bondi did have a particular style. A cross between British seaside resort and Spanish Southern California. Lots of curves. Archways and balustrades.

Something on the rock platform caught my eye. The last rays of the sun beamed on something painted in white on a boulder down there. The crude drawing of a syringe. I pointed it out to Vince.

'Yeah,' he said, as if he'd seen it all before.

'Do kids come down here? Use this spot?' I asked him.

'What do you think?'

We started to head back to the beachfront. A man and a woman in their forties were sitting on another bench. He had his hand on her knee. She didn't seem to mind. 'Seduction in progress, stage two,' Vince announced. Then he looked embarrassed. I was feeling a bit embarrassed myself.

'Let's find a place to drink these beers,' I suggested, changing the subject.

'Good idea,' said Vince, glad to have the subject changed.

The barbecuers were starting to pack up now. It was getting dark, kids had to be put to bed. Vince put the six pack between us on the bench then offered me a beer. Bondi could easily have become as brassy, extravagant and soulless as the Gold

Coast, but it wasn't. You could feel a renewed sense of civic pride. Developers wanted to do the place over with big tourist hotels. Think of all the money and employment it would bring to the area, they'd argue. But then Bondi would lose its flavour and become just another big hotel.

There may have been a renewed sense of civic pride but there was also a syringe painted crudely on a rockface looking out to sea. Vince and I sat looking out to sea as well.

'The reason I was the one who went into the tunnel,' Vince continued, 'was that in my misspent youth I'd done a bit of . . . urban caving.' I knew Vince and Steve belonged to the university speleological club but I thought that meant exploring Jenolan Caves. 'I found the girl in the stormwater drain in Rushcutters Bay park. You know the one I mean?'

'Yeah, I know the one,' I said grimly.

'It was during my time at the Centre. One of the kids came in one day with this anklet. It was leather thonging with beads threaded on it. It looked like the one Tracey wore. We hadn't seen Tracey for a couple of weeks so I asked her where she'd found it. She told me she saw it floating in the water in the drain. So I went and had a look. I went in all the way under the road. That's where I found her.'

'Does that happen a lot, people sheltering underground?'

'Occasionally. Look, as bad as it is in Sydney, at least we've got climate on our side and some semblance of a welfare system. In the tunnels under New York there are whole communities, some with elected mayors. Can you believe it? There have even been babies born in the tunnels over there. Crack babies. There's a whole underground society with different communities, some friendly, some not. There are loners. Men, women and children. Some set up a permanent life under the city. Tap into the electricity supply, catch water from leaky pipes, light fires, eat the rats. Before the rats eat them.

'But as I said, here the tunnels are used more as occasional shelter. The temperature never drops below freezing point in Sydney, there's more space, more air around people. They don't shoot each other over a park bench.'

'But they sometimes die. What had happened to Tracey?'

Vince shook his head. 'There was no way of telling. Kids crawl down into places they think are safe and can't get out. Tracey could have slipped and fell, she could have OD'd, and yes, she could have been killed.'

'My father . . . well, actually no. Someone bearing my father's name died in that stormwater canal. Anzac Day, 1985.'

'Sorry, I didn't realise,' said Vince, extending condolences on behalf of someone I didn't even know.

'Is that the only time you've ever found someone like that?'

'Yes,' said Vince. 'And I must have been all under this city at one time or another. Particularly when I was a student. Steve must have told you about it.' Vince offered me a second beer.

'No. He never did. You weren't one of those Agharti seekers, were you?'

'Pardon?'

'There's supposed to be a subterranean world called Agharti.'

'I don't know anything about that, we were just down there for the buzz.' Kerry had said the same thing. What was it that was so compelling about it? Vince told me how he and Steve had once gone all the way to Bondi by canoe via the sewer tunnel. 'Brown water rafting,' he grinned.

I couldn't resist the opportunity. 'I hope you didn't lose your paddle.'

He saluted me with his beer. Things were loosening up, especially tongues.

'There was another group who called themselves the Drain Drivers. They used to drive minis through stormwater drains. They'd go for kilometres. Under the surface, the city is absolutely riddled with tunnels. What the kids do now is race through the Harbour Tunnel in the wee small hours.' He took a mouthful of beer. 'You know what I'd like to do? Drain all the water out of the harbour, scrape away the surface layer of the streets and just have a good look. You'd see a completely different city. Tunnel City. There are even private ones. You know that pub in the Rocks, the Hero of Waterloo?' I'd heard of it, it was the oldest pub in Sydney. And still functioning. 'Back in the early days there was a trapdoor in front of the bar. Drunks would be dropped through it and pressganged.

Sold to some ship's captain. If you go downstairs there you can see the tunnel that used to lead to the waterfront. Manacles on the wall and everything.' Vince was almost gleeful.

'Why don't we go for a walk?' I suggested. 'We can stick the rest of the beers under the bench and pick them up later.'

Vince was doubtful that the beers would still be there when we returned but he didn't mind. 'Where will we go?'

'As close as I ever want to get to caving,' I said. 'Let's walk along the rock platform, to Needle Rock,' I christened it.

Vince brought one of the beers with him. Just in case. We walked back to the bench where we'd seen seduction stage one. It had now progressed to about stage eight. Didn't these people have homes to go to?

We found a way down to the rocks. My eyes were accustomed to the dark now and besides, the moon was shining so brightly you could almost read by it. I took off my shoes, preferring to feel the way with my feet and giving myself a better grip. I trod on something soft and realised it must have been the clump of rags we'd seen earlier. I put my shoes on again. I didn't want the next thing I felt to be a syringe. We continued round the point, looking down into the black jags of crevices, taking care to jump well over them.

Then it came into view—Needle Rock. An easy landmark for kids if they knew where to look. Despite the fact that I could feel eyes everywhere, we saw no-one down here. And such a romantic spot too. With all that seduction going on up above you'd think some of it would have trickled down here. The rock loomed larger and larger as we approached, much bigger than it looked from the walkway.

The moonlight accentuated the white paint, making it look like the bleached bones of a skeleton. If it was a meeting place, there was no meeting tonight. We strolled over to it. No sign of real syringes. But they could have been thrown down the crevices or out to sea.

From afar, this side of the rock appeared to be straight but now I could see that it curved inwards at the bottom so that you could sit there, lean your back against it, and have a slight overhang protecting you. We moved past it.

At the base of the cliff there were all sorts of little caves. In their womblike way they were almost welcoming. I sat down. Vince followed suit. If I waited here long enough, maybe I would see something. Sand or the weathering of sandstone had given me a softish place to sit. A little damp with the salt air but it was cosy. I could almost curl up and go to sleep. Except I didn't want to give Vince the wrong impression. We were sitting close but not touching.

I wondered what the kids were like who came to the rock, who used this as a place to shoot up. The beach didn't seem to go with the lifestyle. City streets, garbage bins, back alleys, park benches, yes. Being out here with nature seemed too . . . healthy. But the beach was one of the zones in between. The zones where the homeless lived. The zone where my father lived.

We sat there in silence. Talk seemed pointless. The wind blew through my brain, and I became lulled by the chaotic pattern of the crashing waves, the dance of white spray. If there had been conversation, Vince would have pointed out the purely scientific reason for the phenomenon—at waterfalls, wherever water is in this kind of motion, and on the tops of mountains, negative ions are produced. This promotes a feeling of well-being.

Vince's arm came across, offering me the bottle of beer. I took a sip and returned the bottle, our fingers lightly brushing with the action. If we stayed here much longer . . .

'Guess we better be heading back,' I said, standing up and dusting damp sand off the seat of my trousers.

'Guess we'd better,' said Vince.

We began the journey back. Soon the painted face of the rock was lost from view, like the dark side of the moon.

Just as I was about to climb back to the top, a small object came hurtling over the edge. I didn't know what it was but instinctively I stepped aside, pulling my head out of range. It landed on the rock platform. I bent down in the moonlight and saw what it was—a syringe. Vince saw it too. I shot a glance up to where it had come from but saw nothing. I did hear something though—the sound of a car driving away. Using his shoe, Vince rolled the syringe into a crevice.

When we got back to the top the couple on the bench had thankfully gone. It must have something to do with the survival instinct of the species that if sex is going on in your vicinity you kind of want to have some too. I didn't want Vince thinking that because he was here he'd be the one I wanted to have sex with. We were good mates, that's all.

It was getting late now, the air was cooling down. The other cars parked nearby had left as well. It was as if there was not another human being in the world. Like we were standing in the middle of an empty film set. The silent seaside flats, the streetlights, post box, the moon hanging in the air.

When we got back to the bench, by some miracle, the beers were still there. 'One more for the road?' said Vince.

'Yeah,' I said, 'why not? Let's go back to the van though, it's getting cold.'

The van was now surrounded by hoons leaning against their cars, flexing their young muscles, interacting socially, trying to crack onto girls. I didn't want to sit here and have a quiet drink. 'Excuse me,' I said to a guy leaning on the bonnet of the van.

'This yours?' he said, standing up. I had the keys and I was getting into it, what did he think? 'Nice van,' he said admiringly, patting the side as we drove away.

I drove up to where we'd just come from. This way we could have the view without the brisk seabreeze or the audience. Vince handed me the last beer. Again there was the light brushing of fingers. Well, I could handle it. It wasn't repulsive or anything. I was sitting behind the steering wheel, nothing was going to happen.

I don't know if it was the beer, the setting or the fact that he was a social worker, but I found myself saying to Vince, 'You know, sometimes I think I'm better off on my own. In a relationship I feel as if I'm losing myself. I married young, I didn't have a sense of self at all then.'

'And with Steve?' Vince asked softly. This was the first time since I'd ended the relationship with Steve that I didn't close up like a sea anemone the minute someone mentioned his name. 'I don't know. If it's not fireworks all the time, what's the point?'

Vince stretched his arm along the back of the seat. He wasn't actually in contact with my shoulder but his arm would have been only a hair's breadth away. 'I think we expect too much in our society. All this self-fulfilment and individuation and have a good day.' The hand had definitely moved now, resting on my shoulder, his fingers idly drawing little circles on my arm.

'You know what the real problem was?' I said to Vince, and it had only now occurred to me that this *was* the problem because up till now I'd shoved it all to one side, 'Maybe I was too much of myself with Steve. He became like a shadow of me. If I pushed he would bend, if I walked one way he would walk that way too. It wasn't two individuals meeting anymore. It was me and someone who reflected myself.'

'Some people would give their eye teeth to have that happen.'

I kept thinking about teeth as our lips crashed and we started in on some personal caving, exploring the inner recesses of each other's mouth. Meanwhile, our hands had found their way under each other's T-shirt.

Why was my body responding the way it was? Vince was an old mate, that's all. Why were my hands, as if they had a life of their own, feeling their way up his midriff, playing with the hairs on his chest? I don't even like hairy chests.

Although there was no stopping my hands, I managed to unhinge my mouth long enough to say, 'Vince, we shouldn't be doing this.'

'Yes, you're quite right.' Another long exploratory kiss. 'Let's get over into the back.'

There was an emergency board meeting happening in my head, so fast it was over before I knew it. One lone voice shouted yes! and without even taking a vote on it all the others followed suit.

As well as constructing an aboveground city on this site there was also a city under the ground. Replicating the maze of roads that got us around on the surface was a maze of subterranean tunnels and pipes. In the sewer tunnels you could go from Balmain to Bondi without ever coming up above ground. As well as sewerage tunnels there were water tunnels, drainage, mining, electricity, gas, railway tunnels, telephone tunnels, not forgetting the Harbour Tunnel itself. We used them every day, in one way or another. We travelled on trains under the city, pulled water through the pipes every time we turned the tap on or flushed the toilet, sent messages along the cables in underground tunnels every time we used the phone.

Just when you think you've hit rock bottom you discover it's only another layer and that there are more underneath. The surface of the city is merely a skin. Beneath it are the veins carrying life blood, air vents that act as lungs, the sewers a lymphatic system draining away waste products, telephone lines the nervous system transmitting messages for the proper functioning of the body.

In our myths, in our collective psyche, the underworld is a dark and unknown place, because there lurk the monsters with thin wraith-like tendrils that can pull you down. It is the dark side of the mirror. Dante's downward rings that descend into hell.

One day Hades, God of the Underworld seized the beautiful young Persephone and took her down to his realm. Demeter, her mother, got understandably depressed and refused to perform her Earth goddess duties. She ranged around the world looking for her beloved daughter and for as long as she pined there was perpetual winter on earth. Eventually a deal was struck with Hades which meant that Persephone would spend six months of the year in the netherworld and half aboveground with her mother. But first Persephone had to be found.

Why was I thinking about myth and symbolism on a fine morning such as this? Well, you wouldn't want me dwelling on the lowlife night I just had, would you? How could I do that? How could I have had sex with Steve's best friend in the back of a borrowed panel van?

I felt a strong need to wash my sins away. I went into the bathroom, turned the shower on and stood under the hot needles of water. Then I wrapped a towel around my wet hair, dressed, and took a strong cup of black coffee out onto the balcony with me.

If Madalena had voluntarily disappeared the second time there was a good chance that she'd taken refuge in the womb of the earth. She'd been there before for the thrill of it. Now she was sheltering there. In the hard dank spaces underneath; the safe, enclosed spaces. She was somewhere under this city and the person most likely to know the exact location, if anyone knew at all, was Raf.

I went back to his spot on the street but he wasn't there. He had been here recently, though, because The Last Supper had been erased and there were the beginnings of something new.

Maybe he'd gone to the loo and he'd be back in a minute. There were public lavatories in Hyde Park behind St James station. He could easily have ducked in there.

I waited. Sat on the wall and looked across the road to David Jones, the store where the kids and I had shopped for Mina and Brian's wedding present. Its own advertisements said it was 'the most beautiful store in the world'. My grandmother used to take me there on our trips to town. Everyone dressed up to go into the city then, even five year olds like me. We would go to the seventh floor and eat chicken sandwiches for lunch, thin triangles of white bread with the crusts cut off. Then we would come across to Hyde Park and I would try and catch pigeons, a fruitless task, while my grandmother would have a lie down on the grass. Hyde Park, the quiet oasis in the heart of the city.

If he was taking a pee, it was a long one. I walked past the newsstand guy and up the path leading to the men's toilets, a likely place for nocturnal activities if ever I saw one. I hovered around for a while but no-one came in or out.

I walked further into the park, up a pathway bordered with brilliant blue agapanthus standing tall and straight in their skirts of dark green leaves. From my childhood the only birds I remember in the park were pigeons but now there were seagulls, and ibises strolling round poking their long curved beaks into everything.

I wandered over to the Archibald Memorial Fountain. Through the spray of water I kept watch on the patch of street Raf used as a canvas. He still hadn't shown up.

On the central pedestal of the fountain stood a naked young Adonis permanently pointing towards St Marys Cathedral, though why a pagan god should be pointing in that direction was beyond me. Water fanned up behind him like a peacock's tail and surrounding him were male and female figures wrestling, killing, or just plain posing with a variety of horned beasts. The tableau looked like a body-building contest for Olympians. Just what I wanted to be reminded of this morning—naked bodies and horned beasts.

I left the fountain to the tourists and walked over to a chess game in progress. There were huge black and white squares painted on the ground dotted with plastic chess pieces about a metre tall. Chaps sat around on benches talking or watching the game, just as they would have done in Mediterranean villages. Except here we were surrounded by tree ferns and other shade loving plants with large lush leaves. One of the players, a tall lanky man in shorts and a red T-shirt, had his shopping hanging in a plastic bag on a confiscated bishop.

Throughout the entire game neither he nor his opponent said a word to each other. On my way back down the path I watched a dero going through a bin. I caught myself in my old habit—looking but not doing anything about it. Raf obviously wasn't here at the moment. I'd see if I could catch him later. In the meantime, if I wanted to watch homeless men, there was a place where I could look at them in droves.

Matthew Talbot Hostel for Men. The sign was on the corner facade of the brick building, a couple of minutes walk from William Street. Despite the drone of traffic up there the only sound in this quiet street was a radio blaring country music through the doors of a house open to provide some relief from the summer heat. Across the road from the hostel a dero, or rather a homeless man, sat propped up against a wall. Perhaps he was just enjoying the sunshine. Or maybe he was trying for the hostel and hadn't quite made it. He had his arm in a sling and took no notice of me as I entered the hostel.

There were men, young and old, standing round the entrance. I went into a reception area with a curved reception desk of the type you find in old-fashioned hotels. Except the place was a lot more downmarket than a hotel. But not as downmarket as I expected it to be. It was clean, there was a strong smell of bleach, and it had recently been painted—green and pink.

There were three women behind the desk—a motherly woman in her fifties, a woman in her thirties who looked like she might have had a drink or two in her life, and a woman in her twenties who despite the freckles and the ponytail looked as if she could handle any funny business that might arise.

On the wall was a chart entitled Outreach, with photos of

houses and flats and the suburbs they were located in. There were contact phone numbers at the bottom of the chart for those interested in medium/long term accommodation in community housing. Houses in Five Dock, flats in Newtown. It could have been a real estate agent's.

I thought perhaps I'd be walking into Dante's Inferno, that men would be pissing in the corners and dribbling in their beards. Screaming and clutching their stomachs, each in their own individual hell. But it wasn't like that. The motherly woman asked if she could help me.

'Yes,' I said with false bravado, 'I'm looking . . . I'm wondering if my . . .' I had to stop. Inexplicably I was on the verge of tears. I don't know why, but I felt the same as I did in the office of the crematorium when the clerk had said my father's name. Probably a little fragile from the lack of sleep last night.

The motherly woman said softly, 'Would you like to go somewhere more private?' Like a nurse asking me if I'd moved my bowels, a ridiculous expression it seemed to me. I mean, what do you say? 'Yes, I've moved them, I thought I'd put them up round my lungs today'?

Having someone treat me condescendingly was enough to burst the little bubble of emotion that had welled up inside me. 'I'm looking for Guy Valentine,' I stated.

'Is he staff or client?' asked the woman.

'Client.'

'And what's your interest?'

'I'm his daughter,' I announced.

If I thought that was going to open doors I was wrong. 'You must understand,' explained the woman, 'that we respect our clients' confidentiality here.'

'Look,' I said, 'he's my father. If he's here, if you know where he is, I want to see him.'

She spoke through an intercom then turned to me. 'Nadia will be able to help you,' she said.

I had the feeling she thought I was being difficult. I stepped back and turned my attention to the doorway leading to the inside of the hostel, waiting for Nadia to appear. There was a sign which said 'To Left—games room, lounge, dining, kiosk, kitchen, laundry, clothing store. To Right—toilets, showers, proclaimed place, clinic, welfare, sick bay'. The sign was momentarily obscured by a bright-skinned woman with dark eyes, wearing clothes with Aboriginal motifs and big earrings. She came up to the desk and the motherly woman pointed in my direction.

'Hi, I'm Nadia,' she introduced herself to me. Having now passed me on, the motherly woman busied herself with other tasks. Nadia took me through to the right. We passed the clinic where a man was having his eyes tested against a chart with rows of letters, then we went up a ramp to a small glassed-in space marked Proclaimed Area. It looked over a dormitory of beds, three or four of which were occupied by men sleeping in their clothes. The beds were clean and white though none of the sleepers seemed to feel the need of sheets. Nadia sat down in the only available chair. There was a note stuck to the glass wall saying 'If Charlie Holmes wakes up and asks for his money, tell him that Martin has banked it for him. On no account give him the money.'

It was kind of peaceful here, watching over these men as they slept during the middle of the day. Nadia explained that the Proclaimed Area was where the police bring the men when they're drunk and disorderly, or if they look like they might do some damage to themselves. 'Mrs Grimes tells me you're looking for your father,' Nadia said.

'Yes, that's right.'

'Do you think he wants you to find him?' asked Nadia.

The question was ridiculous. Of course he'd want me to find him. I'd rescue him from this place, take him home, give him a nice hot bath, a new set of clothes. 'I'm his daughter,' I said, as if that explained everything.

But apparently it didn't. 'Sometimes having a family member turn up is a disaster,' said Nadia. 'They get upset when they think about them, particularly at holiday times like this, when everything around them blares happy families. It makes them feel all that much worse.' I realised now what was happening. She wasn't helping me with my enquiries, she was *counselling* me. 'It is a point of strength with the men *not* to get in touch with their families because they know their weaknesses. They know the hurt of the past—the guilt they already feel will be compounded if they're reminded of it.'

I heard what she was telling me but it wouldn't be like that with Guy and me. Once he saw me, the years would dissolve away and we would be happy families once again. 'I appreciate that,' I said. 'I just want him to know that I'm here and that I'd like to see him. No strings attached. Perhaps I could just leave a message. If he doesn't want to get in touch with me, OK. I'll accept that.' I knew even as I was saying it that I was lying.

'Look, I understand how you feel,' said Nadia. 'My father was an alcoholic. Left home when I was thirteen. Not an easy age to have your father piss off, let me tell you. He swore he would never leave his children. You see, he'd been forcibly removed from his Mum and Dad. But,' she sighed, 'the pattern repeats itself.'

'Did you ever see him again?'

'Yes,' said Nadia. '*He* got in touch with *me*. So it was a different ball game. I was twenty-seven. I'd already gone beyond thinking he was a bastard for leaving Mum to bring up four kids on her own. I was curious. So I went to see him. He was living in Mosman with another woman.'

'Do you stay in touch?'

'Sporadically.'

I asked her if she could at least tell me whether she knew the name Guy Valentine.

'The guys in the Proclaimed Area, we write their names down in this book, but the others . . . they come and go as they please. Some of the regulars we know, those who've been coming here for years. They pay their eight bucks a night for accommodation, five for a meal. Often we know them only by a nickname. Some of them leave everything behind when they become homeless, including their names.

'But if he's been brought in here to the Proclaimed Area we'd probably have a record of him. Unless there was a volunteer on duty—sometimes, if it gets busy or there's an emergency, they get a bit slack about the bookwork.'

She opened a ledger in which there were handwritten entries—the date, the name of the person, time in, time out, bed number. 'Valentine, was it?'

'Yes.'

She started looking through it, starting with today's date. There was a stack of similar-looking ledgers on a shelf at the side. 'Perhaps I could give you a hand,' I offered.

'Well,' she hesitated, 'we're not supposed to.' But she didn't say anything when I opened the first ledger on the stack.

'How far do the records go back?' I asked.

'Forever. When do you think your father might have been in?'

'Anytime in the last thirty years.'

'Oh,' she said, with a downward inflection. We chatted a bit, her 'charges' slept on soundly, a heavy, immobile, alcoholic sleep filled with no dreams. It was tedious, boring work going through the ledgers but I was used to tedious, boring work. I pressed on, running my eye lightly down the list of names, looking for long surnames combined with short first names. I found one or two that were close, experienced the expectancy of the heart, the slight widening of the eyes, but they proved to be red herrings.

'I'm ready to go now.' The speech was slurred. One of the sleepers had got up and was now standing in front of Nadia.

She glanced down at the book. 'Richard?' He nodded laboriously. 'Why don't you go back to sleep for a little while,' she said.

'OK.' Obedient as a child he climbed back onto his bed.

'They're supposed to stay here till they're sober,' she explained.

Together we went through the whole of the eighties, which was as far back as this particular set of ledgers went. Not once was there a mention of Guy Valentine. I even went through a couple of the ones Nadia had checked to make doubly sure.

'You can always talk to the men,' she suggested. 'Although they may not talk back to you.' She looked at her watch. 'It's just about lunchtime, you'll get a couple of hundred of them in one go.'

This opportunity was too good to pass up. 'Dining room's straight down the corridor, is it?' I said, remembering the sign near reception. I made moves to go.

'Hang on,' said Nadia. 'I'm breaking for lunch now. As soon as Annette gets here I'll come down with you.'

When Annette turned up Nadia escorted me to a huge room at the end of the corridor. Despite the cheery colours, it still looked institutional, like a hospital, or worse, a prison. On one side of the room were long rows of tables full of men eating salads. On the other side men sat in chairs in rows, just sitting quietly or watching the television on the wall. There were old men, young men, relatively well-dressed men, others in an odd assortment of clothes, like pink shorts with a suit jacket. Some were mentally disturbed.

They were men of all shapes and sizes, from all different backgrounds, but they had one thing in common—here in this room they were all well-behaved. The orderliness of them was eerie. Despite the large numbers, there was very little talking. A few of the younger ones who were waiting talked, mucked around a bit, but at the tables there was no animated dinner conversation. There didn't appear to be any imposed order, no wardens or nurses walking around with big sticks.

'It's the different ways men and women are perceived in our society,' explained Nadia. 'Women's refuges are houses, homes. Places of refuge for men are institutions. That way they don't have to relate to each other. Or look after themselves—it's all done for them.' We walked down the aisle between the diners and those waiting. 'G'day, nurse,' someone yelled out. They weren't all that orderly. 'Specially the older blokes,' Nadia continued, 'they're mainly loners. They have mates in here, but out on the street they're solitary. The younger ones hang around together outside though, things are changing.'

There was a queue of men at the far end of the room lining up to get their salads. The kitchen was bustling with activity, the clinking of metal, of pots and pans. Probably for the inevitable cups of tea because nothing they were eating today needed cooking. There were crates of bread, vegetables and other food at the entrance to the kitchen area. 'Donations,'

Nadia told me, 'from bread companies, from local shops. How do you want to go about this?'

I said I'd try the older men first, the ones who would be about Guy's age.

'Rupert is pretty affable,' said Nadia, pointing out a dapper little man in a frayed suit and tie despite the heat.

He was at a table with other men, none of whom were saying much. At the next table was the man with his arm in a sling that I'd seen outside. He hadn't been sunning himself at all, just waiting outside till lunchtime. He was doing a good job of singlehandedly manoeuvring the salad onto a piece of bread to make a sandwich. I walked up past his table. No more comments now, everyone was intent on eating. Quietly, chewing their food well.

'Rupert,' said Nadia, 'there's a young lady wants to meet you. Must be your lucky day.' He looked up from his meal.

'G'day, Rupert,' I greeted him. 'How're things?'

'Not too bad thanks, nurse.' The second time I'd been called nurse in the last two minutes. Did I look like one, or did they think they were in hospital? I declined his offer of half a slice of white bread.

'Rupert, I'm wondering if you know my father—Guy. Guy Valentine.'

'Guy?' he said, 'like Guy Fawkes?'

'That's right.'

'Never heard of him.'

'Short stocky bloke. Curly hair. Probably grey. He used to work for the newspapers.'

'Journalist?'

'Yes,' I said with a glimmer of hope.

'Sorry, nurse, never heard of him. Will you let me buy you a cuppa?'

He was the perfect gentleman, I didn't like to refuse, but if I had cups of tea with all of them I'd drown. 'Thanks, Rupert, another time maybe.'

'Can I take you to dinner?'

'How can you be thinking about dinner when you haven't finished lunch?' I joked.

I moved on. The story was the same all round—no-one knew him, not by that name anyway. A couple of them asked their mates who shook their heads, but mostly they simply answered the questions as if they were filling out a form. The first lot of lunchers had finished now and were getting up to make way for those waiting on the other side of the room.

It was futile, like counting grains of sand. I had the feeling that Nadia was getting edgy. I was taking up time, being a disturbance to the routine. 'Thanks for your help,' I said finally.

'Sorry there wasn't a better result,' she commiserated.

I found my own way back to the reception area, nodded briefly to the women on the desk and headed out the door. There were fewer men standing round now. They were probably off somewhere having a siesta. Except the man with his arm in the sling. He was back out here, propped up in the same place he'd occupied before. He appeared to be sleeping. But I soon found out he wasn't. At the very moment I walked past he stuck out his leg. I very nearly tripped over it.

'He always reckoned he had a daughter,' he said lazily.

I stopped in my tracks. 'Pardon?'

'We never believed him but.'

'Never believed who?' I asked, hoping I sounded casual.

'Shakespeare. That's who you're looking for, isn't it?'

My nose started quivering like a bloodhound on the scent of something. 'Are you a mate of his?'

'Maybe. What's it worth to you to find out?'

'What do you want?'

He looked me up and down as if deciding what I could afford to pay. 'You can start with a six pack.'

'No problems.'

Using his good hand to help himself up, he moved from a sitting to a standing position. 'Let's go, baby.' His gait wasn't as smooth as his patter but I was prepared to go to the end of the earth with him. Well, at least to the end of the street.

We went further than that, however. Round the corner, across the road and up to a pub on William Street. He'd led me there but once we'd arrived he didn't want to go in. 'My money's no good in there,' he said.

'But it's my money,' I reminded him. Nevertheless he still didn't want to go in. 'Anything in particular?'

'Yeah, I'll go for those Colds.'

Very trendy, I thought. I went into the minute bottle shop, pressed the bell to get the barperson's attention, all the while keeping my eye on my new friend. I needn't have bothered, he wasn't going anywhere. He was hanging out for those Colds. Three minutes later I was back on the street with the six pack.

'What are you going to drink?' he asked.

'You're not going to drink all of these yourself, are you?'

'Too right I am,' he assured me.

'OK,' I sighed, 'I'll get some more.' I started back for the bottle shop.

'Why don't you make it a slab. It's cheaper by the two dozen. I'll hold onto those for you,' he offered.

I moved them out of his reach. 'I'll look after them,' I said authoritatively. Once he had the six pack he'd be off like a shot.

I went back in and rang the bell again. The same barperson appeared. His eyes were close together and he had a long drooping nose. The combined effect was that of an owl. But he didn't seem to register any surprise that I was back so soon.

'I wondered if I could return these and buy two dozen instead.'

'No worries,' he said. His accent revealed him to be a New Zealander, and fairly recently arrived. I was dying for him to say six pack but he managed to avoid it. He worked out the difference in price then did something complicated with the till.

Out I came again, carrying the slab. I hoped we weren't going to be walking a long way. He didn't offer to carry it for me but I guess a man with his arm out of action can be excused. 'Let's go and sit somewhere and drink in a civilised fashion,' I suggested.

'I know just the place,' said my friend.

We crossed back over William Street and went down back-streets of Woolloomooloo similar to the ones that led to the hostel. But we didn't go back to the corner that I assumed to be his 'spot'.

'This'll do,' he announced. It was a piece of footpath under the Eastern Suburbs railway line, in roughly the area where I'd seen the two boys joyriding between carriages. It was shady under there and presently unoccupied but judging by the general smell, it was a regular watering hole.

He sat down, leant against the graffitied wall and patted the concrete beside him. 'Well, are you going to sit down or not?'

I sat down and placed the slab in protective custody between my feet. I wrestled one bottle away from its mates and held it out to him.

'Rip the top off for me, will you, baby?' I didn't know how much of this 'baby' business I was going to be able to take but I stuck with it for the moment. I twisted the top off and handed him the beer. He took a long cool swig of it, oblivious to the bit dribbling down his front. He gave a belch of satisfaction. 'Cheers,' he said.

I twisted the top off a second bottle and took a long cool swig myself. Without the dribble. It was refreshing, I could feel the bubbles going all the way down. I figured on beer one for hospitality, beer two preparing the way and beer three to get him going. I was hoping to get away with less myself.

'I guess we'd better introduce ourselves if we're going to drink together,' I suggested.

'Why?' he questioned. 'None of that's important.'

I had a sinking feeling—the bloke was probably just a chancer. Listening to me asking questions in the hostel and working out how he might get a few beers out of it.

'How am I going to put you in my little black book if I don't know which letter to file it under?'

'I'm ready for my second, thanks, baby.' I passed him his second beer. Three beers, that was the limit. If I didn't have something after three beers I was leaving. And taking the rest of the beer with me.

'S. You can put me under S. For Sebastian. But everyone round here calls me The Doctor. Sorry to say, I'm presently without a phone. But you know where to find me. Cheers.' He took a swashbuckling swig of his second bottle. 'You don't look much like him,' he said suspiciously. 'How do I know you're not an imposter?'

I liked that touch—him thinking I was the imposter. A crafty old bugger if ever there was one. I pulled out the photo of Guy. Young and looking very spruce. Wavy hair in a fifties quiff, the short snub nose that David inherited, dressed in a dinner jacket and stiff white shirt. Cadet Journalist of the Year, 1959. I held onto it while Sebastian looked on, silently nodding.

'Well I'll be buggered,' he said softly. He looked away from the photo, down at the ground, as if remembering his own past, his other life. 'No,' he repeated, 'you'd hardly recognise him.' He jerked suddenly. 'Fuckin' bastards. The lot of youse.' Another swig of comforter. Ah yes, that felt better now, the bastards had retreated into the distance. Lost in the alcoholic haze.

I took another swig myself. No matter how many times I reminded myself that this photo was taken all that time ago, it was still the way I saw my father. I looked at the man beside me. Skinny legs with sores on them, broken arm, eyes sunk back so as to be almost indistinguishable in a face of dirt-engrained wrinkles, brushed with beard stubble. A tooth missing, his body odour heavy with the smell of alcohol. Take a good look, Claudia, your father is no longer the man in the photo—he's this one sitting beside you.

Sebastian's head started a slow motion journey to his chest, as if he was nodding off to sleep. Just before it got there he jolted it up. 'Instead of gawping at me, why don't you make yourself useful and pass me another beer?' he said.

I hadn't realised I was staring, it was more that I was lost in thought. I felt suitably chastened. The man had his dignity and I'd just affronted it. I passed him another beer.

'Have one yourself,' he insisted, 'go on.' He nudged me with his broken arm, the sling moving up and down like a wing.

In spite of everything I couldn't help smiling. Another one wouldn't do any harm. Besides, I reminded myself, it wasn't as if I hadn't been practising.

He lifted the beer to his mouth. Beneath his beard I saw the

Adam's apple move as he swallowed. I looked away, at the house across the street, in case he thought I was staring.

'We were mates at one time, good mates. Before the fight. Must be going on for ten years now. We used to kip in that park at Rushcutters Bay. You know the one I mean?'

I took a swig of beer then turned slightly in his direction. Trying to appear casual. 'Yeah, I know the one.'

'Well, one morning he comes at me with a broken bottle, accuses me of rolling him in his sleep. But I hadn't been there at all that night. I'm sorry to say I hadn't been able to make it home. The police had picked me up. The usual—drunk and disorderly. I'd spent the night in the hostel. It's raining like buggery so they let us stay there a bit longer but eventually it was time to go. So I'm coming back the next day feeling pretty good. The rain had eased up, I had breakfast in my belly, a flagon of sherry under my arm.

'But there's no sign of him. I thought he must have gone out looking for breakfast himself. It's harder to find in bad weather, people don't go to the parks, there's no food in the bins. So I'm ready to settle down with the flagon and then I see him sitting under a tree. Sitting there shivering. And I says, "You mad bastard, what have you done with your coat?" Because he's not wearing it. First time I ever saw him without his coat on. Give us another, baby. All this talking, it fair makes a man parched.'

I looked at the slab. We'd made more dents in it than I thought. I must have been drinking my fair share, because I was even warming to the idea of being called 'baby'.

'Claudia? Is that you?'

Oh shit. I'd recognise that voice anywhere. It was Janet. One of the ex-chorus girls who'd twittered around at Mina's wedding. Shit. Of all the people who could catch me sitting under a railway line drinking a slab of beer with a dero, it had to be Janet. Of all Mina's friends she was the biggest gossip. I may as well have made an announcement on the evening news. I kept looking down at the ground.

'Claudia?' The voice was closer now, almost upon us.

'Hello, Janet,' I said tiredly.

'I was just taking a short cut home, I thought it was you.'

'Yes, it's me all right.'

She was waiting for an explanation. But I was under no obligation to give her one. She stared at Sebastian, doing something peculiar with her nose, as if trying to pull it back into her face. Sebastian slowly raised his head to gaze at this apparition. From the toes of the Nikes, the length of the gaily patterned tights, right up to the sunhat. 'Hello, baby,' he greeted her, 'want a beer?'

'No thank you, not during the day,' she said stiffly.

She hung around, still waiting for me to give her an explanation of what I was doing here, drinking in public with a derelict person. But the only sound coming from me was a satisfied 'ah' as I took another mouthful of beer. 'Well, I'll be going then,' said Janet. 'I can see you're busy. Give my love to your mother.'

No need for that, I thought, she'd be on the phone to Mina as soon as she got home. Maybe she wouldn't even wait that long. There had to be a public phone around here somewhere.

Off she trudged, her ample bottom wiggling in the tights. Before she turned the corner she looked back. I held my drink up. Cheers. Sebastian, I noticed, had taken advantage of the situation to help himself to a new one. It was a pity the momentum had been broken, because it took another two beers before I was able to get Sebastian back to where he'd left Shakespeare sitting without his coat on.

'I knew something must have happened, he never went anywhere without that coat. He wore it twenty-four hours a day, slept in the thing. I took the flagon over to him. He had a drink then he said: "Some bastard's stole my letters, Doc. All my letters." He had scraps of paper he'd keep in that coat. And pens. He had a beaut collection of pens. Most of them didn't work but they looked nice. They weren't really letters, he never posted any of them. He'd write things down on a scrap of paper, fold it up and put it in his pocket. What a mad bastard carrying all that paper around. Strike a match near him and he'd go up in smoke.' Sebastian shook his head, thinking of the memory.

'Who took his coat?'

'Well, he thought I did at first, that's why he was dirty on me. Then he said it was the devil. He'd slept in the tunnel that night, the tunnel under the road, because of the rain. There's a ledge you can sleep on as long as you're careful you don't roll over and end up in the drink,' Sebastian guffawed. 'Shakespeare always used to reckon there were devils in there anyway, he'd only sleep in the tunnel when it was really raining cats and dogs. So he's sleeping in there and he hears these noises. He thinks at first it's me so he calls out, "Doc?" Then someone hits him, knocks him out stone cold. Then the next thing he knows he's propped up under the tree and he doesn't know how he got there.'

'What happened after that?'

'Well, we kind of went our separate ways. I know he got Mrs Mason to fix up his Social Security form—that would have been in his coat as well.'

'Mrs Mason?'

'She used to work at the hostel. Not any more though. They've got all these new birds down there.' He reached for another bottle and managed to get the top off it with no assistance from me, the crafty old bugger. Holding it in the hand with the sling and opening with the other. 'Cheers,' he said.

'Cheers.'

'He'd never go back to that place, you know. Never went back. I stayed away a few nights but then I went back. Kipped there for years after.'

'And now?'

'Na, I give it away. I've got another little place, all to myself. It wasn't really the same without Shakespeare.'

'Where did he go?'

'Last I heard he was up Surry Hills way,' he said, as if Surry Hills was miles away in the country, instead of about two kilometres. Still, I guess when you're on foot and you stick to your own territory it may as well be on the moon.

'Last you heard.'

'Yep, last I heard.'

'When was that? Recently?'

'Depends what you call recent, doesn't it? Couple of years ago.'

I didn't remember my conversation with Sebastian verbatim, there were huge gaps which I filled in later to give it some semblance of coherency. What I remembered was the place, the coat, Mrs Mason, that something had happened to my father the night he 'died'. Drunk as I was by this stage I kept saying these things over and over in my mind because I'd need them for later, when I was sober.

I stayed on to finish the slab with Sebastian—at least I think we finished it. I remember doing some dancing. I remember that in particular because I'm positive his arm came out of the sling. Then it got dark and for some reason we had this bright idea of going back for another slab. I remember the bright red traffic lights at William Street, then the bright blue light of the police car. And I remember telling the young officer that I was a PI and that I was doing undercover work. Fishing around for my ID and not being able to find it. 'Sure,' he said, 'and I'm Matlock.' I don't know what possessed him to say that, he was much younger than Matlock.

I remember the bright city lights, Sebastian and I sitting in the back of the police car being driven around like royalty. And then standing in a place with lots of noise. I think I was making most of it. The cops handing over forms and some- one—a nurse?—asking me my name. I started to tell her about the undercover work but she wasn't interested. Sebastian was there and then he went somewhere else and I was looking at a room. Proclaimed Area. I'd seen that this afternoon, in the Matthew Talbot Hostel. It was just the same only the colours were different and instead of men on the beds there were women. No way I was going to lie down there, I'd never slept in a room with more than one bed in it in my life and I wasn't going to start now.

'Where . . . am . . . I?' I demanded, in a slow, controlled voice, the sort of voice school principals use when they come across a nest of children playing with matches.

'It's all right, calm down,' I was told.

'Ring a cab for me,' I said imperiously. 'One passenger. Going to Balmain.' At least I knew not to try and drive my car. Come to think of it, I couldn't remember where my car was. My vision homed in on a phone. I lunged towards it and tapped out the cab company number that I thought I knew off by heart. Why wasn't anyone answering? A woman approached. Ah, help at hand.

'Do you have a home to go to?' she asked.

'Of course.' I reeled off the name of Jack's pub.

'You live at a pub, eh?' They didn't seem to believe me.

'Yes, look it up in the phone book, ring Jack up, he'll vouch for me.'

Someone did use the phone. Because the next thing I knew I was being escorted to the door where a cab waited.

'I'll be back,' I announced ominously.

Another ride through the bright lights of Sydney. Then suddenly we were outside the pub. I gave the driver some spare change. He said it wasn't enough. I handed him my wallet. 'Help yourself.' I remember seeing him take a ten dollar blue plastic note out and handing the wallet back.

'Evening, Jack,' I said, foolishly passing through the public bar where all the regulars could see me.

It was Marty who helped me up the stairs, damn it. He was always such a smartarse, I'd never hear the end of this. 'Thank you, that'll be all,' I dismissed him when we got to my door. I fumbled around for half an hour trying to get the key in the lock. I must have succeeded because when I woke up it was daylight and I was in my own bed. Thankfully alone.

B oy, did I feel seedy the next day. It was mid-morning when I woke up. I'd slept for a good twelve hours. Didn't make me feel any better though. I felt like a member of an extinct species suddenly waking up and finding out it was the twenty-first century. I thought at first I was still under the railway bridge with Sebastian because I could smell the same smell. Then I realised it was me. I was sweating beer. Casual sex with an old mate one night, getting drunk and disorderly with a dero the next, what was happening to me? It was that panel van. I had to get rid of that panel van, give it back to Danny before it led me further astray. If only I could remember where I'd parked it.

I stumbled out of bed and into the shower. Washed my hair, turned the hot tap off and stood under the cascade of cold water wondering yes, why *do* female private eyes have so many showers? It took a few seconds to penetrate my hair but soon I felt the cold beating into my brain, hopefully clearing out the cobwebs, though why a spider would want to spin a web in my brain was beyond me.

I pressed Play on the answering machine. The first message was from Mina wondering where I was. Oh God. Dinner. Last night. I was supposed to go over there for dinner last night.

'Mum? It's Claudia.' She was so relieved to hear my voice, she thought something must have happened to me. Well, obviously Janet hadn't got to her yet. 'I'm sorry. I got caught up in something and I couldn't phone.' She asked me if I was all right. 'Yes, I'm fine,' I lied, 'it was just something routine.' She said Brian wanted to talk to me, perhaps I could give him a ring at work. 'Yes, OK. Bye now.'

I dressed then went up to a cafe in Rozelle for some bacon and eggs. I could have had them in Balmain but I didn't want bits of tomato and alfalfa sprouts decorating my breakfast. I wanted grease, and plenty of it.

The cafe reflected my mood—seedy. It looked as if nothing had been moved since the 1950s. There were Coke ads on the wall that must be collector's items by now, chipped laminex tables, and a vase of plastic flowers on the counter. There was only one other person in there, a grey man who may have been a homeless person himself. Maybe he wasn't grey, maybe he just needed dusting. He ate very slowly, intent on his task.

My bacon and eggs came, with a pot of tea and a chipped mug. This was living. Being a coffee addict I rarely drink tea but tea seems to go with the bacon and eggs. There was a bottle of tomato sauce on the table but I hadn't sunk so low I'd put tomato sauce on fried egg. Blood and guts. I sat the egg on the buttered toast and stuck a knife into the yolk, letting it run into a yellow pool. Fortunately the white was firm. A snotty white that morning and I would have lost it. I cut off a piece of bacon and toast with egg yolk and began my breakfast.

It hit my belly with a thud and stayed there. I had the feeling that it had actually pasted itself onto the wall of my stomach. Food again. I'd recently had a dollop of sex and here I was still eating—dollops of grease. So much for the food and sex theory. It wasn't food as such but the type of food. What was I doing eating greasy bacon and eggs in this seedy cafe when I could have been having foccacie and good coffee in any number of trendy cafes? Because I was trangressing. It had started right back in Melbourne with the cake and cream.

I looked over at the man in the corner. He could have been a wax dummy except that, like the men at the hostel, his mouth was moving, slowly, methodically chewing his food. And somehow with food, with this breakfast at least, I had slipped below the veneer of civilised society into another world. The sub-world, the underground. Life on the bottom rung. Perhaps I would never find my father but last night I'd experienced the kind of life he'd led. That's why I'd sat under the railway bridge with Sebastian and got ripped, that's why I was sitting here this morning. But I didn't want to live my father's life, I wanted to rescue him from it. I left the second piece of toast, paid my money and went on my way. I had work to do.

From Rozelle I went into the city. On the footpath by St James station was the outline of an idyllic tropical rainforest, refreshingly cool in the blazing summer heat, even if it was only chalk. Raf's new work had progressed but the artist was nowhere to be seen. It was early afternoon. I waited but he didn't show up.

I drove up to the house in Darlinghurst and knocked on the door. There was no answer. The music I'd heard on my previous two visits was absent. It looked like everyone was out. Which, in a way, was probably just as well. I wanted to speak to Raf on his own, and I didn't want him forewarned, didn't want the household letting him know someone was asking after him.

He wasn't at his painting, he wasn't at Darlinghurst. But I hadn't run out of possibilities yet.

I drove to Glebe, heading for the railway tunnel that, accord-ing to Kerry, the Agharti group used as a meeting place. The former goods train line in Glebe runs right the way through to Darling Harbour. Part of the line is visible from White Bay but what with everything else happening around that area at the moment, you can pass by it every day without even noticing. What motorists pay attention to now is the work in progress on the new suspension bridge over Glebe Island Bridge. Or the way the former wheat silos on the other side of the road have been transformed into Olympic art—classic columns with sportspeople in various poses. Sometimes you'd see the artists at work, miniscule figures on frames. It was like watching Michelangelo's minions working on the Sistine Chapel. As I drove round White Bay and into Glebe I wondered whether any of that was Raf's artwork. Public art. From what Kerry had told me it was the kind of thing he'd do.

I parked the van in Glebe Point Road. There was a gradated grassy slope between Glebe Point Road and Bridge Road. I walked down it, past neat little terraces with shady gardens. A high wind whistled in the row of poplar trees. Wafting up on the wind was the hum of the Bridge Road traffic and the sounds of the city. There was a park bench, rarely used, a long strip of playground with swings and slippery dip. Through the trees I could see the trawlers moored at the Fish Market across Blackwattle Bay. Behind that the Harbour Bridge and tall city buildings. Blinding glittering light bounced off them from the glaring sun. The last thing I saw before going down the final set of steps was the railway bridge crossing Bridge Road. It curved in towards the city—from this angle it appeared to run right into the Centrepoint Tower.

The wire fence had a gap in it at one convenient point. I thought of the wire fence alongside the stormwater canal in Rushcutters Bay. Same dilapidated fence, same overgrown weeds. I walked through the weeds, up the grade, swung over the low metal wall beside the rusting tracks and landed on the chunky gravel. If I turned right I could walk along the track, aboveground, to Darling Harbour. But I turned left and crunched along to the wide gaping hole of the tunnel.

Coming into it from bright sunlight the tunnel seemed to swallow you up. It was not a feeling I enjoyed. I don't mind heights but I don't like being underground. Even though the tunnel was two tracks wide, I felt claustrophobic. I could think of a lot more fun ways of getting thrills than this.

I had only just entered the tunnel when a huge flapping thing suddenly appeared out of the darkness. I automatically ducked but still felt the breeze as it screeched past. A bat. Flapping out into the sunlight like the proverbial bat out of hell. I calmed down. The noise of my feet crunching on the gravel must have scared it. It wasn't heading for me on purpose, I reassured myself; I'd disturbed it, that's all. It was getting out of there, which is what my instinct told me to do as well.

Instead, I walked further on into the darkness. There was the odd flattened drink can on the ground, old electric wires and cables. It all looked as if it had been here a long time. I didn't really expect to come across a meeting of Raf and his Agharti worshippers but the tunnel would perhaps reveal something. Occasionally there were alcoves where railway workers presumably took refuge from a passing train. I walked on, crunching gravel underfoot. The whole floor of the tunnel was covered in these chunks of gravel which in places completely obscured the railway sleepers. What did they do when they had their meetings, bring cushions?

I trod on something softer. I shone my torch down to find I was standing on the remnants of a hay bale. As if this was a barn rather than a railway tunnel in the middle of the city. Though the tunnel seemed to be a country of its own I remembered that in the outside world, Harold Park Raceway was not too far away. Horses, hay. Would people be carrying hay bales across the park? Someone must have.

I moved on. I could hear the faint trickle of water, it felt cooler. Coming from the left side of the tunnel. I shone the torch again. Between the tracks and the wall of the tunnel ran a narrow drain. Water also ran down the walls in places leaving mineral deposits that looked like dirty stalactites. Surely I must be midway now. I looked back. The circle of light, the place where I'd entered the tunnel, looked far away. The light at the other end was faint and wan. Maybe if you were fifteen, maybe with a whole bunch of people, this would be fun.

I tried not to think about the fact that there were tonnes of earth pressing down on me. I don't even like going into a police station. What was I doing in this claustrophobic place? I remembered childhood fears of the dark. Now I was in the pitch black it struck me that there was a good sound reason for them. In the childhood of the species we made our homes in caves. But you never knew what other species also called that cave home, what creature might be lurking in the darkness at the back of the cave, whether there was any back to the cave at all. One step too many and you might plummet blindly into a gaping black void. I wondered whether a scream would echo deafeningly off the walls or just get swallowed up in the darkness.

This was ridiculous, I was scaring myself. The hangover

probably wasn't helping. But the light at the other end of the tunnel did seem to be getting fainter and fainter. This couldn't be, my mind was playing tricks on me. I went on, staying on the tracks, keeping the metal beneath my feet. If I stayed on the tracks I'd be all right. Kerry had said they would explore any kind of tunnel—railways were an obvious one, but there were Telecom tunnels, the stormwater canals, a whole host of tunnels and pipes conveying services to the city. Even the optic fibre super highways were carried underground.

There was a dull, faraway sound. A train approaching? How did I know for sure this was a disused tunnel? Maybe they'd started using it again. I felt as if I'd been in here for years. I strained my ears but the noise faded away.

I kept the torch on all the time now because the light that was faintly visible at the other end of the tunnel had disappeared. I came across another alcove, this one deeper than the rest. There were recesses of darkness that the torchlight didn't reach. I stepped off the track and came up close to the wall. The alcove had a small door in it, swung open to reveal a power box. The door looked as if it had been in that position for a long time. The rusty remains of a seat were in front of it. Everything was utterly still and inert.

I swung the torch to the wall opposite. There was a similar alcove on that side, yet somehow it looked different. I crossed over the tracks. The first thing I saw were the butts of candles on the ground near the wall, candles that had burnt away almost to nothing. I shone the torch directly into the alcove. Onto a faded chalk drawing.

I don't know why it took me by surprise—after all, I was half-expecting to see some evidence of the Agharti gang. It was a drawing of the same peculiar keyhole entrance as the photo I'd seen in the book. As the tattoo I'd seen on Kerry. Although the darkness had preserved the bright colours of the chalk, the seepage of water had started a process of disintegration. I'd obviously located the meeting place but discovering it didn't help me any. What was I to do? Leave my name and phone number on the wall for Raf? The candle butts were dusty. The place didn't look as if it had been used recently anyway.

I heard a loud rumbling noise coming straight for me. Automatically I pressed myself against the wall, lost balance and fell backwards into the alcove. It sounded like a plane. A plane coming right through this tunnel. It boomed louder and louder then faded away. I stood up, panting. Relax, I told myself. If you can hear a plane that loud it means you're almost out. I shone the torch along the tracks and followed the beam. In the distance I could see shapes looming in the darkness, blotches of trees and shrubs. I could hear cicadas, distant traffic, signs of the outside world.

The quality of the air changed and it wasn't long before I walked out of the tunnel. But everything was different. There was the faint smell of smoke and a darkness in the air. I could make out the track extending over a series of support arches through Jubilee Park across the storm-water canal and on forever. I clambered down the siding into the park and kept going, across the walkway over the canal. An orange armchair sat half-submerged in the water of the canal. The park was expansive, I could see for miles. I walked to the road and hailed a cab back to where the van was parked. It was taking the long way round, but once through the tunnel was enough. I had absolutely no inclination to repeat the experience.

The dead-end underground, the hangover, brought me forcibly back to my other obsession. Matthew Talbot wasn't the only hostel in Sydney, there were others. Some of them in Surry Hills. Another snippet of the conversation with Sebastian came online. Surry Hills was where my father had shifted to. And he may have specifically mentioned Swanton Lodge because the place seemed vaguely familiar. It wasn't a lot different from Matthew Talbot except that it didn't cater exclusively to men; they took women as well. I walked in, hopefully looking better than I felt.

I breezed up to the desk, trying a slightly different approach this time. 'I'm here to see Guy Valentine,' I said, as if it was a business appointment.

The woman looked at me as if the name rang a bell. 'Ye-s,' she said, 'just wait a minute, will you?'

I was taken aback, not anticipating such a quick result. I didn't expect him to actually be here right at this moment. I thought about leaving a message and then walking out. Did I really want to have the reunion with my father in the reception area of a hostel?

The other woman at the desk was smiling at me, ready to start up a conversation. I smiled back, not enthusiastically enough for her to start talking to me though. It didn't seem as busy here as it had at Matthew Talbot, perhaps because it was a quiet mid-afternoon period. There was the sound of metal buckets and mops in the corridor, and the same strong smell of bleach I'd noticed at Matthew Talbot.

'Excuse us.' The bucket and mop had made it into the reception area, manoeuvred by a gentleman with black eyebrows and grey hair swept straight back from his face. I moved aside to let him get on with the job. He was whistling, enjoying his work.

The woman came back carrying a ledger. Alone. I expected to see a short stocky man with her but there was no-one. 'Did you say Gay Valentine?'

'No, it was *Guy* Valentine.'

'Hmm, that's odd,' she said. 'We had a Valentine in here last night but in the women's dorm.' She placed the ledger on the counter. 'Only here for half an hour though.'

Oh God, no wonder the place looked familiar. When I'd said last night 'I'll be back' I hadn't realised how prophetic those words would be. Well at least no-one would recognise me, unless the night shift doubled up and did the days as well. Upside down I could read the comment: 'Refused to stay.' Yes, I remembered that bit. The cleaner had now started mopping up around the desk. I moved out of his way.

'This isn't Guy, it's a longer name than that. It looks like . . .' she squinted her eyes, peering. 'What does that say, Robyn?' she asked the other woman at the desk. 'Is it Caroline?'

The other woman peered at it as well. 'Looks to me like Claudine,' said Robyn.

'Actually, it's Claudia,' I said, putting them out of their misery. 'It's me.'

'You were in Proclaim last night?' They weren't surprised—they got all sorts in here—just baffled.

'That's right. Let me clear things up for you. I was in Proclaim briefly last night, that's over and done with. This afternoon I'm here on an entirely unrelated matter—looking for my father whose name is Guy Valentine.'

But they were still baffled. The mix-up with the names, it was all too confusing for them.

'Guy,' I repeated to their blank faces. 'Shakespeare,' I said as a last resort. 'He used to hang out at Rushcutters Bay, had a mate called Sebastian.'

They stood there slowly shaking their heads. So many names, so few beds.

'That's the trouble with you professionals,' the cleaner addressed the women. 'They keep swapping youse round so you don't stay in one place long enough to get to know anyone. He used to do this job, Shakespeare. Gawd, he was so slow.' He chuckled to himself as if it was a private joke.

I forgot the women and turned my attention to the cleaner. 'He worked here?'

'Sure did. Volunteer. Same as me. You've got to put something back into it.' He went on with the job, whistling and sluicing water around and throwing that mop to the ground as if it were a bull.

I moved away from the desk and started following him round. 'How long ago?'

'How long ago what?' he said, his mind completely back to the task in hand.

'How long ago did Shakespeare work here?'

'Ooh, let's see now.' He pulled the mop through the wringer. 'Two, three years.'

'Do you still see him?'

'No. I reckon he lost interest. He just dropped off. They often do. No commitment,' he said disparagingly.

'Do you know where I can find him?'

'Not really. He used to walk to work so I assume he lived round here somewhere.' With a quick flourish he finished the reception area. 'Ask them,' he said, meaning the women at the desk. 'It must be on the records somewhere. Excuse us.' Off he went to plough other pastures.

I returned to the desk. Presumably the women had overheard most of the conversation. 'Could you tell me his address?'

''Fraid not,' said the first woman. 'We can't give out that sort of information about staff members, volunteers or otherwise. We do about clients—we have to give addresses to police and Social Security, so we figure, why not family members, members of the public. But I'm sorry, not with staff.'

'I'm sure he's been a client at some stage,' I cajoled. 'Could you do it on that basis?'

She smiled. 'If you'd like to leave your name and address, perhaps we can pass it on. That's the best I can do,' she said regretfully.

It wasn't the best they could do. 'Look,' I said, presenting her with an alternative, 'you don't have to tell me the address but could you at least tell me if he is on your records so I know this isn't all a wild goose chase?' I stood there, feet firmly planted on the ground. I may have refused to stay last night but this morning they couldn't get rid of me.

'Well . . .' She brought out another ledger from under the desk.

What was it with all these ledgers? We were living in the Information Age, didn't they have all this on computers, databases? She was shaking her head. 'I'm sorry, he doesn't appear to be on our books.'

'Are you sure?' I said. I felt like seizing the book out of her hands and looking through it myself. I mean, they did have trouble making out my name in the Proclaim register.

'We get so many volunteers through here,' she explained. 'Clients who dry out, are full of good intentions. They work here for a couple of days then they're back drinking again. I mean, we'd have someone like Stan on the books,' she said, referring to the cleaner, 'because he's been a regular, but I'm afraid we have no record of your father.'

I wrote my name and phone number on a piece of paper. I could have given them my business card but this wasn't business, it was personal. And knowing I was a private investigator would only complicate things. 'If you hear anything, could you let me know?'

'Sure.'

I walked towards the corridor. 'I'll just say goodbye to Stan,' I said and disappeared before anyone could call me back. I found him in a room marked Laundry. 'Hi,' I said, holding my hand out to him, 'I'm Claudia. Guy . . . Shakespeare's daughter.'

He wiped his hand down his trousers. 'Pleased to meet you, Claudia.'

'I've left my number at the desk. If you happen to run into him, or you see anyone who knows him, can you let them know there's a message for him here?'

'No worries,' he said.

I walked out into the streets of Surry Hills again. If he was here two or three years ago, he could still be here now. Within walking distance of Swanton Lodge. I could walk in ever-increasing circles from where I was standing right now and doorknock every residence in the area.

There weren't many residences around the Lodge, it was businesses, rag trade premises, a few Chinese clubs, secondhand books and music stores. Perhaps I could just walk around the area, I was bound to run into him. I headed up Campbell Street, crossed over Crown. Before I knew it I was up behind Taylor Square. I walked through a back alley full of crumbling little houses on one side and the garbage from Oxford Street restaurants on the other.

Taylor Square had always had its coterie of homeless men despite the trendy cafes springing up around it. Cafes with that blotchy paintwork that cost the earth and could have been done for nothing by a five year old left alone with a box of paints on a wet afternoon. The cafes also had bentwood chairs and tables on the footpath to cater for the long hot summer. Sitting at the tables were elegantly pale-skinned people wearing flimsy dresses, singlets with deep armholes, big socks and workboots, talking about art galleries and eight millimetre movies. No-one seemed to be talking about the smoke in the air. In doorways between the cafes lay men who showed absolutely no interest in any kind of conversation at all.

There were ways of finding out where people lived other than knocking on every door and wandering round the streets. Social Security. He was on it once, he may still be on it.

Bernie was my Motor Registry contact, he'd been slipping me bits of information over the years and in return I'd been slipping him bits of money. In fact I think I must have paid for the renovations on his house.

'G'day, Bernie. It's Claudia.' Bernie went through his usual routine of trying to chat me up and I went through my usual routine of asking about his wife. Then we got down to business. 'You wouldn't know anyone in Social Security, would you, someone interested in augmenting their disposable income?'

'I might do,' said Bernie. 'Depends what you want done.'

'I've got a name, I need an address. Last known address. And it'll probably be sickness benefits,' I added.

'OK, I'll see what I can do,' Bernie said. 'It'll have to be money up front for this one.' Between ourselves, Bernie and I had gotten to the stage where prompt payment didn't matter. Often I didn't pay him till after I had billed the client. Payment to Bernie was part of what is euphemistically known as expenses.

'I'll get a quote,' Bernie suggested.

'I don't need a quote,' I said. 'I want the job done, whatever it takes. I know the person in question was drawing Social Security in 1985, the search can start there. I want a current address and anything else on record. I'll pay the going rate. Plus I suppose you'll be wanting a small commission.'

'Well,' said Bernie, 'you know how it is trying to put a kid through private school.'

'I'm sure you're doing it tough, Bernie.'

We worked out the nasty business of payment then I gave him the name. For the first time in his life, wise-cracking Bernie was stuck for words. 'He's a relative?' he asked tentatively.

'Father.' Bernie was a mate but he wasn't a friend and I didn't feel any compunction to go into the details. 'I'd like it as soon as possible, Bern.'

'It's already done,' he said. It must have shaken him because he signed off without his usual 'cop-u-lator'.

The bushfires had reached Sydney. By the time I got back to the pub everyone was talking about it. 'City Under Siege' read the headlines. Eight hundred kilometres of New South Wales coastline was burning, from the Queensland border down to Bateman's Bay. Sydney was in the middle of it. The leafy North Shore suburbs were ablaze, as were the suburbs to the south. At the beginning of the week there were forty fires, now there were 148. Four lives had been lost, homes destroyed and thousands of people were being evacuated. Already a hundred million dollars worth of insurance was being claimed. It wouldn't take long before this figure would more than double. 'The oven door of Hell opened', began one article as the hot, blistering, north-west winds, uncommon in this season, whipped the fires on. Now you could smell it on the air. The fire was no longer limited to the bush on the periphery of the city but racing up its veins as well.

In the south a fireball had jumped the Woronora River and swept through Como and Jannali. I thought of Rosa in Lugarno. All that was separating Como from Lugarno was the Georges River. I'd stood talking to her on her old timber jetty jutting into the Georges River. A fireball couldn't jump a river as wide as that. Could it?

News of the bushfires occupied almost all the newspaper space, eclipsing all else. So I almost missed a small paragraph at the end of the In Brief section. A decomposing body had been discovered in the back of vacant premises in Leichhardt. I probably would have read it then promptly forgotten about it except that the premises were on Parramatta Road. I remembered the 'To Let' signs on my way to La Giardinera. It had to be one of them. I wondered whether the body was already there the day I walked by.

I took the newspaper upstairs with me, thinking about the effect heat might have had on the rate of decomposition. One would imagine that a body would decompose quickly because of the heat. However this heat was unusually dry. It seemed an irony, the giant tornedo of fire engulfing the city while at the calm centre of it, one lone body lay decomposing.

I woke the next morning to the sound of the phone ringing. I got to it just before the recorded message took over. It was Brian. Immediately I felt guilty. Mina had told me yesterday that he wanted to speak to me and I'd completely forgotten about it.

He'd run a check on Grimaldi as I'd asked him to. He was going to call with the results of that but now something far more interesting had cropped up. Would I like to drop by and see him? He felt like getting out of the office and away from all this bushfire business for five minutes. Perhaps we could meet in a cool dark corner of the Rose and Crown.

I didn't go there often but Brian did. It was the place where I'd first met up with him after not having seen him since I was a child. The pub closest to his work, a civilised sort of establishment that used to have little bowls of nuts at the bar for the customers. I remember Brian telling me a few months ago that the place had 'gone off'. Instead of nuts they'd started serving potato skins.

Nevertheless, when I arrived at the Rose and Crown he was sitting at his table with a bowl of potato skins in front of him. He had his jacket off, sleeves rolled up and tie loosened. Beside him was an orange juice in a long glass chock-full of ice. I ordered a mineral water. 'Have a skin,' he said, offering me the bowl.

'Thought you preferred nuts,' I pointed out.

'Well, you've got to roll with the punches,' he said philosophically.

I took a skin and dipped it into the sour cream and chive dip. Overhead a fan was moving the air around, such a nice change from the creepy cold of airconditioning.

Brian had a briefcase on a chair beside him. It was new. 'Wedding present,' he said when he saw me looking at it. 'Don't know how I got by all these years without one,' he said with a touch of irony.

'So what did you find on Grimaldi?'

'I had a company search done. He owns a few properties around Leichhardt but he's small fry. Has some interesting friends though.'

'Fabio?'

'That name didn't crop up. I mean, really, Claudia, without a surname it's pretty hard going.'

I took a sip of my mineral water, letting this gentle admonition wash over me.

Brian reeled off a few names, most of them Italian. 'You've probably never heard of any of them,' Brian said. 'They don't get their names in the papers. And because they're Italian I don't want you thinking they're Mafia. Let's call it multiculturalism. The old Anglo-Celtic network is no longer the only game in town. It's mostly white collar but if you have a close look at that collar you'll find grime. It seems Grimaldi's job is to wash away some of that grime.

'A couple of years ago he was going broke. The height of the recession, it was happening everywhere. But instead of declaring bankrupt, his fortunes suddenly improved. Now I don't know all this for certain, but based on the company links, a bit of hearsay, and what I know goes on elsewhere, I think someone must have helped him out. In return for favours that were fairly small at the time but gradually got bigger.'

'Very interesting,' I remarked.

'Ah, but you haven't seen the most interesting bit.'

Brian flicked the briefcase open and took out a photocopy in a clear plastic protector. 'There was a small news item they ran yesterday, but you probably didn't even notice it.'

'The body in Leichhardt,' I said.

Brian was impressed.

'I always read the small print,' I told him.

'Well, the premises belonged to Grimaldi. And this was found on the body.' He lay the photocopy out in front of me. 'It's from one of the police photos.'

The background was dark and grainy, but in the foreground was a square of white. A book of matches, and diagonally across it La Giardinera. I recognised it immediately. There'd been one just like it sitting in the unused ashtray the day I had lunch there.

'I believe the police have questioned Mr Grimaldi but not well enough to find something to hold him on.'

'Who was the deceased?'

'Not yet established beyond a shadow of a doubt but the contender is a Leichhardt man whose neighbour phoned the police about a week ago. She was complaining about his dog running loose round the neighbourhood. But forensic thinks he's been dead twelve, fourteen days, maybe longer, allowing for the dry weather that's probably slowed down the process of decomposition slightly.' If the time of death were pushed back a day or two, it would coincide precisely with the day Madalena disappeared.

'If Grimaldi was involved he wouldn't have left evidence that could implicate him, surely,' I pointed out.

'You wouldn't think so. Maybe someone wanted it to look that way, or maybe the guy's not very smart. Do you know him?'

'Not well enough to give him an IQ test.'

If I had money on it, I'd be backing Fabio. This could easily have been one of his 'odd jobs'. Question is, who did he do the job for? As well as working for Grimaldi, Fabio was working for his uncle, whoever that may be. 'Do you have a list of Grimaldi's business associates?'

'Indirectly. I've got the company directors. You can work it

out from there. What's the job, Claudia, you cleaning up
Leichhardt?'

'Not unless I have to. I'm looking for a girl who's gone
missing. Grimaldi's daughter. I'm hoping the father's business
interests have nothing to do with it, but as you know, nothing
is ever simple.'

'Kidnap?'

'No.' I finished off the mineral water. 'Your blood's worth
bottling, Brian. Thanks.' I got up to go.

'When are you coming round for dinner?'

'You're getting to sound just like Mina,' I said. 'Look, things
are rather busy at the moment. I don't want to make an
arrangement and have to break it.'

'Found any of your father's mates, yet?' he asked innocently.
So Janet had phoned.

'Yes, as a matter of fact.'

'Has it helped?'

'Yes. It's helped.'

'I don't suppose she said anything, but your mother's worried
about you.'

'Isn't she always?' I laughed it off.

If Brian hadn't been married to my mother, I would have
openly discussed my search for Guy with him. But it was all
different now. I wanted to talk to him about it but it was no
longer appropriate. It would just make things awkward. If I
passed on what I now knew about Guy, the cosy little life Brian
was building with Mina would crash to the ground.

When I got outside to the panel van the top of it was covered
in black grit. Chunks of cinders falling from the sky. I called
Lugarno but there was no answer. I don't know whether Rosa
had an answering machine, but the phone rang on and on.

I drove to Leichhardt. La Giardinera was closed. The door
locked and the closed sign showing. I went round the back.
There were no cars in the yard. I went up the stairs to find
that door locked too. I put my ear to the door. Inside it was
quiet as a grave.

On my way back to the pub I stopped at Danny's. The
Daimler was sitting there, like a cat waiting for its owner to

come home. Giving me the cold shoulder. I'd been away too long and it was annoyed. That wouldn't last long. They always come round in the end. I walked over to it. The paint job had been done. Danny was right—you could tell.

Danny came out of the workshop wiping his hands on a rag. 'It's the best I could do,' he apologised.

'I love it,' I said. 'In fact, why don't you do one down the other side as well?'

Danny couldn't believe it. 'Mate. This beautiful piece of machinery. What are you trying to do, turn it into a hoon's car?'

'What about dark green and reddish brown? Federation colours. That'd go well on a European car.'

'You can't be serious.'

I don't know what it was but I was suddenly looking at the Daimler in a different way. I felt strangely liberated. Why the hell did it have to look exactly the way it was when it came out of the factory or wherever it was Daimlers come from? I put this to Danny.

He gave me a look as if the question was so preposterous it didn't even call for an answer. 'It's a Daimler, not a Monaro. You know how many Daimlers this age there are in Australia? You could count them on one hand—even with a couple of fingers amputated. I won't do it for you, Claudia. That's that.'

Putting a stripe down the other side would have to look like the lesser of two evils. 'You got any of that paint left?' I asked.

'A bit.'

'It's going to look odd down one side only, isn't it?'

'OK, OK. I'll do the stripe. But that's all. No more talk of painting it two colours, all right?'

'Agreed. So I can keep the van a bit longer?'

'You don't want the LTD or the Saab? They're faster.'

'I'm not going anywhere in a hurry. The van's fine.'

'Suit yourself.'

I'm sure Danny thought I'd gone mad. I was beginning to wonder about it myself. It was just a stage I was going through, the extreme behaviour of the last few days. A couple of nights' quality sleep and I'd be back to normal.

'The guy—Fabio—with the Chrysler. Remember we were talking about him last time?'

'Yeah, I remember.'

'I know you said you didn't have an address but do you have a surname? A contact phone number? Surely you've got an invoice, something like that.'

'I doubt it. I'm a mechanic, not a secretary. I hate all that paperwork. I keep most of the records in my head.'

'So what do you do when it's tax time? Mail your head in, like John the Baptist?'

'I don't know John the Baptist, I'm a Muslim. I stick all the scraps of paper in the office in an envelope and give it to my accountant.'

'How much was the paint job?'

'Getting the colours, mixing the paint, the labour . . . '

'OK, Danny, give me a round figure. I don't need the complete inventory.'

'Seventy bucks.'

'Seventy bucks! For a line of paint half a centimetre wide?'

'That's a fair price, I'm not putting anything on it. You're a regular customer.'

I knew what he was saying was right. It was just that lately the Daimler had become a bottomless money pit. I wrote him a cheque. Sometimes I pay him cash but I have to have something to claim as a tax deduction.

'A hundred and fifty,' I said, giving him the cheque. 'The second stripe's not going to cost as much as the first because you've got the paint already. The rest of it is to buy half an hour of your time to look around the office and see if you can come up with anything on Fabio or the Chrysler.'

'It's that important, huh?'

'It could be. You can ring me on the home number or the mobile.'

I returned to Raf's painting. Once again there'd been progress but the artist was missing. What did I have to do, watch the place twenty-four hours a day? I went over to the newsstand. Every newspaper had FIRE! on it in bold black letters.

I don't know if the guy remembered me from before or not, but he was amiable enough. We got talking about the painting. Then the artist. He told me Raf had gone, that he'd usually left by this time of day. Mostly he worked here during lunch hour, that's when he got the best crowds. I bought the afternoon paper. It felt crisp and dry, like a desiccated leaf. One more degree of heat and the city would spontaneously combust.

When I got home there was a message from Bernie asking me to 'give him a ring sometime'. It was noncommittal, hard to tell from his tone of voice whether the news was good or bad. It was too late to ring him at work and I didn't want to ring him at home. I had a shower to cool off and opened the French doors. It didn't make a blind bit of difference to the temperature.

I tried Rosa again. No answer. I tried her at John and Anna's but all I got was the answering machine. Where was everyone, had they suddenly gone on holidays? I tried La Giardinera and got the answering machine there as well. The recorded message gave the hours of opening and invited the caller to give name, time, number of diners and a contact phone number if they wanted to make a booking. It was dinnertime. Why wasn't anyone there?

I tried driving to Lugarno but the police and fire brigade had set up roadblocks and I couldn't get through. I came back to the pub in search of a few quiet beers. They weren't that quiet—I was surrounded by conversation on all sides. The word on everyone's lips was fire. They were talking about Ash Wednesday when seventy-two lives were lost in Victoria and South Australia, they were talking about the 1967 bushfires in Tasmania. I overheard the argument about eucalypts needing fire to burst open the seed pods, about spontaneous combustion. The stories of vandals sending kites into the air with their tails alight, whether a boy who had been caught deliberately lighting a fire should be charged with murder. Then they got onto other disasters. Granville. Cyclone Tracey. No-one mentioned the floods of 1985.

Three beers and I was still stone cold sober. But hopefully it would be enough to give me a good night's sleep. I went upstairs and got into bed.

At 4 am I was jolted out of bed by the smell of smoke. I saw a brown haze everywhere. Jesus, the pub was on fire! I raced downstairs, into the bar, into the restaurant. But there was nothing burning. The smoke was coming from outside. In the north-west there was a dull red glow in the sky. The wrong direction for it to be the light of dawn.

I went back upstairs and closed the French doors in an attempt to keep the smoke out. It made the room as hot as a furnace. And didn't make a difference to the smoke. It found its way in, under the doors, through every little crack. Softly and silently its long wispy fingers crept into our rooms, our clothes, our hair, all the way into our lungs, our bodies. Whether you were sleeping or awake, you had to breathe it in. We had no choice, there was no other air but this.

I woke up just after nine with the same smell of smoke in my nostrils, feeling decidedly unrefreshed. I reached for the phone and tapped out Bernie's number.

'It's Claudia.'

Bernie started explaining that the price had gone up. The job had taken longer than anticipated. As if he was a builder I'd employed to do renovations.

'Is there a result?' I asked.

'Are you prepared to pay?'

'Of course I'm prepared to pay,' I said impatiently.

'Then there's a result.'

Bernie told me that his contact had examined the records from the present back to 1985, for sickness benefits. There was an address for a Guy Francis Valentine c/- the Matthew Talbot Hostel but it changed in 1987 to a private address in Surry Hills. Then in 1990 the sickness benefits had stopped. Bernie's contact had then looked at unemployment and other kinds of benefits till it finally occurred to him to try the old age pension.

I could have kicked myself when I heard him say that. It was so obvious. Why hadn't I suggested that in the first place? This was where he had found the address. It was still current.

Since 1990 Guy Francis Valentine had been drawing old age pension cheques. And was still doing it.

In those scanty records, change of address and change of pension, was the story of my father's life, clearly laid out before me. 'And?'

Bernie knew what I wanted to hear next but he wasn't saying it. 'Claudia, if it was just between you and me, there'd be no problem. But . . . well, the person wants to know I've got the money before he'll give me the address.'

'How much is it? I can drop the money over right away.'

Bernie told me how much it was. God, if I thought the Daimler was a money pit it was nothing compared to this.

'Yeah, I know,' said Bernie. 'And that's just what my contact's asking. I haven't put anything on top for myself. Seeing as how it's your father.' Bernie sounded almost embarrassed.

'Thanks Bernie,' I said, 'I appreciate that. I'll be there as soon as I can.'

'Give me a call when you're near the building. I'll come out for a cigarette.'

The Department of Motor Transport, now known as the Roads and Traffic Authority, is in Rosebery, a working class area with few houses and lots of industry. Though the name has changed, the building is still the same. As directed, I gave Bernie a call on the mobile as I approached Rothschild Street. He told me to meet him around the back and gave me quite specific directions as to where he'd be. He'd walk along the street a little, to be away from other smokers also cast out of the building to carry on their dedication to the drug. I wondered if workers in the WD & HO Wills tobacco factory, not all that far from here, were allowed to smoke in the building.

Bernie didn't have to be that specific, he's not difficult to spot. As soon as I turned the corner I saw him. The bald head, heavy-rimmed glasses and Russian doll shape were all there trundling along the street. Bernie's shape always gave me a surprise, he had such a thin voice.

I cruised along till I came up level with him. He leaned in the window. I showed him the bills so he could see it was the right amount, then he put them in his pocket. 'You won't be needing a receipt, will you? I've left the book upstairs.'

I looked at him with dry humour. 'What about the address?'

'Right. I'll go and ring him. Copulator, Claudia.'

'Bernie,' I said, 'get in the car. You can use my mobile.'

He looked around furtively.

'For heaven's sake, Bernie, it's the address of an old age pensioner, not the French Connection.'

He got into the car. I switched the mobile onto hands-free mode so I could hear what was said as well. Bernie tapped out the number. It occurred to me that the contact might become difficult, that he wouldn't hand over the address till he actually had the money, but he must have trusted Bernie. He simply asked if Bernie had counted the money and when Bernie said he had, the contact gave him the address. I didn't need to write it down, it rang out loud and clear in the van and finally tattooed itself on my brain.

'Mission accomplished,' said Bernie with a flourish. He got out of the van and lit a cigarette.

'Thanks, Bern, I'll be phoning you. Oh, I've got something else. If you're interested.'

'Sure.'

'American Chrysler, personalised plates—FABIO.' I spelled it out for him.

'Fabio?'

'You know him?'

'Isn't he one of those romance cover models?'

'I doubt it would be the same one. How do you know about romance cover models?'

'My wife reads them.'

Sure, Bernie, sure. As soon as he was gone I grabbed the street directory and found my father's street. I left the street directory open on the passenger's seat and drove off, heading for Surry Hills.

B ut at the first set of lights I caught sight of my own reflection in the side mirror. My eyes had the intensity of a crazy person. What was I doing racing up there like that? It was coming on lunchtime, the best time of day to catch Raf. I'd waited thirty years to find my father. One more day wouldn't hurt.

He was there. This time Raf was there, working on the tropical rainforest scene. His face was partially hidden by straight black hair flopping forward. He was dressed completely in black, apart from a dark blue velvet waistcoat with a silver thread through it.

I put some money in the upturned hat. 'I saw your Last Supper, it was really good.'

'Thank you,' he said graciously.

'What's this one called?'

'It doesn't have a name yet.'

'What about "The Garden of Agharti"?'

He stopped what he was doing. 'You know about Agharti? So few people seem to have heard of it.'

'Oh yes,' I said, 'the kingdom under the earth. Do you believe it could exist here, in Australia?'

'All things are possible,' he hinted, returning to his drawing. 'Thank you,' he said in the same gracious voice as a passerby dropped some coins into the hat.

'Is it possible for someone to live under the ground, do you think?'

'Of course. If there's air, something to eat and drink. In Agharti there is vril light which makes plants grow. According to the legend those people were completely self-sufficient.'

'What about under Sydney? Is it possible to live in the tunnels under the city?'

He looked up again, starting now to get the idea that I wasn't just a passerby asking idle questions.

'Kerry told me you and Madalena were friends.' He didn't say anything. 'Do you know where she is?'

He was colouring in an area of green, rubbing the chalk over and over in the same place, giving himself something to focus on rather than the question I was asking.

'No.' But he did. He knew exactly where she was.

'Is it Fabio? Is that who she's worried about?' A muscle in his jaw tensed.

'Raf,' I bent down close to him. 'Is she all right? Just tell me if she's all right.' I was as close as I could get to him without actually touching. He kept chalking in the leaf, not looking at me. Some more coins were dropped into his hat but this time he didn't acknowledge it. I stayed in close, I could almost feel his body heat.

'Do you know what it's like for Madalena's mother, can you imagine what she's going through?' He wasn't answering but he could hear me all right. I squatted there for a minute more then decided I'd pushed it far enough. I didn't want to bully him into talking, didn't want to use any tactics that might associate me with Fabio. I stood up. 'If you see her, please ask her to call her home.'

'I don't think I'll be seeing her. Like I said, I don't know where she is.'

I walked away. Into Hyde Park and down the path as if that was the end of it. But it wasn't.

I waited. By the fountain from which I'd watched this spot before. He continued with the drawing, occasionally looking up and thanking people for their donations. For seventeen minutes. Then he pocketed the money and put the hat on, pushing his hair behind his ears. He stood up, looked around, then walked into the station. I made my way back and joined the trickle of people entering the station.

St James station was built in the 1920s and would have been very stylish then. The pedestrian tunnel leading into the station was done out in cream tiles with bottle green trim. Every so often there was an arched opening into a parallel tunnel, and a smaller opening at ground level, like a cat door.

Raf walked along with a light step, overtaking an old lady slowly making her way with the help of a walking stick. She kept to the wall so as not to be a traffic hazard, but nevertheless a young dude cut it too fine and sent her off balance. Right into my arms. I managed to steady her. But it had given her a fright. 'Oh, oh,' she started sobbing loudly. People turned around to see what the fuss was. People including Raf. I was looking straight at him. He saw me and ducked through a nearby archway. I wanted to go after him but the woman was clinging to me as if I was a life-support system. Shit. 'It's OK,' I assured her, 'just try to keep walking.' No, she didn't want to walk, she wanted to lean against the wall.

Of course, by the time she'd recovered, Raf had long gone. I went through the same archway into another pedestrian tunnel and followed it out to the street. He wasn't back at the painting, there was not a sign of him. I came back into the station and looked around. He'd completely disappeared. He could be anywhere.

'I'd like to see the station master,' I said to one of the guards.

'Is it a complaint?' he asked.

'No, not yet.'

'Through there and up the stairs, first door on the right. You can't miss it.'

He was right. You'd have to be blind to miss the 'STATION MASTER' sign on the door. Through the glass panel I could see the station master at his desk, stacks of folders neatly arranged in front of him, others in overhead racks. He looked up when I knocked, put his pen down and came to the door.

He was a pleasant-looking man in his mid-thirties, crisp

white open-necked shirt with long sleeves buttoned up at the cuffs.

'Good afternoon, my name's Claudia Valentine.' I told him I was a geography teacher researching a project on urban transport. Did he have any maps or diagrams of the station?

'You're keen,' he remarked, 'doing this during the holidays.' He reached up to one of the racks and plucked out a large plastic folder. On the cover it said 'ST JAMES STATION'. Just as he placed it on the desk his phone rang. 'St James,' he said, turning the folder round, inviting me to have a look. The folder was a bit like a school project itself. Everything neatly set out in plastic envelopes in the ring binder. Timetables, engineering specifications, statistics for commuters, tickets sold. And maps.

One map was of the station and the area surrounding it—Elizabeth Street, St James Church, Macquarie Street— dotted lines indicating the pathways of Hyde Park. It mapped the pedestrian tunnels from Elizabeth Street and St James Road and the below-ground fan rooms. It also gave the plan of the station, the turnstiles and the platforms below.

Another diagram was of the stations and tracks in the inner city, from Central to Circular Quay. It was comforting to see the complex maze of city tracks set out so simply. I noted with interest that at the Circular Quay end of St James station there was a tunnel that appeared to lead nowhere.

'How are you going?' Having finished his phone call, the station master was turning his attention back to me.

'Fine. What's this?' I asked, pointing out the dead-end tunnel.

'There'd be a few of them under the city. Built at the beginning of the century. It was probably going to be one of the tracks on the eastern suburbs line. They were thinking of it even back then. Only took them fifty years to get around to it, then they put it through Martin Place rather than St James.

'Some people reckon General Macarthur had secret head-quarters down there during the war but I've been down there, I don't think so. There's no evidence of it ever having been used. There's a big pool of water at the end of it, that's all.'

'Easy to get into?'

'It's not accessible to the public, of course. But staff go down there.'

'Regularly?'

'When something needs doing. We have people doing maintenance work on the lines that are used, but it'd be years since anyone went down into that particular tunnel. No need.'

'Thanks for showing me this,' I said, 'it's been very helpful.'

'No worries. Do you need to photocopy anything?'

'Not at the moment. Thanks.'

Raf had spotted me, he'd be wary, alert. On the lookout. He may even have been watching me right now. He was going to lead me to Madalena but not today.

The address I had for my father was a block of flats opposite a threadbare piece of grass that was supposed to be a park. There was a bench on it, presently unoccupied. It looked like a good place for a kip. A couple of kids skateboarded along the footpath beside the park. Brothers by the look of them, the younger one trying to keep up with the jumps the bigger one was doing with ease.

The block of flats looked like Department of Housing accommodation. A monolithic redbrick cube with rows of small windows. There was a low redbrick fence around the perimeter and grass inside that was better kept than the grass in the park. Despite the hot dry weather, despite the fires, someone was watering this patch of lawn. The windows had some signs of individual difference, attempts to personalise, to make the impersonal structure more like home. Some of the windows had curtains—lace, faded Marimekko designs from the sixties, a checked blanket in one case. Some windows were open, others closed. Some had vases of flowers—hard to tell from the outside whether they were real or artificial. A couple were obviously bathroom windows with toothbrushes sticking their heads out of thick mugs.

Guy Francis Valentine's address was flat 2. I walked into the vestibule. Flats 1, 2, 3, and 4 were on the ground floor. Everything in here was pretty quiet. All the doors looked the same. I went to flat 2. I stood there ready with my hand up to knock but at the last minute found it surprisingly difficult to do. I listened at the door but no sound was coming out of this flat. I gave a light little tap. No answer. I tried a harder knock. Still no answer. Except for the kids outside on their skateboards this could have been a ghost town. No-one came in or out of the flats. Somewhere in the distance was the sound of talkback radio. I went out of the building but stayed inside the fence.

Number 2 was on the street side of the block. I wondered if my father might be incapacitated, whether he was given this flat because he couldn't climb stairs. I walked across the grass and looked in his window. Despite the attempts at beautification that I'd observed at some of the other windows, the inside of this flat look institutional. Neat, tidy, institutional. The floor was cork tiles with a piece of mustard-coloured carpet in front of a TV set. There was a tiled coffee table with a TV program neatly to one side. Even the small plate with a crust of bread and a butter knife resting on it looked neat. A comfy lounge chair, orange and mustard swirls with slightly frayed edges where the hands rested. The only sign of life was a yellow canary in a cage swinging on a miniature trapeze in the corner of the room. It may have been singing but I couldn't hear it from here. There were curtains at the window, a plain brown material pulled back to let in the light. I tried the window but it was locked.

What the hell did I think I was doing, breaking into my father's flat? I crossed over the street and sat on the park bench, looking at the dry crisp grass. There was still the smell of smoke. The brown haze hovered over the block of flats, kept up there by the heat of the building. Everywhere you looked the sky was full of it.

A minute later I saw the familiar red and blue uniform of Australia Post. The postwoman had on a hat to keep the sun off her, a bag on her back and a stash of letters in her hand. She deposited the letters into the row of letterboxes for the block of flats.

The skateboarders had gone, the odd car drove by. The canary was a good sign. Guy couldn't be too far away if he had a pet to look after. Also, given the general neatness of his flat, he didn't look like the kind of person who would leave his breakfast plate unwashed for very long. At an intersection a few streets away I saw a bus pass by. And finally a sign of life from inside the building. A woman in down-at-heel slippers and lank grey hair held back by a couple of bobby pins came out and looked in the letterbox of number 12. Out of it she pulled a long, window-faced envelope. She shuffled inside again.

From the direction of the passing bus two men approached. They were both elderly, one small and neat-looking with a good head of grey hair and a slight limp, the other completely bald, which made his small round face on a large body look even smaller. Both of them were carrying shopping bags—not heavy items, just the kind of shopping you do on your way home from somewhere. Or if you live alone and get by on the smell of an oily rag. Two nice old gents, battered about by what Life had dealt them but cheery in spite of it. They were walking along at a leisurely pace, the big one bending his head a bit to hear the story the little one was relating to him. When they got to the low wrought iron gate to the flats they opened it and walked in.

'Coming up for a cuppa?' said the big one.

'Yeah, in a minute,' said the little one, 'I'm just going to check the mail.'

'No point in me doing that, no-one ever writes.' It wasn't a whinge, more a light-hearted joke.

'The government writes to you. It's Thursday, you mug. Pension day.'

'Jeez, how could I forget! Check mine for me will you, Guy.'

'Sure thing, Charlie.'

He went to the row of boxes and came away with two letters similar to the one the woman had received. He walked up to the front door and gave one of the letters to Charlie, then both of them went inside and closed the door.

From the minute they'd entered the front gate everything had proceeded in slow motion. He was smaller, thinner than I imagined but it was him. Neither of the men had as much as glanced at the woman sitting on the bench. There was no flying towards each other as it happens in the movies, the atmosphere didn't thicken with emotion. I just sat there.

There was some movement behind the window. Then it opened a fraction. It must have been quite hot in there but when you live on the ground floor you close the windows when you go out. If he caught sight of the woman on the bench now, he didn't come back for a second look.

I stood up. All I had to do was cross the road and knock on the door. He was home now, there was nothing stopping me. Except myself. As I stood alone in the now deserted street, all the years of my life dissolved away and were reduced to these few seconds. He was not the young cadet of the year, the face that I remembered from childhood. Neither was he the dero lying in the street, the one I would rescue and take home and give a good bath. He'd rescued himself. It was time for me to do the same. He was just an ordinary person, an old man living in a flat, looking after himself and his budgerigar. Watching TV with his TV guide neatly on the table. He had a life and I was no part of it.

I stood there, on the point of leaving. I took a few steps. If he were to look out the window now, right now, maybe I would nod hello to him. Just nod in a neighbourly fashion then walk on. Perhaps he would pop his head out the window, looking down the street after me, wondering. Wondering, but never quite sure.

But he didn't do any of that. Nothing happened. For all I knew he had already gone upstairs to have his cup of tea with Charlie. I continued on down the street, got in the van and drove away.

I had a stiff drink at the pub, then went upstairs. There was a message for me to ring Rosa's house. I rang.

'Yes, hello?' It wasn't Rosa who answered.

'Who is this?' I asked.

'Who is this?' the voice repeated back to me.

'It's Claudia Valentine, I'm looking for Rosa Grimaldi.'

'Ah, Claudia,' the voice sounded relieved. 'It's Anna Larossa here.'

'Where's Rosa?'

'She's at the hospital, Concord Hospital. She's been there for two days.'

'What's happened to her?' I said, alarmed.

'Not to her, to her husband. There's been an accident. He's been shot.'

'Been shot?'

'At the restaurant. There was a fight with that boy, Fabio. It's very bad.'

'What was the fight about?'

'We don't know. Arturo is unconscious. The woman who works in the restaurant, Dora, she heard the fighting.'

'And Fabio?'

'Disappeared.' Disappeared.

'Rosa won't come home, she won't leave Arturo's side. Perhaps it's just as well. It's terrible here. John is hosing down the house in case the fire jumps the river again. There's white

201

smoke, like mist. You can't see more than five metres in front of you. People look like ghosts.'

They may not let her through the roadblock even if she did try to come home. I was just grabbing the car keys when the phone rang. I hesitated, undecided as to whether to pick it up or let the machine deal with it. I waited for the recorded message then heard the caller identify herself as Sofia Theodourou.

I wrenched up the phone. 'Claudia Valentine. Hello.'

'I'm sorry to bother you,' she said, 'we've got an unidentified, a girl about fifteen. With a tattoo on her arm.' My blood ran cold. 'Do you know how we can get in touch with the parents?' Sofia asked. Oh God.

I told Sofia about Arturo. 'I don't know if the mother would be in a fit state to come down to the morgue.' I offered to do the ID. I knew it had to be someone who knew the deceased but I felt as if I knew Madalena. I knew her family, I knew her friends, I knew her from the photos. And I would certainly recognise the tattoo if I saw it.

'Sofia, I'll be there in ten minutes. I'll give you a contact number for the mother and do an unofficial ID at the same time. I'm sure under the circumstances this would be all right with the family.'

I got in the car and drove. I was speeding, I don't know why, it was fruitless. If I'd wanted to speed I should have done it before. If I had devoted the hours to looking for Madalena that I'd devoted to looking for my father I might have found her by now. Guilt weighed heavily on me and I hoped for a reprieve. I hoped it wasn't Madalena, that Fabio hadn't got to her. Then I felt sick at heart and ashamed of myself—who did I hope it was, if not Madalena? There was a girl lying dead in the morgue. She was someone's daughter.

There were television cameras outside the Coroner's Court when I arrived. The foyer, though, was virtually empty. Whoever the cameras were expecting hadn't yet arrived. Or hadn't yet emerged from the court. Camera operators lounged against cars emblazoned with TV channel logos. They didn't bat an eyelid when I walked by.

I walked straight through to Forensic Medicine and asked for Dr Theodourou. She was expecting me and came as soon as they paged her. She looked tired. 'The fires,' she said. 'They're all around our area. The police have told us to prepare for evacuation. My husband is packing things up, in case we have to leave.'

I thought of all the roses, of Kirby's carefully controlled patch of garden. The fire running rampant, unrelentingly destroying what we build around us to make us immune to the forces of nature.

'Has it come to that?' I asked as she led me down the long, familiar corridor.

'If they don't get some relief, we'll be the next to go.' She took me into a room with a TV screen.

'I have no problems looking at the body directly,' I informed her.

'As it's unofficial, it's probably better that you see the video rather than the actual body,' said Sofia. 'Some relatives prefer to do it that way anyhow. They feel more comfortable. It's the way most of us experience dead bodies—on a TV screen.'

I lay the photos I had of Madalena out in front of me. 'What happened?'

'Hit and run. Last night. In Kings Cross.'

It could have been Fabio. Shot Arturo then went looking for Madalena. And found her.

'No details on the vehicle?'

'No.'

'OK,' I said, 'let's start it.'

Sofia set the machine going. I felt my stomach cave in. It was the hair. Same colour, same wavy texture as Rosa's. The camera travelled around the face covered in blood. It was hard to distinguish the facial features and I didn't want to have to look any closer than I already was.

'Can we go to the tattoo, please?' I said.

Sofia fastforwarded the video and picked it up again as the camera swept down the right side of the body. She held on the tattoo. It was a phoenix surrounded by flames. I started breathing again. Nothing remotely like the keyhole tatoo that Kerry and Madalena had.

'Is that the only one?' I asked. 'Nothing on the other arm?'

The camera swept down the other side. There was no other tattoo.

'It's not her.'

Sofia looked even more weary than she had before. She put her hand up to her forehead as if to rub the weariness away. It would make things simpler for her if I was able to give a positive ID. They could start to package the body up, put it away and go home.

Was this how it had been in 1985, in the floods? Hindley out there in the rain, wanting to get back to the cosiness of the police station. It might not have been Guy Francis Valentine but it was some other old dero. What difference did it make? We were all going to die some day. In the meantime a quick identification would make his paperwork easier.

'It's not the same tattoo,' I insisted.

Sofia rewound till we were back to the face. She had more experience than me of distinguishing facial features beneath the distortions of blood and injury. She held the frame on a frontal view and compared it with the photos I had laid out in front of me.

Then she handed the photos back to me. 'There's no point getting Mrs Grimaldi down here. Shit.' She rubbed her forehead again, grimacing. 'I've got to take some aspirin. I've had a headache for days. All this smoke.' She flipped the video out of the player. 'I'm sorry, do you mind seeing yourself out?'

I walked back up the corridor and through to the Coroner's section. I wasn't feeling in peak condition myself. There was a canteen of sorts, a room with a few functional tables and chairs. I was sure they wouldn't have anything alcoholic but even a cup of bad coffee would do at the moment. On the wall was a sign which said: 'Catholic Women's League is responsible for this canteen and is staffed by voluntary workers'. There was something wrong with the grammar but I couldn't be bothered working out what it was.

A woman in her sixties was buttering bread, presumably in

preparation for lunch. Sandwich fillings—chicken, ham, tomato, shredded lettuce—sat in small trays behind glass. To one end of the counter was a basket of fruit—apples, oranges, bananas. There was also an array of chocolate bars and sweets. 'Black coffee,' I said.

She stopped buttering bread and got the coffee ready.

'Thanks,' I said, handing her the right change. I went and sat down at a table. It was quiet outside in the foyer, I wondered if the TV cameras were still in the street.

I felt depressed. The body wasn't Madalena, I should have been breathing sighs of relief. But it was someone. Unidentified. Somewhere someone was waiting for a girl who would never come home.

I could hear voices outside. The hair was the same as Madalena's, there was a tattoo, even if it wasn't the same tattoo. Perhaps from the back Fabio . . . The voices got louder, coming this way. I looked up and saw men in suits.

One of them was Russell Hindley.

When he saw me he looked daggers, face clenched. Like he wanted to take out that .38 Special and shoot me on the spot. But he didn't try anything. He walked on by, constrained by the circumstances. He couldn't flex his muscle in the Coroner's Court the way he could in a quiet backstreet.

Then other suits came in, lawyers judging by the expensive dark fabric. They ordered coffee and hung around, idly chatting, kings in their castles, talking freely in front of the servants as if we didn't have ears. 'Someone planted a bomb in that court, they could wipe out what's left of the old gangs.'

'Or at least wipe out their lawyers.' This raised a chuckle. 'I notice Harrington's kept himself scarce.'

'Probably picking his tomatoes.'

'Is that what he ended up doing, growing tomatoes? Finally put all that bullshit to good use, did he?'

'I notice his little mate, Hindley, is here though.' If my ears weren't pricked already they certainly were now.

'He wasn't involved in any of that, was he?'

'He was at Kings Cross, same as Harrington. You think it doesn't rub off?'

A woman's voice cut across the low rumble of men's conversation, a voice I knew. I looked towards the door and saw Carol come in, talking to a male colleague. What was this, the annual Policemen's Ball? Carol stopped short when she saw me but at least she didn't walk out again. She looked, wondering what I was doing here, and not all that pleased to see me. She excused herself from her colleague and came over.

'Claudia?'

'Carol?'

We both wanted to know what the other one was doing here. I went first. 'I've been visiting Forensic,' I said. 'It's never pleasant in there, as you know. On my way out I decided to sit down and have a cup of coffee. It was quiet when I arrived, then suddenly it's the most popular place on earth.'

'Big event, there's media outside.'

'Yeah, I saw them. What is it?'

'Inquest into the disappearance of Edward Leonards.' I recalled the name. Vaguely. Carol jogged my memory. 'Allegedly involved in the Sweetie's scam.'

Sweetie's Icecream Parlours. 'Ah.'

'But that would have been years ago. Why are they having an inquest now?'

'Someone upstairs is pushing for it, new broom sweeping clean.'

'And fortunately, most of the people who could get swept under the carpet are no longer around,' I remarked. Carol declined to comment. 'Are you involved in this matter?' I asked Carol.

'I've been gathering information, yes.'

'The trip to Melbourne?'

'Yes.'

'And Hindley, what's he doing here?'

'I suppose as an ex-officer of the Drug Enforcement Agency he might have an interest in the matter,' Carol admitted begrudgingly. I had a feeling that Hindley's interest went back further than that. 'I'd love to stay and chat with you, Claudia, but the court is resuming in a few minutes and I need to speak to my colleague.'

'It's an open inquest—open to members of the public?'

Carol could see where this was leading but there was nothing she could do to stop me. 'Yes,' she sighed.

'Good,' I said. 'See you in court.'

Before entering the court, members of the public and others had to undergo a security check. Staffing the checkpoint were two sheriffs, dressed in blue with the sheriff insignia on the sleeve. I placed my bag on the table provided and walked through the frame. I felt as if I was about to board a plane.

For some reason I beeped. The male sheriff asked me to extend my arms while he caressed my aura with his metal detecting device. Then the female sheriff asked me to open my bag and show her the contents. There was nothing much in my bag, a notebook, pen, lipstick, the photos of Madalena, a Ferry Ten ticket. Nothing lethal.

I went into the courtroom, a brown brick interior with mustard-coloured wall panelling. It was set out like a theatre, with rows of seats for the audience and a partition separating them from the onstage players. The players were: the coroner, sitting up at the highest table like a king; on the next level down sat the witness at one end and the coroner's assistant at the other. Lower down, with their backs to the spectators, were the legals. On the right, members of the print media sat taking notes, and to the left were the witness's minders. Carol was in this area as well.

As well as members of the public who'd come along for the show, there were 'interested parties' sitting in the gallery—big men in tight suits or short-sleeved white shirts. Moustaches, hair longish at the back. They'd survived the seventies but not by much.

The witness was a balding man in a light blue suit and a bright paisley tie. Some people are born with it, others never attain it. Addressing him was a barrister. Trim black beard, one of the dark blue suits I'd seen in the canteen. 'Now, Mr Glasser,' the barrister started.

'Excuse me, for the purposes of this court the witness will be known as Mr Jones,' interrupted the coroner.

'Now Mr *Jones*,' said the barrister sarcastically. 'In your statement you say that a dinner took place at the Fry 'n' Fish on 26 March 1985 during which Edward Leonards was discussed. Is that correct?'

'That's correct.'

'And what was the nature of that conversation?'

'Dennis said something had to be done about Leonards, he'd become a loose cannon.'

'And by loose cannon you mean . . . ?'

'Well, he was getting out of control. He'd kill anyone. If he didn't like the colour of your tie he'd kill you. He was stupid, going round asking people if there was anyone they wanted knocking off.'

'This was almost a month before Leonards disappeared?'

'That's right.'

'So why did Dennis wait so long?'

'Dennis never killed him. Dennis never killed anyone. He was going to talk to Harrington about it, that's all.'

'By "Harrington" I take it you mean Detective Richard Harrington as he was at the time?'

'That's correct.'

I shifted seats so that I was sitting right behind Carol. I bent over and whispered in her ear, 'Carol, come outside.'

She sat there frozen, as if she hadn't heard what I said.

'Do you think I'd drag you out if it wasn't important?' I tried again.

She'd heard. Without turning around, she quietly stood up, went through the motions of bowing to the coroner and went outside. I did the same.

Not surprisingly, Carol was fuming. 'This better be good, Claudia. You'd just about have to be able to tell me what they did with Leonards' body to have dragged me out like this.'

'He's at Rookwood, in the Crematorium wall.'

Everything stood still for a minute then Carol understood what I was getting at. 'You can't be serious!'

'Think about it. I didn't make the connection at first because I was out of the country when it happened. Leonards was last seen a month after 26 March. That puts it pretty close to 25 April, doesn't it? Anzac Day. Dennis Carey goes to see

Harrington. Harrington arranges a little send-off for Leonards. Both Harrington and Hindley were at Kings Cross at the time. And the night of the twenty-fifth, Hindley was on duty.

'I don't know the exact sequence of events but let's say Leonards is brought to Rushcutters Bay park. He might already have been unconscious when he arrived. Hindley and Harrington both know deros frequent that park. It's Anzac Day, they're going to be tanked, passed out. Easy, they think, to grab some ID off one of them and plant it on Leonards. Hindley fills out the Report of Death to the Coroner, saying the body is that of Guy Francis Valentine. The body is cremated, never to be found. Except there's one thing wrong with it—Guy Francis Valentine is still alive and living in Surry Hills.'

Carol had started off shaking her head but by the time I got to the end she was at least listening. 'You've found him?' she said.

'Yes.'

'What was it like? What did he say?'

'We didn't speak.'

'What do you mean, you didn't speak?'

'He didn't see me. I left without making contact.'

Carol was waiting for me to explain further. Perhaps over a drink, a game of pool, but not now.

'You could go and see Guy, ask him what he remembers of that night. Ask him what happened to his coat. But there's even more telling proof right here in this building. Blood samples. Leonards must have relatives. See if they're prepared to have a DNA analysis. See if they get a match with the specimens taken from the man Hindley identified as Guy Francis Valentine.'

Carol was thoughtful. 'Leonards had a son, I believe. Living in Madagascar. I'll think about it while I listen to the rest of the proceedings. You coming back in?'

'No,' I said. 'I've got to get back to work.'

I was at the fountain in Hyde Park with my hair pulled back, wearing the round-rimmed glasses I'd worn at La Giardinera. It didn't take much to change your image. I was standing vigil, watching Raf. When he moved, I would move. I would follow him to the ends of the earth and there I would find Madalena. Nothing would get in my way. I wouldn't be stopping to help old ladies in distress or doing any other type of good deed.

The perfect image of summer that this place represented the first time I stood here had switched into its own negative. The sky was brown and the reflection of light off the billowing smoke had turned the tall city buildings a blue of hyperreal intensity. The only reason the cloud hadn't drifted down to the ground the way it had in the outer suburbs was because the heat from the buildings kept it hovering. Gotham City. Behind the smoke the sun was a red ball of blistering heat. It was only midday yet the light resembled a garish sunset. If hell had a waiting room, this was it.

The mood had changed too. Instead of a relaxed holiday feel there was a recklessness, as if everything was out of control. In the midst of this Raf was methodically working on the rainforest. It was almost finished now. He leaned into a pool of blue–green chalk, attending to some detail. A few people watched him work while others walked respectfully around the painting rather than straight across it.

I watched him all the way through lunchtime, changing position once or twice in case he looked over this way. He never did.

It was 2.45 when he finally made a move. He pocketed the money, put his hat on, walked to St James station. Down the stairs and into the pedestrian tunnel he went, then into the station proper. Before passing through the automatic turnstiles he went over to the old-fashioned milk bar and bought two Cherry Ripes. Two. While he was doing that I bought a train ticket. He went through. I hung back for a minute then passed through the turnstile myself.

The platform had enough people on it to make me feel inconspicuous. Raf was standing right down one end. The train from Circular Quay pulled in, the automatic doors opened and passengers got out. Raf waited to get on. I walked onto the train, three doors up from him. The guard signalled and the train started to move. I looked back. The platform was now empty. I had no idea where he'd be getting off so I set out to locate him before we got to Museum, the next station. I moved progressively through the carriages.

He should have been three carriages away but there was no sign of him. I went right to the end of the train and still couldn't see him. Perhaps he didn't get on the train after all. But there was no-one left on the platform when the train pulled out.

He wasn't on the train and he wasn't on the platform. There was only one other place he could be. In the tunnels. The realisation came as no surprise. Subconsciously I'd known from the start that he hadn't got on the train, I just didn't want to admit it because that meant I had to go into the tunnels too.

I got off at the next station and waited for the train going back to St James. On the return trip I put my hands to the window and looked out. There were lights every few metres, similar alcoves to the ones I'd noticed in the Glebe tunnel, and archways that went through to other tracks. They all flashed by in seconds.

The train pulled in at St James. I got off but instead of going up the stairs like everyone else, I hung around the platforms. There were two—southbound and northbound. In between was a kind of trough where a track might once have run. At the end where Raf had been waiting, the tunnel entrance of the former track was blocked off by a white timber wall. In the wall was a small door that appeared to be locked. Perhaps it was the aborted tunnel I'd seen on the map.

It would be easy to slip down off the platform and into the tunnel. Best time was when a train had just pulled in, people milling around. No-one would notice. And if there was a train in the station already, there'd be no danger of meeting another one in the darkness of the tunnel. But you couldn't stay there long. This was part of the City Circle. There were trains coming all the time. Raf would know this. He was the tunnel king, he would know his way around.

I looked at the timetable. There was a train from Circular Quay due in two minutes. The next one from that direction would arrive seven minutes later.

I stood in the place Raf had stood. The train from Circular Quay was dead on time. People got off and others got on. The disembarking passengers started making their way up the stairs. The guard looked up and down the platform then gave the all-clear signal. A quick look around, a deep breath, then I slipped down onto the tracks and walked into the darkness.

A metallic smell invaded my nostrils as soon as I entered the tunnel. Behind me the lit-up area of track at the station was still visible. I pressed on, hugging the wall.

Raf wouldn't have stayed in this tunnel long, there'd be too much traffic. But somewhere there would be an archway leading into the aborted tunnel. There was also the strong possibility that once down here I might stumble into tunnels that weren't on the map. I had seven minutes before the next train. I hoped I would find the other tunnel before a train came zooming along this one.

I continued on, feeling my way along the wall. I didn't want to use my pencil torch unless I had to, didn't want to alert him to my presence if he was up ahead. I heard a soft scratching and felt something run over my hand. Automatically I withdrew my hand. Only a cockroach I assured myself, just like the ones at home.

According to the diagram the boarded-up tunnel ran parallel to this one for a while, curved east, then abruptly stopped. I must have been at the place where it curved away because suddenly, instead of feeling the wall, my hand felt thin air. I turned the torch on briefly. There was an archway leading into the other tunnel. I switched the torch off again. In those few seconds I'd seen walls streaked with grime, a bit of faded graffiti here and there. Oddly comforting, the fact that someone had been down here to do this, even if it was years ago.

There were no actual train tracks in this tunnel, I could walk freely. Nevertheless I was reluctant to leave the security of the wall. Through the cold oppressive silence I could hear little scurryings and the occasional drip of water. As I felt my way along I began to notice that in places there were streams of wetness. I hoped it was water. My eyes were getting accustomed to the dark. Up ahead the quality of the darkness was different, glistening almost. Was this the pool of water the station master had referred to? If it was, things weren't looking good because I hadn't seen any signs of Raf.

I turned the torch on again. It *was* water up ahead. But nothing else. This was a wild goose chase. Perhaps Raf was still on that train. How stupid of me to have got off. To be down here. I kept on, towards the water, thinking how futile this all was. I left the torch on. There was no reason not to, no-one was here to see it.

Not only was there a pool of water, there was a patch of sand in front of it.

And in the sand there was a print. I shone the torch directly on it. It had been made by a heavy shoe, a workboot worn by railway workers. Or by inner city kids. Something caught my eye. A spot of cobalt blue. Blue chalk, of the type Raf used.

The footstep was facing in the direction of the water. I shone the torch into the water. There were dark shapes in there. I reached in and felt a piece of iron, part of a rail track presumably, then a pick. Workers' equipment left behind after work on this tunnel was abandoned?

I waded in a bit further, and suddenly I was in over my head. I started treading water, then made my way to the end wall.

The water was just as deep here but at least I had the wall for support. I shone the torch down into the water and at the bottom of the wall saw a different shade of darkness. I dived down. It was an opening through to the other side. I remember Vince and Steve talking about caves with water in them, that sometimes you had to go under water to get from one cave to the next. But what would I find on the other side? Was there a place where I could come up for air?

My heart was thumping so hard it was creating ripples in the water. Was it my heart that was making the muffled sounds I could hear? I counted to four, trying to bring my heart beat to an easier pace. I pressed my ear to the wall. A whispering sound and behind it a dull whoosh. It would be OK, all I had to do was swim through to the other side. It was perfectly safe. I could have a look then come back exactly the same way.

So I did it. I wriggled through the opening, swum in a direction that I hoped was up, then burst through the surface, gasping for air. I fished the torch out of my boot. It flickered for a second, long enough for me to see walls that seemed to be glittering with crystals. Then the light petered out.

Somewhere I could hear the dull whoosh, louder now than it was on the other side of the wall. Was it traffic passing overhead? Everything else was still, and the whispering had ceased.

I kept swimming forward a few strokes till I touched the ground again. It wasn't sandy here as it had been on the other side, it felt like chunky gravel. I stood up, took one step and then the ground gave way. I heard a snap then felt my ankle in a vice-like grip. I was caught in some sort of a trap. The messages of pain began coming through. A searing circle around my ankle. I tried to pull my foot free but it wouldn't budge.

'Is anyone there?' I cried desperately. I felt overwhelmed by panic. Trapped beneath the city. Up above in the streets no-one would hear my silent screams. No-one knew I was here, no-one was going to come looking for me. In the darkness I could smell my own blood. If I died down here no-one would ever find me.

I breathed, to keep the panic at bay. My foot was caught in a trap, that was all. There was no other damage. There was a way out, I just had to stay calm and think of it.

The darkness that deprived me of sight seemed to sharpen other senses. Something, or someone, was close by. I couldn't see what it was. It was as if the atmosphere suddenly thickened somewhere to my left. I put my hand out and groped the air. I touched something, something that instantly shrank away. There was a sharp intake of air. It could have been me.

Then, in amongst the cold blackness, I smelled it. The scent of jasmine. Perfume. Soft and warm as the body temperature of a human being.

'Maddy? Raf?'

There was no answer. But someone was there.

'Maddy, there's been an accident. Your father is in hospital, he's very badly wounded.' My words seemed to get eaten up by the darkness. Yet still I could feel an alertness in the air.

'Is it Fabio you're worried about? Is that why you're down here? The police are looking for him, I don't think he'll bother you. In fact he's probably left the country.' I tried to keep my breath even but it was coming in fits and starts. I felt nausea creep up from my stomach and flow all over me. A ringing in my ears, then nothing.

I was dead. I had been through the dark tunnel they talk about and now I could see the warm welcoming light. It was just the way they describe it in books. I groped for the light, I had to reach it, had to keep it in view. This was it, the final stage in the death experience.

My mouth was dry, the ringing had returned to my ears. Sensation. My ankle, instead of being surrounded by fire, now felt like ice. The vague blotches of light and dark came into focus. I could see now that the light was a kerosene lamp. Above it was a face. Raf's face.

'You fainted,' I heard someone say. Now another face came into view. It was Madalena. More gaunt, sharper-featured in the lamplight than in the photo. But it was Madalena.

I attempted to stand up. Slowly, tentatively. But when I tried to put weight on my left foot pain shot up my leg like a howling wind.

'You better sit down,' Raf said. He put the lamp on the ground and now I could see my surroundings. What I thought were crystals was a mosaic in broken glass. The walls were covered in it. A work of art. Raf's underground gallery. He sat me down on a mattress. The whole place looked quite comfortable. Mattresses, cushions, candles.

'Did you come all this way to tell me that my father's in hospital?' asked Madalena.

I had to smile, despite the circumstances. 'Your mother hired me to look for you. Before any of that happened.'

'Hired you?'

'I'm a private investigator.'

'Really? Mum hired you? What did my father think of that?'

Not Dad. My father. The distant one. The same way we referred to Guy.

'He didn't know. At first.'

'But Mum'd never do anything without his permission.'

'She did this time. Why didn't you at least let her know you were OK?'

'I was going to but then something happened.'

In the course of time Madalena told me about it. She had a cosy little hiding place down here, centrally located even if it was lacking a few facilities.

'What do you do for food?' I asked.

'Mostly we go out to eat,' said Madalena.

While the place was comfortable, the idea of having to swim through that pool to come in and out didn't appeal to me greatly.

'There's another way,' said Madalena. She picked up the lamp, took it over to one corner and shone it on a metal ladder ascending up a shaft. The street's up there,' she said. 'At night when there's no-one round, we use that.' I wished I'd known about this back entrance before I'd embarked on the journey through the tunnel.

'Sorry about your ankle,' Madalena apologised. 'We set it up like that in case he followed me here.'

'I don't think there's much damage done,' I said. But I was pretty keen to get out of there and have it seen to. I didn't want to end up with tetanus. Or worse.

'We'll take you up the ladder,' said Raf. 'Tonight, when it gets dark and everyone's gone home from work. It comes out near Druitt Street. This shaft is part of the old hydraulic power system that used to operate in Sydney. Or you can go out the same way you came in.'

'I'll wait,' I said.

Before going to Coogee for dinner I told Mina that I'd twisted my ankle so she wouldn't be alarmed when she saw the bandage on it. Or the walking stick I was using. I felt about a hundred. My punishment for being annoyed at the old lady who thwarted my first attempt to follow Raf.

I had intended to get a cab over, but Brian offered to drop in on the way home from work and pick me up.

'Are you familiar with a hydraulic power system that used to operate in Sydney?' I asked him as we drove towards Coogee.

'That's a blast from the past. There used to be about thirty kilometres of pipes around Sydney at one time, pushing high pressure water to power lifts, cranes, operate sprinkler systems, open bank doors. Sydney Hydraulic Power Company. Now isn't that a name to conjure with. Why do you ask?'

'Oh, no particular reason. I just like to keep in touch with what goes on in this town.'

'I presume since you're having dinner with us that you've finished your job?'

'That's right.'

'Is she back home, the missing girl?'

'Depends what you call home. She's staying with friends in Darlinghurst at the moment. She'll probably stay there till school goes back.'

'Has she been in touch with her mother?'

'She has. Her mother wants her home, of course, but Madalena's not ready to go. A lot has happened to her in the last few weeks. Amongst other things, she turned sixteen. So unless she's in moral danger she can live where she likes.'

Brian parked the car outside a block of four seaside flats, each with a balcony. Mina was standing on one of the balconies, waving. Brian helped me out of the car. I tried to be gracious about it.

'What happened in Leichhardt?' he said, as I hobbled up the drive.

'You know the body that turned up in the vacant premises? It was a local who played cards at the restaurant. He ran up a debt, a few thousand.'

'Gee, they're strict. They topped him for a few thousand?'

'Fabio was looking for an excuse. Grimaldi was losing it.' I recalled Grimaldi at the restaurant, drinking straight from the bottle. 'So his business associates brought in Fabio to teach him a few elementary business principles. Maddy caught the tail end of that lesson the day she went to see her father.'

'And I suppose she thought her father was a mild-mannered clerk in an office.'

'Well, a mild-mannered restaurateur, anyway. She heard raised voices behind the door and her father say, "Get rid of it. Just get rid of it." She thought maybe she'd called at a bad time.

'She's on her way out when she sees Fabio coming down the stairs carrying a rolled-up carpet—with a hand dangling out the end of it. Can you believe it? The guy's been watching too many movies. It's OK, Brian. I can manage the stairs,' I said to stop him trying to lift me up by the elbows.

'He sticks the body in the boot and then he sees Madalena in the alleyway. By the look on her face he knows he's got a witness. He tries to run her down. She flees. To Darlinghurst. She can't go home because she thinks her father ordered the killing. Things weren't that good between them anyway.'

I told Brian about the brother who had drowned. 'She always felt that he blamed her for it. Brian, for God's sake. Let me do it on my own, it's good therapy.' Brian mumbled apologies and said he was only trying to help. I apologised as well and said I wasn't used to being an invalid.

'Anyway,' I said, continuing with the story, 'after a few days she settled down a bit. The phone at Darlinghurst had been cut off because the kids were late paying the bill so she went up the street to phone home. Her mother wasn't there. On the way back to the house she saw Fabio at the door. And that was it. She couldn't go back. She went to the safest place she could think of—underground.'

'How did Fabio know to go looking in Darlinghurst?'

'Well, some of her friends from the house had gone to Lugarno the next day and picked up some things for her. She'd given them the key. She thought perhaps Fabio had followed their car back to Darlinghurst.'

Mina had left the door open. The smell of garlic and basil wafted out. Delicious.

'The father's still in hospital. He'll live but I don't think it'll be business as usual.'

'And Fabio?'

'So far, he's the one that got away. If he made it in time before customs were alerted, he's probably back in the old country. He would have had to leave the car behind, though. That would have hurt. Hi, Mum.'

As Mina kissed me on the cheek I smelled Ashes of Roses talcum powder. 'You don't look as bad as I thought,' she said gaily. 'Fancy doing that, all that time you've been living at that pub, going up all those stairs, and now you've gone and twisted your ankle. You weren't drinking, were you?' she asked anxiously.

'Not on that occasion, no.'

I handed her a bottle of the Minchinbury champagne that she loved so well. 'Oh lovely,' she said. 'I'll just pop it in the fridge to chill up a bit. Come through and I'll show you the photos of the honeymoon. I've got them all laid out on the table for you. I took seven rolls,' she said proudly. 'Two hundred and fifty photos for you to look at. Some very interesting cloud formations.'

Mmm, great. I could hardly wait.